JESSIE WINTERSPRING

A Feel-Good Small Town
Time Travel Romance

Editors: See acknowledgment / Special thanks

Cover by Miblart

To my favorite grandfather, *Lolo* Julio, I wish I could go back in time to be with you again. That said, I hope you aren't sharpening your *itak* and waiting for the day you can intimidate my husband, like you did with every boy who got close to me. Thank you for all the love *Lolo,* I will always return to our precious moments. Please keep watching over me from up there with the stars.

Author's Note

This story includes depictions of traumatic events such as child neglect, domestic violence, off-page sexual assault, parental death, a car accident, and a house fire. Reader discretion is advised for those sensitive to these topics.

Prologue

JUST LIKE HIM

November 9th, 1955, Alicante Jail

Eighteen-year-old Celestina gripped her handbag tighter as she stepped inside an eerie stone corridor, a single guard leading her toward one of the cells. He called through the bars to the man inside, who sat up on the metal bed and raised his head.

Celestina staggered back.

The guard put a gloved hand on her elbow. *"¿Estás bien?"*

She wanted to say "*Si*, I'm okay" and hide her emotion but her lips locked and her eyes widened when the prisoner turned his handsome oval face toward her. Her breath caught as her heartbeat sped up on seeing his dark-gray, hooded eyes—just as she remembered them from eleven years ago—but when a sneer appeared on his bow-shaped lips, she withered inside. This wasn't the same man who raised her.

He got to his feet and place his hand on the bar separating them. *"¡Hola! Hermosita,"* he said, the disgusting smile never leaving his face.

She hated his insulting compliment. Hated how his eyes traveled down the length of her body. She struggled not to squirm, feeling as if an army of ants had crawled under her skin. But she endured it, looking him straight in the eyes. "*¿Eres* Ángel Castro Rivera?"

The man's face lit up, his leer widening into a menacing smile. "*Sí.*"

She swallowed, her throat sore from doing it so many times since leaving Beniardà. "*Soy,* Celestina. *Hija de* Maria Josefa De la Mota."

Ángel's smile faded for a second before returning. "Well," he drawled, his flirty tone gone, "daughter of Maria Josefa, why are you here?"

"I'm your daughter."

He looked at the guard, who shifted and turned toward the exit, but Celestina grabbed the hem of his uniform jacket, forcing him to stay.

Ángel sighed. "So, *mi hija*, what do you want from me?"

Good question. What did she want from him? Her mother turned thirty-three two months ago and, in her drunkenness, told her where her biological father was and that he looked just like her *papá.* And so, here she was after so much trouble proving her identity and so much preparation.

The corners of her eyes stung, and her stomach churned. Ángel not only looked like the man who lovingly raised her, he sounded just like him. And worse, they shared the same name.

Her mother warned her that this man, her father, would never care about her or why she existed. Maria Josefa was right, this man and her *papá* looked identical, but she was wrong about everything else. They were not the same at all. Her *papá* was caring, but this father in front of her was a criminal. A prisoner. Murderer. He'd taken multiple lives and was nothing like her *papá.*

What am I even doing here?

"I wouldn't mind having some fun with your body," he said as she turned on her heel, "just as I did with your mom. Although she was years younger than you then. She was what, uh, *catorce? Sí, sí,* she was fourteen. Oh, how good she felt."

Celestina turned back, raising her bag. Because of this brute, she never knew a mother's love. Because of him, both she and her mother suffered every day. She needed to hit him at least once to release years of pent-up anger. But the guard grabbed her arm.

"Time to go," he said.

"*¡Monstruo!* I hope you die here!" She almost growled as the guard pulled her away.

Chapter 1

Leonardo

October 17th, 2020

I grabbed the key that hung beside the door and glanced over my shoulder at the kitchen. "*Abuela, ¡me voy!*"

My eighty-two-year-old grandmother popped through the kitchen doorway, wearing her favorite sunflower apron and holding a ladle. Even though wrinkles dominated her face and her once-brown hair had turned white, I could still see the beautiful young woman in the black and white pictures she used to show me when I was a kid.

"Where are you going, Leo?" she asked.

I pocketed the key. The three tiny sixty-four-year-old pompoms from the keychain plopped out. I pushed them in before answering. "Just a little walk, *Abuela*."

"Okay. Don't stay out too long. Dinner will be ready in less than an hour. I'm making *paella de marisco.* Be home on time." The grimace must have shown on my face because she lifted the ladle and pointed it at me. "Now, *hijo*, I know you didn't like it when you were a little boy but you're twenty-nine now. You must eat what is served."

"But, *Abuela*—"

"Mariposa ate a lot of seafood during her pregnancy, so I can't understand why you dislike it."

I chuckled. My mom's craving and my dislike for it had become an inside joke in the family. "*Lo sé.*"

"*Bueno.*" She smiled. "Go take your walk, and don't get lost!"

I chuckled again as I walked out into the cooling Spanish afternoon. The entire village was small enough that you couldn't get lost if you wanted to.

Beniardà was part of the Alicante province, but many Spanish citizens didn't even know it existed. The village was surrounded by tall mountains, and fog just loved to collect here, like steam from a cooking pot. Constant cleaning was a must if one didn't want to see the mold thrive.

My grandparents left this quiet *pueblo* for the busy city of Valencia after getting married, but over sixty years later they moved back to their childhood village. I visited their home often, at their invitation.

"*Te veo,*" I told the street cats, bidding them goodbye and petting one of them as they rushed off to greet Rosetta, a woman in her early seventies carrying their meals. Rosetta was a daughter of a baker. My grandparents say cats had always surrounded her. Now, in her older age, she takes care of the strays, so they ignored everyone else the moment she showed up.

I smiled at her, and she smiled back before telling the cats to calm down. Their meows echoed as I walked past the water fountain with

'1955' in big dark writing etched on it, followed by the *pueblo's* crest and 'Font Vella.' It was one of Beniardà's beautiful spots.

It was 2020, but everything about the village almost looked the same as the photographs in my grandparents' home. Except for the *plaza* and La Penya, a historical landmark in Beniardá. La Penya was a short *paseo* lined with wooden benches and large flowerpots on both sides. It had a panoramic view up to Benimantell and Castillo de Guadalest, and down to the reservoir with its hypnotizing dark-turquoise water.

The road had cobblestones but during my grandparents' youth it was nothing but earth, and not a single bench in sight, so they sat on mounds where the railing now stood. However, the *pueblo* kept its unique charm, transporting me back in time the moment I walked around its small narrow streets and rows of stone houses. It was as if time stood still in this part of Spain.

Not far from me, two kids jumped down from the swing at the playground. It wasn't a bad thing for me, a city boy, to be stuck in this sleepy village. I loved the tranquility the *pueblo* brought compared to the bustle of the big city. It soothed the nerdy part of me—the part addicted to anything 80s, both film and music. I swear, I'm an old soul trapped in modern time. Well, except during the summer festival in late July and early August. They made so much noise. Enough to make me pray for Hell, or for someone to throw rotten eggs at the screaming crowds who partied until dawn.

I kicked a small stone, which tumbled along and clattered off something when it landed at the bottom of the largest group of trees, where lustrous fall leaves covered the ground in beautiful orange and yellow hues.

When I kicked another stone in the same direction, it happened again. This time, I investigated.

Dry leaves rustled beneath my feet as I walked closer—a sound I loved. I cleared the area where the stones landed and clicked my tongue. They had bounced off a bottle buried in the soil between the tree's giant roots. Only the bottom of it was visible, its glass a faded blue, matted with grime from being there for years, if not decades. Something about it piqued my interest. I had nothing else to do anyway, so I looked around. A branch beside the nearby *lavadero,* where the locals did their laundry many years ago, and where the fountain water drained, might be just what I needed.

Yes, this will do.

I grabbed my phone out of my pocket. The charging cable and its wall plug dropped to the ground. After I got stuck in Madrid two years ago with a dead phone, I decided never to leave home without my charger. If I'd had the cable, I could have charged it in my car, but if I'd had the plug, I could have charged it at a gas station before I got lost. Lesson learned: always bring a charger when you travel.

After I snapped a photo of the bottle with my phone camera, I set about excavating it with the branch. At first, I was cautious and gentle but picked up the pace when I noticed a piece of paper inside it. The small bottle had a shape I'd never seen before—slim at the top and bottom and wide in the center. It had a rusty metal cap, which I twisted, but it wouldn't budge. Of course not. It could never be that easy.

A stone wall separated the forest from the *lavadero*, so I brought the bottle over to it, took a deep breath, then slammed it against the wall. A strange sense of relief surged through me as the glass shattered. I wasn't one for adventure when I was younger but something about this piece of paper had me excited. It was the size of my thumb, and slid out onto my palm. I checked the area to ensure the sound of breaking glass hadn't drawn anyone's attention, then focused on my prize.

The letters had faded but were readable. From their elegant strokes, I got the feeling that a woman wrote it:

> *I wish to have someone who understands me and will love me for me.*

The writing had a red smudge under it. A lipstick? The playful side of me immediately kicked in. "Well, sweetheart, too bad I'm the one who found it." I kissed the paper and winced when it sent a static charge through my lips. Then, before I could gather my thoughts and realize how impossible it was for a piece of paper to conduct static electricity, the remains of the bottle glowed in my hand. I let it go, and it smashed on the hard asphalt ground.

I stumbled back, prepared to take off running, when a firm hand pressed my back. Before I could make sense of the situation and turn to see who pushed me, a powerful force dragged me toward the pieces of glass. I fought the pull, with no effect. It was as if gravity had latched onto me, and no amount of struggle against it mattered. A blinding brightness overpowered my sight, and the commanding energy enveloped me, leaving me no choice but be drawn forward, toward the broken bottle, though I couldn't see a thing.

What the hell is happening?

The pull grew stronger, and I felt weightless and pulled in multiple directions at once.

Crap, *Abuela* is going to think I ran away because of the dinner.

Chapter 2
THE WISH

October 6th, 1956

Under the giant tree near Beniardá's *lavadero*, nineteen-year-old Celestina sat with her treasured blue heart bottle. She didn't bother straightening her wild curls like she used to do. Today, she was there to mourn.

The dry, colorful leaves on the ground rustled as she reached into her bag, and the moment her finger touched the edge of the paper, she shifted from the sting that shot through her finger. Drops of red appeared when she pulled her hand away. She'd gotten a paper cut.

She brought her finger to her lips and sucked the blood, her eyes prickling as tears threatened to fall. If only she could explain the hurt in her heart the same as the sting of her finger, she'd feel a lot lighter. If only she had someone who understood her. If only she knew how to make real friends. But, at nineteen, she had learned none of the social skills needed to do so. Unusual, yes, but the situation with her mother didn't help. Her mother, who only knew how to drink, shout, and beat her, had prevented her from speaking or playing with other people since she was seven. Other than her visit to jail last year to see her real father.

In a *pueblo* where everyone knows everyone, no secret stays hidden. Because of this, she couldn't help but wear a mask. Her visit to her biological father was one of her attempts to know more about herself, but just remembering the experience made her sick.

She looked at the paper, tore away the piece with blood on it, and scribbled with tears marring her vision:

> I wish to have someone who understands me
> and will love me for me.

She inserted it and screwed the metal cap in place, then hugged the bottle, whispering her goodbye.

Siesta was almost over, and the last thing she wanted was someone seeing what she was about to do. They were already wary of her, and she didn't wish to make it worse. She looked around and listened for any distant voices. Once sure the area was clear, she lifted the trowel and marked the ground between the big roots of the tree, apologizing and thanking it in her heart.

"You see, Tree, I must protect my bottle. It's the only thing my *papá* left me." She dug into the dirt. "*Mamá* wanted to get rid of it. So, it would be a great honor if you could keep it for me."

The wind blew, with orange and gold leaves dancing their way to the ground. She completed her digging, secured the bottle in the hole, covered it, and offered a small prayer.

It might be laughable if anyone knew but she prayed that her *papá's* words about the bottle being able to grant wishes were true.

After her solo ceremony, she got to her feet and took a deep breath, the wind blowing her wild hair across her face. She threw one more glance at the "grave" of her bottle and gasped when a glowing light came from beneath.

She got down on her knees and dug it up. The paper was gone, and a light swirled inside like someone had trapped it. She looked around again, readied herself for whatever may happen, and unscrewed the cap.

The light poured out like liquid, swirling to the ground.

Chapter 3

LEONARDO

I'd no idea how long after I was sucked into the ground that my consciousness cleared but, when it did, I found myself in the dark. I say dark but, somehow, I could still see, though I couldn't tell if I was looking with my eyes. It was scary how comfortable I felt—despite being bodyless. It was almost like nothing, yet everything at the same time.

Sounds filled my head. Lots of them: people calling my name; a baby's cry; a dog barking. Visuals came, of me as a baby, grabbing a handful of my mother's light-brown hair as she looked down at me. I laughed with her. My half-Filipino father's face switched from stoic to loving as he looks at us. I missed them both so much.

My grandparents didn't speak about them. It's my fault they died. My grandparents never blamed me but I spent my whole life mourning them. I regretted that one moment of carelessness so much, and wished I could rewind time and stop myself from crossing that road. If I could, they would not have sacrificed themselves for me.

A powerful force, equal to when I got sucked in, cut short my trip down memory lane and pulled at me. At least the first experience prepared me, and I was almost excited as my body slid out of the dark. The light came first, followed by physical sensations as my feet touched the ground. For a fraction of a second, I was naked, the chilly wind sprouting goosebumps on my bare skin before my clothes materialized, and the weight of things inside my pockets returned. I inhaled, filling my lungs with fresh Beniardá air, and listened with joy to the chirping of birds and the calming flow of water from Font Vella.

How long was I in there? Why did it feel like forever?

I scanned my surroundings, my gaze stopping on a young woman. She stood with her back to the wall, wore a gray plaid dress, had unruly dark curls, and familiar steel-gray eyes that were wide and full of fear, wonder, and excitement. Then I saw the bottle in her left hand, a replica of the one I smashed, only hers was shiny and new.

Her posture was rigid, and before I could assure her that I meant no harm, she sprinted away from me, her feet pounding up the hill past Font Vella. She cast a single glance over her shoulder as the distance stretched out between us.

"What a strange experience," I said, scratching my head. I pulled out my phone, needing to free it from the rolled cable. Four-thirty-seven in the afternoon. Huh? I was sure the time was five-forty when I stepped out of the house.

Did I accidentally adjust the time backward? I sighed. Too many mysteries. I'd better go home, eat *Abuela's* paella, and sleep this whole thing away.

I walked back without paying much attention to my surrounding but stopped outside my grandfather's house. The flowerpots at the door looked different, and the blue door was now brown. What the...? The wall paint looked new too. I pulled out the key from my pocket and inserted it into the lock. It clicked. I blew a breath of relief, half-expecting it not to work.

"*¿Abuela*?" I called on entering. "How did you guys paint and dry the wall so fast...?" My voice trailed off as I walked down the hallway, my mouth falling open on seeing the framed photos on the walls. All black and white. I didn't recognize anyone in them, except for the young portrait of my grandfather. As my gaze wandered, my body numbed. The house layout was the same but the whole interior was different.

My heart pounded, and I struggled to gain a full breath. I did my best not to panic but the more I saw, the more my bones turning to jelly. When I open the closest room—the bathroom—the shower stall was gone, the mirror was too small, and the large tub had been replaced with a small antique sitting tub.

I closed the door and opened it again, hoping it had been a hallucination, but the tub was still there. It looked like the type used for babies, only larger. I slammed the door and stumbled my way into the living room.

Am I in the wrong house? I recognized some of the furniture but so much had changed. The cozy red sofa had been replaced with a gray and black one, and the glass coffee table was now an opaque wooden one.

I looked up at the framed photos above the rustic wine rack. A strong pang hit my chest at the realization that my parents' photographs were gone. My head spun. When I thought about it, the entire house felt foreign. I couldn't smell the faint floral scent that always lingered in the air. The flowerpots that adorned the corners of the room were not around, and the space smelled like musk and dried plants.

"*¿Abuela?*" I called, whipping around and striding into the kitchen. Another strange room but I no longer cared. My parents' photos were our most-treasured possession. How could they just tuck them away? It didn't make sense. None of this made sense. How could they change and replace so many things in the house in such a short time?

"*¿Abuela?* Where are you?" I searched for her in two more rooms.

Nothing.

I climbed the stairs to the bedrooms, hoping to find them, knocked on their bedroom door and opened it when no one replied. I wished I hadn't. What welcomed me was a mountain of mess. The room had no bed and looked more like a stockroom. My head hurt.

Maybe all this will go away after I lie down for a while.

I stopped outside my bedroom door, confused at the sound of music filtering out. How? I don't have a radio or TV in my room.

The music stopped and a man said, "And now, after so many requests from you folks, here's the new hit: *You Belong To Me*, by Jo Stafford," and with that an oldie from the 50s played.

Did he say 'new'? I almost laughed, except I couldn't feel the muscles of my mouth. I couldn't feel my body.

A woman's silky voice filtered out next, paired with a light clicking of heels. I groaned, tired of surprises. "What now?"

I opened the door, ready to see anything, but froze when I found a young girl wearing a tight top and a knee-length floral skirt dancing with my shirt.

I sighed. Resigned. "*¿Quién eres?*"

She stiffened, then threw the shirt on the bed and smoothed it out without looking at me. "I was folding your clothes. You're paying me to clean your house and take care of the laundry. So, that's what I'm doing." Her hands moved so fast as she folded the shirt, set it aside, and grabbed a new one from the basket at the foot of the bed. "You got back early. I thought you would be at Font Vella with your friends after work?"

I stayed quiet, wondering what I should do. A young woman was in my room, talking about things I had no idea about. Paying her to care for *my house*?

"Who are you?" I repeated. "And what are you doing here?"

She stopped folding the laundry and laughed, though her voice quivered. Then she turned the radio off and faced me. She was beautiful, her skin smooth with olive undertones that glowed against the warm beige of the walls. Thick lashes accented her large almond eyes, and her heart-shaped face was framed by cascading waves of rich brown hair. She looked like a living poster from the 50s, and also looked a bit like my mother, especially when she raised a reprimanding finger at me.

"Now, Alonso, I know I may have overstepped my boundaries and cooked you a meal, too, but you should be thankful! Look at my generosity with kindness. Don't treat me like a stranger."

As I listened, observing her movements, my body stiffened, then weakened as I realized who the stranger was. "*¿Abuela?*"

She gasped and put a hand to her chest, so hard I heard a thud. "*¿Abuela?* I'm only nineteen. You should know better than to call a young woman your grandmother." She stared at me for a long moment. "Why are you asking who I am?"

"I need to know. *¿Eres, Maria Isabela?*"

"*Si, soy* Maria Isabela Jurado Portes. You know that."

But Maria Isabela Jurado Portes was my grandmother's full name before marrying *Abuelo*. What the hell? And before I knew it, the words slip out of my mouth: "What in the devil?"

Chapter 4

THE STRANGER

Isabela clenched her fists as she listened to Alonso's words. An uncomfortable tightness formed in her chest. It offended her when he addressed her as "*Abuela*." He had been calling her "*Bella*" lately instead of Isabela or Isa, which everyone else preferred because there was just too many Marias in the village. Still, for a long time before that, ever since the first time she'd plucked up the courage to approach him, he'd called her "kid." Well, he'd been sixteen when she was nine but was the only one in his group who called her that. Now, she was done with school and sometimes helped on the farm. She was an adult. However, *kid* still sounds better than *Abuela*.

Am I behaving like an old woman?

She looked down at herself, then back up again. "Alonso, more than calling me *Abuela*, I hate that you're breaking your promise!"

His frown deepened. "Promise?"

"Yes. Your gift for my nineteenth birthday is a promise that you won't curse. At least not in front of me."

"Look, *Abuela*, it's nice of you to show up in my dream but calling me by *Abuelo*'s name—"

"I ask you again, who are you calling '*Abuela*?' I'm nineteen!" Tears welled up and she blinked them away. "*¿Qué te pasa?*" she asked, her voice shriller than she'd intended.

"What? There's nothing wrong with me." He touched his forehead. "But I must have hit my head hard without knowing it. Or the strange experience at Font Vella is making me dream crazy things."

She stared at him, worried. "What happened in Font Vella?"

He shook his head, as if to empty it. "Not important. Now, get out of my room." He stepped closer and grabbed her shoulder. It was then she noticed, though the man looked like Alonso, this wasn't him. He was taller, his hair lighter and longer. This man was disheveled and a few years older than *her* Alonso. Something about him seemed out of place.

She swiped his hand away and stepped back, looking him up and down. What a sloppy man, with his shirt sticking out of his jacket. And his hair looks as if it has never been combed. How odd. Everyone carries a comb these days.

"*¿Quién es usted?*" she asked, keeping her tone more polite than his had been.

He gave her a lopsided smile, and that made him look so much like *her* Alonso. "My name is Leonardo, and, as I told you, *Abuela*, I am your grandson."

She balled her hands into fists, her blood pumping like never before. "You can't be my grandson! I'm not your *Abuela*. I'm not even married yet. One more time and I'm going to—"

"*Si, si, si.* Now, *por favor,* get out." He grabbed her by the shoulders again and shoved her toward the door, her heels scraping the stone floor as she pushed back, with no effect because he was so strong. "This has to be the most realistic dream I've ever had," he said.

She looked back over her shoulder. "That's because you are not dreaming. You are in the wrong house!"

He laughed. She whirled around and sidestepped her way back into the room, grabbing a hanger to protect herself. She'd no idea who this Alonso look-alike was but she wouldn't let him do what he wanted in Alonso's home. It would be her home one day, and she couldn't allow some crazy person, possibly a drug addict, to stay and ruin it.

When he tried to grab her wrist, she turned away and swung as hard as she could with the hanger. He jumped back but not fast enough, its tip scraping his cheek. That left him looking stunned. He reached for his face, the action slow, and stared at his bloodstained fingers. His whole body stiffened and he looked at her with horror. The stranger looked hurt, as if she had betrayed him.

Guilt gnawed inside her, and "*discúlpame*" hung on the tip of her tongue, but she banished it and scolded herself. She was not obliged to apologize. Not when she was defending her future home.

She held the hanger tight, aware that she was trembling, doing her best to prepare for what he might do after she'd hurt him. Her mouth was dry and her throat tightened as she took a deep breath. Even with the fear, and her heart thundering, she kept her chin up and her gaze level. She could not let him see how terrified she was. "If you don't want more of that, get out of Alonso's house!" She lifted the hanger and lunged at him.

"Wait, *Abuela*!" he cried, raising both hands in surrender, but she would have none of it. The word *Abuela* wouldn't let her. This was personal now.

"I will not let a trespasser do what he wants when I'm around!" She stepped forward, brandishing the hanger in wild swipes. He stumbled back, and she chased him as he ran out of the room and down the stairs.

But then he stopped at the bottom and grabbed her wrist. "Okay, okay, I'm sorry for calling you '*Abuela*,' but you look like her. At least, when she was younger."

He let go and stepped back, keeping both palms facing her. She looked him over and lowered the hanger. He didn't seem dangerous at all. "I already introduced myself. You must know your grandmother's name, no?"

A wry smile dimpled his cheeks. "Her birth name is Maria Isabela Jurado Portes. But everyone calls her Isa."

Heat flushed into her face and she lifted the hanger again. He stepped back through the hallway, covering his face with one hand.

"I don't know what's going on. I thought this was a dream, but I'm telling you the truth. And I live in this house!"

He lowered his hand and fumbled in his pocket, which was when she whacked him across the head, thinking he might be reaching for a knife.

She backed away but stopped when he pulled out a key. The key to the house, with three tiny pompoms.

"This is my home, too, *Abuela*."

She walked up to him, her steps tentative, and took the key, then felt around her skirt pocket and chuckled. "Nice try. I don't know how you did it but you stole it from my pocket." She dropped the key into her skirt pocket and pointed at the door. "Out."

He looked lost. "*Abuela, por favor créeme.* Please, believe me."

The loving way he said "*Abuela*" warmed her heart. He sounded desperate but his words came with real affection. If she were an old woman, she would be glad to have him as her grandchild. She groaned inside, feeling bad for this confused man. Instead of whacking him again, she put the hanger down on the table and gave him a gentle shove.

"I'm really sorry, Leonardo, but you can't be here. This isn't even my house."

"What the hell is going on?" he whispered, letting her push him out.

She wondered, too, but a stranger inside Alonso's house with her would create so much misunderstanding, which she'd rather avoid.

Once he was out of the house, she watched him walk down the path, his pace slow, his head low as he shook it. He seemed confused about where to go, so she called out to him and waited for him to turn around.

"If you have no place to stay, go to the church. They might help you. Tomorrow, you can try dropping by the *ayuntamiento*." She pointed at the narrow street toward the government office. "Keep going that way."

With a downcast look, he gave her a nod and went on. With that, she shook her head and ignored the guilt tapping at her heart. She closed the door and pulled the key from her pocket. The three yarn pompoms—one blue and two red—danced after she shook the ring.

She'd made it the same day Alonso entrusted her with his spare key after her birthday three months ago. There were no others like the ones she held.

"Hmph, he thinks he can fool me by showing the key?" She laughed but froze when she noticed an identical keychain with pompoms hanging at the mounted key holder beside the door. "*¿Que?*"

ﾉ̀

Isabela's voice had sent Celestina hiding around the corner of Alonso's house. She was a socially awkward person, and tailing someone through the narrow streets of the *centro* was unlike her. However, she felt like she had to do it, because while she'd been terrified when the man came out of her bottle, her curiosity got the better of her.

Is he really a man? He can't be human. Maybe he's a ghost? Or from another world? She remembered what her *papá* had said before he left: "*Celest, this is a magical bottle. It will make you travel to places you want the most and make your dreams come true.*"

She looked in the direction the man went after Isabela had pushed him out. He'd used a key to enter Alonso's house, or did he use magic?

With all she'd seen up to now, he had to be a genie. Yes, her genie in the bottle.

Maybe he can grant my wishes?

She paced around and took a couple of deep breaths, then steadied herself, becoming determined.

He is my genie, so he must grant me at least three wishes.

With tentative steps, she moved out of her hiding spot and turned toward the street leading to the church. She needed him to come with her. The question was, how to do it without scaring him, or, better yet, where was she going to get the courage to ask him before he vanished again?

Would he be far ahead now? She hurried down the street to the center of an intersection, where the road forked to different alleys. He could have taken any of them, or entered the church. She paced back and forth in front of the building, her short heels echoing louder than usual on the cobblestones as she tried to decide where to turn first. Her heart took a flip when she saw him up ahead. He looked dejected, moving away from the church as he walked up the hill.

When she took a step to follow him, her bottle held to her chest, all she heard was "Leonardo!" before someone ran into her from behind. The two of them tumbled to the ground, the person's protective hand around her as they rolled. The air was pushed out of her when she ended up on her back, under her assailant. A woman.

"*Perdón, ¡discúlpame*!" the woman said. "I was in a hurry and couldn't stop myself in time. *¿Estás bien*?"

When the woman sprang up, Celestina saw that it was Isabela. She looked at her outstretched hand before noticing the stain on her leg. "B-blood," she said.

Isabela followed her gaze to a long scratch on her knee. She laughed. "Oh. *¡Que fiasco!* But what about you? Are you—"

Celestina jumped to her feet and strode away, scanning the hill for her genie.

"*¡Espera!* Celestina, wait!"

She didn't, sprinting off instead, her eyes stinging from tears of annoyance. It was the first time she'd spoke to Isabela, who was as wonderful as she'd imagined. How embarrassing, though. Isabela was the friendly girl next door, who everyone liked, while she was the strange girl from the edge of Beniardá, with no close neighbors, no friends, and locked up most days. Her mother forbade her from going to church, but fearing a stronger punishment would befall her, she snuck out on Sundays and attended mass. Everyone stayed away from her, except the priest, who was always kind.

Determined to change her situation, she hugged her heart bottle tight to her chest as she ran. Every story she'd read about genies, they always gave three wishes, and she knew what she was going to ask from her genie.

One: the ability to socialize comfortably and finally make friends.

Two: since she couldn't wish for someone to love her, she would ask for her mother's happiness.

Maybe if *Mamá* was happy, she would stop her cruelty towards me.

The third she hadn't decided but knew it would come to her in time.

Chapter 5

LEONARDO

Confused didn't come close to how I was feeling, with my thoughts all jumbled. My brain was numbed. Reality felt unreal. At this time, nightmares seemed preferable.

At first, I convinced myself I was experiencing a hyper-realistic dream, but I'm realizing now that I was wrong. It wasn't just my grandparents' house that had changed—the entire village was different: the color of houses; how changed the streets were; and some homes were not even built yet.

The La Penya beside *Abuelo's* house didn't have cobblestones.

How could I have missed that?

Abuela's thrashing forced me to accept reality. What choice did I have? This wasn't a dream—it was real.

I took my smartphone out of my jacket pocket and unlocked the screen. No network connection.

When I reached another intersection, nature called. One road led into an area of Beniardá I've never been before and another went toward Font Vella. I tucked away my phone and stood in front of some bushes, opened my fly, and released the pressure with a contented sigh.

A gasp nearby almost made me wet myself. I zipped up as fast as I could, looked around, and saw a girl retreating. That girl. I recognized the gray plaid dress, and her dark curls fluffing in the air as she hurried off. She was the one who ran from me after that weird bottle experience. The girl who reminded me so much of someone, but I couldn't put my finger on it.

I thought about following her but decided against it, needing to solve a more pressing matter: being trapped in this crazy world. The sky was cloudless, and though the sun had set and the streetlights were lit, it wasn't dark yet. What to do? My head was blank. I'd never been the thinking type, always preferring to go with the flow; it was my way of coping with problems. I worked in a travel agency, and only needed to do what I'm good at—socializing. But I had a feeling I needed to use my brain this time.

"Argh! What a pain." I shoved my hands into my pockets.

"You should wash your hand first!" a woman said, her voice shaky.

She stood about twenty feet away from me. A cold feeling washed over me. It was her. There's no way I wouldn't recognize the woman I'd been obsessed with as a young boy. I didn't earlier, but I'm sure of it now. The girl in the black-and-white photo with my grandmother now stood in front of me—in full color. The beautiful girl I secretly nickname Purrball. My first crush.

"Celestina?"

Her skin lost its color as I moved toward her, and her breathing became shallow. Yet she stood tall and still.

"How...do you know my name?"

"You're Celestina De La Mota, correct?" I took one more step, approaching her as I would a stray cat.

She opened her mouth, gripping the odd-shaped bottle so tight it looked like it would break. I was six feet away from her when her face turned bright red. When I took another step forward, she stiffened. On my next step, she took two steps back.

"It's okay. I only want to talk for a bit." One more step. "That bottle—"

She didn't wait for me to finish. As she spun around and ran from me, her heels made sharp, clicking noises on the ground. I sighed. Enough, I won't play her game again.

I walked back toward Font Vella. Maybe if I lingered there long enough, this crazy experience would end and I'd return to my normal life, leaving this strange, indescribable situation behind.

As I approached another intersection, a group of giggling girls walked by. They were laughing at me. I turned and looked after them. All three wore dresses, their skirts full, with belts that accentuated their small waists. Different but similar to what Celestina wore.

"Is it a costume day?" I remembered that the girl who looked like *Abuela* also wore a similar style. The kind I saw in old films or videos set in the past. "Yeah, maybe this is some Beniardá event I'm not aware of." But then another group of young girls, dressed in tight tops and swing skirts, walked by.

One of them looked like a younger version of Rosetta. She was about eleven years old, with freckles and fiery red hair. She stopped and offered a snack to a cat lazing above the stone wall.

"Rosetta!" her group called out, and an icy feeling trailed down my back.

What the hell is going on? How could Celestina, Rosetta, and my *Abuela* be so young? I walked faster to the fountain, drank the refreshing spring water and washed my face. I couldn't handle this anymore. It was too much. Even at home, I never watched mystery films or shows because I hated being forced to think so hard.

"What kind of costume is that?" a man asked, followed by a couple of laughs.

I lifted my head and looked around. Eight guys with a variation of swept-back hair looked at me. They sat on the side of the fountain, smoking and grinning like I was some sort of clown, except they were the ones looking like they stepped out of a 1950's film set.

"*Shh, es un turista,*" another said, laughing with everyone.

I stared at them, dumbfounded. They just called me a tourist. Me? Then, *bang!* Like a bullet to my brain, I realized I'd not seen familiar faces around yet, other than the two young women from an old photograph and the young-looking Rosetta. Everyone else I'd encountered were strangers.

Impossible.

I scanned the faces of the men in front of me and stopped, open-mouthed, at another familiar face—again from the photo.

"*Abuelo?*" I blurted out, prompting everyone to burst out laughing. They pushed each other and slapped their legs, then turned to the man I'd just spoken to.

"You look too old for your age. *El chico turista* mistakes you for his grandfather!"

More laughter, more shoving and teasing.

One man stood up and laid an elbow on my shoulder. I moved away and bumped into the man who looked like my *Abuelo*. Unlike when I called the woman back in the house *Abuela,* this one's reaction felt menacing. Even with the chilly wind, sweat prickled my skin under three layers of clothing.

The man inched closer, and despite being taller than him, I felt intimidated. I took a deep breath.

"*Mira*, I didn't mean to call you my grandfather, okay? I've been having the strangest last few hours. The only reason I blurted out '*Abuelo*' is because you look so much like my grandfather when he was younger."

The man just stared at me, and I swallowed hard, my heart thundering. His hard expression and aggressive demeanor reminded me more of a gangster than a young man hanging out with his friends.

"Look, I'm sure you know about him." Everyone knows my grandfather—a bad-boy farmer in his youth. Beniardá's own James Dean, according to my grandmother's stories. "His name is Alonso Suarez Barros."

I expected him to nod and relax, but my comment made things worse, and he looked like he really wanted my head off my shoulders. His friends, laughing earlier, now stood and surrounded me, no longer smiling.

I'm not a small guy, and I was confident I could fight a couple of these guys, but with eight of them, I was sure I'd be cleaning the ground with my blood. I waved my hands, desperate to make him understand. "I'm not looking for trouble." I looked at his friends, then back at him. "I'm telling you the truth. You must know Alonso, right?"

"*Soy yo.* You're facing him," he said, speaking for the first time.

¡Mierda!

Amid my confusion and attempt to calm everyone, someone grabbed my arms from the back.

"Don't hurt him! *Por favor,*" a woman said as I turned to defend myself. Celestina? Purrball. I thought I was being attacked.

"He's my distant relative, coming to visit," she said.

What? My grandparents are the only relatives I have left.

She kept her grip on my arms, so I leaned closer to ensure only she would hear me. "Are you trying to help me or stop me from defending myself?"

Her grip tightened. "Don't move," she whispered. "You mustn't use your magic on anyone in the village."

"What?"

Her eyes widened, pleading. "Shh!"

Magic? What the hell is she talking about? Do I look like a wizard to her?

They all looked at each other, then at her.

"Celestina, let me go."

She let go and stared at me, still wide-eyed. "You really know who I am?"

"You just said he's a distant relative, coming to visit," one guy said.

"Right, of course." She forced a laugh before straightening, then hooked her arms on mine.

Wow, she was good at hiding her fear. I smiled. I'd never encountered anyone this...amusing. She was an adult, but her reactions were that of a girl.

Abuela said Celestina was mysterious, feared, and admired. To me, she seemed more like a street cat, wary and curious. Her fearful eyes were always alert, her body positioned like she was ready to flee at any given moment. *Abuela* was right about her being special, though. Thanks to her intervention, I doubted these guys would beat me, which eased my anxiety. They'd been fooling around earlier. I'm sure I could persuade them to let everything slide.

I cleared my throat to speak but another one of Alonso's friends stepped over to him.

"Guys, don't you think *El Chico Turista* and Alonso look related?"

Everyone gave the two of us a weird look, and all responded with slow nods. The cheeriest of the group punched his open hand, then pointed at Alonso and me. "You're right! They could be brothers. Same face, eyes, nose, skin tone."

More nods. Their hostility towards me seems to have vanished.

"Except *el turista* is taller," another added, "and seems to have woken from a nightmare."

More nods and laughter.

Celestina gripped me tighter.

If they only knew how much of a nightmare I was in. *Abuela* used to tell me that, after I reached puberty, I looked like my grandfather. I always gave her a smile and joked about it but never put much thought into it.

But coming face to face with him, my *abuela*, and now Celestina, forced me to think that maybe the impossible had happened. Did I really travel into the past? The thought of it sent a shockwave through me. Oh god, how do I go back?

My brain hurt from thinking too much, and my heart thundered, my chest tightening to the extent I suspected I was going to faint. At this point, I was glad Celestina was holding my arm.

Chapter 6

THE NEWCOMER

Alonso studied the stranger in front of him. His friends were right, the man looked a lot like him. However, no matter how similar they were, he and this stranger couldn't be related. He was an only child of his deceased parents, who were born and had died in the village. And everyone knew how loyal they were to each other. Even if he'd been unaware that infidelity was going on between his parents, the village would have caught it. He was certain he had no half-siblings. His mother was also an only child, and his father's sister had two children—and this stranger wasn't one of them.

As he observed the man whispering with Celestina, he couldn't deny the similarity, and how strange it felt. But he had no reason to doubt the girl, who barely stepped out of her house. When she did, it was to go to mass. She and her shut-in of a mother never associated with anyone, making them both infamous and somehow feared by the village folk. For Celestina to run to Font Vella from her isolated home, that said a lot.

The two couldn't seem to agree on whatever they were discussing. Celestina caught him off guard when she turned to him, reached for his collar, and pulled him down. No other girl besides Isabela dared to touch him. She looked at him for a long moment, then whispered, "He's my genie. I need him to grant my wishes."

His neck went cold. "Genie?"

She nodded. "He came out of my favorite bottle."

This time, he nodded back, amused. Celestina was about nineteen, but unlike Isabela—who openly pursued him, like a woman—she was a little girl inside. Pity bubbled up within him. *It's probably because her mother keeps her locked up in their house and won't let her mature.*

Okay, let's play along with her game. He looked at his friends. "*Me voy.*" Then he walked away.

"*¿Que?*" the twins, Arturo and Adalberto, said in unison. They looked at each other and grinned, like it was a joke only the two of them seemed to get.

Juan Martin, who had snuck behind Celestina and the stranger, stopped to look at him. "You're going where?"

"With them," Alonso replied, gesturing with his thumb. He turned to Celestina. "*Está bien, ¿sí*?"

She nodded. "Of course, it's okay." Then she muttered something to the stranger and dragged him away from the group, a little too eager.

"Are we that scary?" he asked. Celestina tensed up and shook her head.

"She's scared of everyone," the stranger said.

He chuckled. "Done muttering now that a girl saved you?"

"Don't provoke him!" Celestina said. She pushed him away until his back was against a wall. "I told you, he's a genie! I saved you and your group because I don't know what kind of magic he's capable of."

He looked at the man, who seemed put off at the sight of him. Or was it because he'd spoken to Celestina? He put an arm around her and the heat in the guy's eyes intensified. Interesting. She seemed to have turned to stone, so he let go of her. "Does your genie know you're the master?"

A tint of red colored her cheek. "Of course he does!"

"Okay. So, what do you plan to do? You obviously can't bring him home. I doubt your mother will welcome him."

Her mouth opened, and she looked at him, like she had only thought of it. It surprised him how easy she was to read. He might be bad-tempered but everyone feared Celestina more than him. From his point of view now, however, she was nothing more than an ordinary girl.

"What are you going to do?" he asked. "Anything I can help you with?"

"Yes, come with us to get the bottle."

"Huh?"

"The bottle he came from. I'll ask him to get back in there so I can bring him home."

He snorted but stopped himself from laughing. Things were about to get interesting. He wanted to see the stranger's reaction when she asked him.

When she went back and spoke with him, Alonso followed her and extended his hand. "I can't call you, '*El Turista,*' like my friends. I'm Alonso."

"Leonardo."

They shook hands, the man's grip tight. He squeezed back, and Leonardo did too. In the end, both sets of knuckles were white until Celestina grabbed his wrist. Next moment, Isabela jumped around a corner beside them and grabbed Leonardo's hand.

"I need to talk to you."

Alonso zoned in on Leonardo's wrist. He wanted to break the part Isabela held and bring her home with him. She turned to him. "That's fine for the both of you, right? I only need to speak to him privately for a short time."

He gave a casual nod. Celestina did the same but in a more enthusiastic way.

"I have to get my bottle," she said. "I left it over there!" She pointed in the general direction of a small *nispero* garden down the hill to Font Vella.

She left without another word. He had a feeling he would soon behave like a madman if he stayed, so he touched Isabela's arm. "I'll go look for it with her."

Celestina picked up the heart bottle from under one of the *nispero* trees.

"Is that *the* bottle?"

She stiffened on hearing Alonso, just above her head, leaning so close his heat was on her back.

"*Si*. It is." She straightened and took a few steps away before meeting his gaze. He was as scary as the rumors said and just as handsome. Now she had somehow grown used to his presence, and could look him in the face, she saw what everyone else did: he and Leonardo looked alike, but that was where the resemblance ended. Even though she didn't know either of them, the short time she had observed them was enough to define how different they were. Alonso was prickly—he put people on edge. One would feel the need to handle him with care. A sharp blade who would cut you if you touched him the wrong way. While Leonardo...

Oh, Leonardo... She hugged her bottle. Leonardo was like the wind. Gentle, approachable, easy-going. She grimaced. Because of his carefree attitude, she didn't seem to know how to get a hold of him. *I must make him return to the bottle before he escapes.*

"Should we get back now?" Alonso asked. The earlier amusement in his eyes had vanished as he craned his neck to look back the way they'd come.

"Are you worried because Isabela is alone with Leonardo?"

"No. I need to get home. Bella has the key." He walked up the hill before her, and she wondered if he truly wasn't aware that he'd been playing with the key in his hand this whole time.

She knew how much Isabela liked him, having declared it in front of the girls in school when they were thirteen. But, right now, she was probably the only one who was aware that Beniardá's bad boy was jealous of the newcomer.

"Leonardo is my genie. He won't care about Isabela."

Alonso continued striding ahead, and she let him go.

The moment Celestina and Alonso were out of view, Isabela lifted the key she took from Leonardo. He looked at it but didn't take it back. She liked him even more. "Who gave this to you?"

"Didn't you say that I stole it from you?" he asked, smiling.

"Just answer my question."

"You won't like the answer."

She stomped her foot. "*¡Respóndeme!*" she demanded, shaking the keychain.

"My grandmother."

"Did she tell you why she made it?"

"Yes."

Her legs trembled. "Why?"

Leonardo leaned on the wall behind him and pushed his hand into his pocket. "Why do you want to know?"

Instead of answering, she took out her keys. "I made this. And I don't remember making two sets."

"No way!" he exclaimed. His face lit up with excitement, then fell. "No way," he repeated, now dejected. "I can't believe I really time traveled."

She stared at him. "You what?"

"I'm from the future," he said, now looking at her as if he'd known her all his life. "I suspected it, but I kept shoving it aside. Then I met *Abuelo* and Celestina, and now, thanks to that,"—he nodded at the keychains— "it's finally confirmed." He lowered his gaze. Even though nothing of what he said made sense, she reached out and rubbed his head. He looked up and pulled her into an embrace. "*Abuela,* what am I going to do? I'm sure you're so worried about me by now."

"I'm not!" she shrieked, pushing against him, but he was too strong. She cleared her throat. "Let go of—"

"Let go of her!" Alonso's roar could have woken the dead and forced the living to play dead if they saw his vicious expression.

Leonardo set her free and mumbled an apology. "I was referring to the future you," he said, but his words didn't matter to her. Alonso might commit his first murder if she didn't do something.

She smiled and walked up to him, blocking his path. "Leonardo only confused me with someone else."

His gaze fell on her. *"¿Tu tambien?"*

"*¿Que?* What do you mean with '*you too*'?"

He didn't reply and now looked at Leonardo, who walked after her. Run away. *¡Idiota!*

"Stay there!" she commanded, looking over her shoulder and using her whole body to stop Alonso from attacking. "Alonso, why are you angry?"

He stood still, and seemed to be searching for an answer himself. It was then Celestina passed them and went straight to Leonardo, panting.

"Hurry and get in!" she cried, holding out the bottle to him.

The look of confusion on his face was priceless. He gazed at her with unblinking eyes before pointing at the bottle's tiny opening. Celestina nodded. Isabela felt Alonso vibrating. He was looking at Celestina with a smile, controlling his laughter.

"Get inside," Celestina said.

"Yeah, get in, Leonardo." Alonso erupted into laughter.

Isabela found nothing funny. She had spent so much time observing Alonso since childhood, noting how he was often angry, but Celestina turned his anger to laughter in seconds. "What's so funny?" she asked.

"Just watch." He put an arm around her shoulder, a gesture he had never made before. And, just like that, her jealousy melted away. She leaned on him and watched.

"Inside?" Leonardo said.

Celestina nodded.

"The bottle?"

Celestina nodded again.

"How?"

"Use your magic!"

Leonardo leaned closer to Celestina. "What magic?"

"I don't know. You're the genie here."

"A genie? Me?" He rubbed his disheveled hair, making it even messier. "And I thought I was confused when I got here. You need help."

"Yes, I do! And you're going to make it happen with your magic."

"Look, Celestina, I don't know why you think I can do magic, but the only piece of me that can fit in that bottle is my thumb!" He reached for the bottle but Celestina pulled away without letting him touch it.

She stomped her foot. "I saw you come out of the bottle!"

"Huh?"

"I did! Now, get in. We have to talk in my room."

"I can't, you crazed Purrball."

"Purrball?" Alonso echoed in a trembling voice, laughing out loud. This time Isabela joined him. The whole thing was funny.

"I'm telling the truth!" Celestina said. She marched toward them and stomped on Alonso's foot. He jumped back and crouched, groaning.

Isabela covered her mouth, thinking Alonso sort of deserved it.

"I saw it," Celestina said. She glanced back at Leonardo before sprinting down the road, no doubt heading for her house.

Isabela looked at the puzzled Leonardo. "You don't have a place to stay, do you?" He shook his head. "Then come with me."

Alonso shot up. "*¿Porqué?*"

She left his side and walked toward home, waving for Leonardo to follow her. "*Vamonos,* Leonardo."

"Bella, *espérate—* "

"See you later, Al!" she said without looking back, failing to bite back a smile, and loving his reaction.

Chapter 7

FAMILIAR STRANGER

The white stone walls and gray roof of Celestina's house were like any other home, except that hers had an unfriendly air. It kept people away. Made them uncomfortable. Unwelcome.

She held her breath as she twisted the backdoor knob. It was unlocked, just as she'd left it. She hated going out without her mother's knowledge but, this time, she had no choice.

Earlier that day, during the *siesta,* her mother arrived drunk and barged into her room. It was *Papá's* death anniversary, and because of that, she'd forgot to lock her door. Her mother's expression soured at the sight of her crying over the heart bottle her *papá* had gifted to her a short time before dying twelve years ago.

"Haven't I told you, I don't want to see anything from that man?" her mother slurred as she snatched the bottle from her.

She pulled it back, enraged, and her mother grabbed a broom and struck the back of her leg. The pain sent her to her knees but she hugged the bottle, determined to protect it with her life. She expected a second hit but it didn't reach her. What came instead was the sound of her mother snoring on her bed.

For years, she had no idea why her mother hated her *papá* so much. She'd burned every memory and photograph of him. And, thanks to that, there was nothing left of him other than the bottle.

She remembered *Papá* sitting beside her at night, telling her stories of his adventures, about parallel universes, and time travel, and about meeting her mother in another lifetime. Those versions of her mother were something she wished to see—happy and loving.

His stories are what she clung to when he would vanish without notice, only to reappear a few weeks later with more stories to tell. She loved him so much. He made her feel important. Her mother fed her, dressed her, and gave her a roof over her head, but never made her feel loved. *Papá* was her protector. Whenever her mother beat her, starved her out of anger, and verbally abused her, her father was there to comfort her and keep her safe.

Still, the verbal abuse was the worst. Words left the deepest scar in her heart. *Papá*, however, made everything better. Then, one day, after going missing for two weeks, he materialized in the center of the living room, looking much older and with a gunshot wound in his stomach.

"Papá, ¿qué pasó?" she said, tears streaming down her cheeks. She was seven years old, and though she didn't know how terrible the situation was, she knew it was bad. He was drenched in blood and pale as a sheet. "I'll go call for help," she said, with no intention of calling her mother from the farm. She would not be much help. The woman always shouted at her *papá* whenever he was around, and never failed to remind her how useless she was, just like him.

She turned to go but he grabbed her wrist and placed the heart bottle in her hand. "Celest,"—*Papá* was the only person who called her that— "Celest, this is a magical bottle. It will allow you to travel to places you want the most and make your dreams come true."

A moment she would never forget. So long ago now. She sighed and took her mind back to today's events, remembering the bewildered look on Leonardo's face. He came out of the bottle. She saw it. But it didn't mean he knew it. Or maybe she was so desperate to hang on to *Papá's* words that she actually imagined the whole thing?

Logically speaking, it would be impossible for a man to fit in the bottle, but she'd seen her *papá* magically appeared. The stories he told her couldn't only be for entertainment.

She shook her head. Her *papá* wouldn't lie.

He really jumped through time and visit parallel worlds. He'd vanished right after giving her the bottle and a letter for her mother. She placed her open hand over her heart—the pain never went away. No matter how many times she tried to forget his words, they still rushed back to her:

"Celest, I will be honest with you because this might be the last time you see me. I'm not your real father." Her seven-year-old mind couldn't grasp much of what he was trying to say back then, but he went on, saying that her real father did something horrible to her mom. He told her he'd paid her mom to go along with the lie so he could take the role as her father. *"And, most importantly, I did it because I love you. Te quiero, mi niña."*

For years, she'd wondered what he meant. The man she knew as *Papá* was someone who only looked like her biological father—the man living in prison.

That man had the same name, the same face, but was a stranger. A man who sneered like a maniac when she'd introduced herself as his daughter. A stranger who wanted to "have fun" with her.

How dare he tarnish the memory of her *papá*. She wanted to claw his face until he was beyond recognition. Punch his neck to make him sound different from her beloved *papá*. She'd stepped out of that place broken but determined to earn her mother's love. However, nothing she did changed anything.

She dropped onto her bed and hugged the bottle. "*Echo de menos, Papá*. I miss you."

Celestina peeked out of her room at eight-thirty p.m., sure her mom was already in bed.

Her bottle needed to be hidden in a place it was less likely to be found. Under the mattress was too obvious. In her closet was no good. Nowhere in her room was safe. The kitchen. She remembered the large flowerpot with fake fabric flowers her mother had made. Handcrafts were one thing she'd inherited from her.

She tiptoed to the kitchen and sighed upon seeing the leftovers from what she'd prepared earlier still on the table. Ever since she'd learned to cook when she was eight—thanks to old recipe books belonging to her *Papá*—her mother stopped making food for the both of them. Although her mother was still cold toward her after visiting the prison, she'd stopped being so angry when sober, which was a welcome change.

Confident she was alone, she lifted the fabric flowers and placing the bottle at the bottom of the pot. She then brought the leftovers back to her room with a glass of water, ate in silence, and went to bed with a smile.

"*Papá*, I found someone. He came out of the bottle. Tomorrow, I'll speak to Mamá to let her know that I'll go to the *centro* from now on. I want to see him again," she said before drifting off to sleep.

"We're here," Isabela told Leonardo, motioning to her front door. Noises filtered out, of plates and cutlery as her mother got dinner ready, her father's laughter from whatever book he was reading, Jorge's stomping feet as he ran around, and Rodrigo snapping at their younger brother.

But Leonardo didn't seem to pay attention to it—he only looked back, and she could guess where.

"You live close to each other?" he asked.

She smiled. "Yeah." Alonso lived three houses up across the road. From her bedroom window, she saw him go out each morning and return from work each afternoon. She fell in love with him when he was eighteen, admiring the hardworking boy who nearly dropped from exhaustion after working in the field all day. All she wanted was to make him feel better, and she often brought meals for him. Her mother, who pitied him for losing his father to cancer, and his mother a short time later in a car accident, let her deliver the food. They called her feelings "puppy love." But here she was, eight years later. She had the same desire to be by his side—stronger than ever—because now she wanted to be with him forever.

"You didn't tell me that in the future," Leonardo said, his voice soft. It seemed more to himself than her.

Observing him this close made her wonder why she felt safe being with him, despite knowing him for less than half a day. She didn't even know his full name yet.

Hmm, why? She looked at him from top to bottom and wondered if she might have the same feelings for him as she had for Alonso. Her stomach churned the moment the idea entered her mind. Can it be true that he's from the future?

She put her hand in her pocket and felt the two keychains. It was hard to believe, but him coming from the future seemed plausible. She held the keychains tight and sat on the doorstep. Their keys were the same. That itself would be impossible—unless she'd given them to him. And she'd never do that. Unless they somehow knew each other—in the future.

"Leonardo." She tapped the step when he looked at her. He sat beside her, like an obedient boy, and she nearly reached up to ruffle his hair. It was a thing she did whenever Jorge was acting cute. But Leonardo was a man older than her. Yet she couldn't stop looking on him like a boy. She didn't even feel uncomfortable when they squeezed close together. It was crazy. She needed to solve this mystery before it drove her insane.

"¿Abuela?"

"¿Si?"

Ugh. She hated how she responded without thinking, as if it was the most natural thing to be called Grandmother.

"What year is it?"

She laughed. "It's 1956! Don't tell me... You want to ask about the month next?"

"Yes, what month are we in?"

October, she almost replied but held herself from voicing it out. "Are you serious?"

He rested his elbows on his knees and gripped his head. "I really did time travel."

She exhaled. It was too crazy to believe what he'd said but she couldn't ignore his distress. And the keychains.

"Leo, about the keys—"

He perked up and looked at her with excitement.

"What?" she asked, leaning away.

"*Abuela* always calls me that, or *hijo*."

She sighed. It was the most natural nickname for his name, and it was pretty common for older relatives to call the younger boys *hijo*, especially parents. She let it slide. They'd get nowhere if she let him take the lead in their conversations.

"Let's say that your grandmother gave you the keychain—"

"She did."

"Okay. Did your grandmother ever tell you the story behind the three pompoms hanging on it?"

He looked her in the eyes and shook his head. "Mom did."

"Your mom?"

"She's your daughter."

"My...what?"

He chuckled. "Sorry. She *will be* your daughter."

She was aching to correct him but decided against it. "Okay. What did your mom tell you?"

"She said *Abuela* made it to celebrate the day *Abuelo* trusted her with his spare key. It thrilled her because, after being in love with him since she was eleven, he finally let her take care of him." He looked at her. "Are you all right? Are you cold?"

She shivered, but not from the cold. She'd told no one about the keychain. And yet a stranger was telling her story. "And w-who is your...*Abuelo*?" she asked. Please say Alonso, please say Alonso, please say Alonso! "*¡Dime!*"

"Whoa, you're really fiery, *Abuela,*" he said, but she glared at him and he held his hand up. "*Bien*, I'll tell you. Stop glaring. It's scary. Who else would you be in love with anyway?"

"You mean, Alonso? Ha! Nice try. Anyone in the village can tell you that. You think you'll be able to make me believe you came from the future because of—"

"Here," he said, reaching inside his jacket and taking out something flat. A black thing filled the palm of his hand. "What's that?"

"Cellphone," he replied, touching the shiny black surface. It lit up, sending her up on her feet, her heart hammering. He tapped around the bright screen. "Ah, here it is." He pushed himself up off the step.

She stepped back. "What is that thing?"

"A cellphone. Future technology. Look..." He held it up and showed her the screen. She winced, then stared at the picture of a young couple on it.

"Future," she whispered, dying of curiosity, but it was scary too. A screen that showed colored photographs.

"Come on, *Abuela,* this won't harm you. Or are you afraid that I'll prove I'm telling the truth?"

"But why would you want that? Me knowing the future?"

"I already told you."

She steeled herself. "Okay, okay. Show me." She stepped closer and studied the woman with long brown hair and a man with shoulder-length brown hair. "What's with their hair?" she asked.

Leonardo chuckled. "That was the most popular hairstyle in the seventies. It's called feathered hair."

She scrunched her face. "Feathers? What are they, *pájaros*?"

He laughed. "That's exactly what Mom said. You told her when she first styled her hair that birds are the only ones with feathers."

She stared in awe as he showed her more photos of the couple by sweeping his finger across the screen. It was like magic. The images convinced her. She had no choice. No matter how much of a headache it gave her, she couldn't deny that he had something out of her time.

As she looked at the photo of the woman with feathered hair, she couldn't hold back a gasp. "*Es mi hija,*" she said without a doubt. She could see herself in her.

Leonardo smiled. "Yes, she's my mom."

"What's her name?"

"Mariposa," he replied, the same time as the name popped into her head.

"What was she like? Was she a good mother to you?"

A bittersweet smile appeared on his face. "She was wonderful. She was good at mixing drinks. My dad said that she was the most talented barista, and he fell for her because of it." Isabela didn't remove her focus from Mariposa, her heart longing for the faraway future in Leonardo's story. "However, Mom was a terrible cook but she could make everyone eat her food with her stare. I think even *Abuelo* was scared of her."

At that they both laughed. Then she sighed. "But this doesn't prove that I'm your—" Again, her words were cut when he stopped at an old but colored photograph of a smiling woman in her wedding dress, her hair a little different from how she wore it now. She was in her mid-twenties.

"It's me!" she cried, grabbing the cellphone, almost pressing the screen to her eyes.

"Yep, the day of your wedding." He touched the screen, and the next picture came up. Her eyes watered on seeing the man standing next to her outside Beniardá's church.

Alonso.

She looked at him. Everything felt overwhelming and unreal. But, more than anything, she was relieved to have an explanation about why he felt familiar. She opened her arms and hugged him. "Oh, I'm so happy to meet you, *mi nieto*!"

He stiffened and leaned back. "You know, I kept calling you *Abuela*, but a nineteen-year-old calling me 'my grandson' is weird."

She laughed as she let him go and gave his shoulder a playful slap. "You're saying that now?"

Chapter 8

LEONARDO

The moment our laughter died down, I looked at my young grandmother.

Young grandmother—that sounded so wrong, but it was the only way I could think of her. "*Ab—*" I was about to say it again but her calling me *"mi nieto"* rattled me more than I could admit. So weird. "What else can I call you instead of *Abuela?*"

"I might be young but I'm still your grandmother. If you don't want to call me '*Abuela*' anymore, then say my name." She shrugged. "Simple."

Wow. Now I know where I got my easy-going traits from. But picturing myself calling her Isabela was bad enough—bringing myself to do it was worse. "I can't."

She sighed. "Okay, you can call me Bella. Only Alonso calls me that, so it won't feel as if you're disrespecting me."

I don't think so. I noticed the daggers my grandfather sent when his gaze landed on me as he entered his house. I pissed him. Calling *Abuela* a nickname he called her would be asking to get stabbed in my sleep. I give up. "Can I just call you Sabel?"

"Suit yourself," she replied, stepping up to the door and pushing down the handle. She held the door open for me. The low ruckus inside from earlier became loud and clear.

A man, not much older than Alonso, with dark hair, passed by. I stepped back.

"Isa, *cierre la puerta*, you're letting cold air in."

"I have a visitor, Rodrigo."

"Okay, let them in quick. The heat is rushing out."

"It's just one. Leo, come along."

"Not Alonso?"

Isabela frowned. "Why? You think Alonso is the only man who will visit me?"

The man stepped back just in time to see me step into the house. Like many houses in Spain, the entrance hallway connected straight into the living room.

He snorted. "I'll never ever visit you if you're not my sister." She opened her mouth but her brother turned to me and extend a hand, "Rodrigo. Isabela's older brother."

I know. I've seen him in so many photographs. Like *Abuela's* parents, he will grow old and die in Beniardá. Single forever. But, Jorge, the youngest, though he never became famous, joined a band and went on tour around Spain, earning a decent fan base playing in bars and hotels. He will brag about it to his grandkids. I looked around for the brat, who should be about thirteen by now, and found him in front of a shiny walnut brown antique radio in the living room, humming with a music I've never heard before.

"Leonardo," I said, taking Rodrigo's extended hand.

"Last name?"

Isabela looked horror-struck.

"Arevalo," I said, leaving out Barros, my middle name and *Abuelo*'s last name. I'm sure it was what made *Abuela* panic a bit, though I was glad to see relief in her eyes now.

Rodrigo nodded. "*Encantado.*" He turned to scold Jorge for singing louder than the radio. Their mother stepped out of the kitchen, telling them to quiet down. She told Isabela to help now she was home.

They left me standing in the corridor, wide-eyed and not knowing what to do. Hey, I'm in the center of a moment no one in my time has seen. I just saw my great-grandmother as young as my grandmother. It was both exciting and a bit creepy. But did *Abuela's* mother even notice me? Could it be that I am only visible to people my age or younger?

I shook my head and got a strong urge to take out my phone, wanting to update my social media accounts. Then the reality hit me: there was no way I could. No signal. People hadn't even invented the first cellphone yet. It would be about two decades before Marty Cooper lead his team to produce the prototype. I couldn't just take it out and expect them to react like *Abuela.* Now that I thought about it, she truly was an amazing woman. No wonder *Abuelo* told me that no one could match her.

Fluffy dark curls flashed through my mind, with Celestina's eager eyes looking at me with expectation. I shook the image away.

My gaze landed on *Abuela*'s father. He put his book down and beckoned me to sit on the sofa diagonal to his armchair. The moment I sat, he introduced himself as Pablo and his wife in the kitchen as Juliana. I gave him my name, but my focus wandered toward the two brothers. Despite the large age gap, they behaved like two little kids, fighting over the radio. Jorge wanted to keep listening, while Rodrigo wanted to switch it off.

"You dress strangely," Pablo said.

I straightened in my seat and gave an awkward laugh. "*Si,* I get that a lot."

He nodded once. "I've never seen you before. Are you a tourist or one of Alonso's friends?"

Claiming to be my *Abuelo's* friend was risky. I went with being a tourist. It worked, leaving a heavy silence between us.

"So, why are you with my daughter?"

Abuela! I cried inside, and, like an answer to my prayer, she popped her beautiful head out of the kitchen to invite everyone into the dining room. I jumped up, ready to flee to her side, when a knock on the door caught her attention. I was stuck with my inquisitive great-grandfather. His eyebrows furrowed as he studied me.

Rodrigo tapped my shoulder. "*Hombre, vámonos.*"

I practically skipped to follow him but froze on hearing *Abuela's* voice.

"Alonso, why are you here?" she asked, inviting him inside.

His gaze shot toward me and I got the firm impression he wanted to choke the life out of me but, as soon as he took everyone else in, he offered them kind greetings before looking back to *Abuela*. "*Un accidente.*"

Rodrigo tapped my shoulder again, urging me to follow. I caught a few words of *Abuelo* explaining that his meal slipped out of his fingers and his plate broke. It was impossible to catch the rest of his story as Jorge crisscrossed between Rodrigo and me, belting out some old Spanish song. No, it was new, and Rodrigo, not a fan of the song, scolded him.

Great-Grandpa Pablo welcomed my young *Abuelo,* and Great-Grandma Juliana stepped out of the dining room to rush everyone in for dinner. She noticed me for the first time. "Oh, we have a new visitor!" I liked the cheeriness in her voice.

"Isa's new friend," Rodrigo said.

"How can you carry a plate of food carelessly?" Isabela asked Alonso. "Your hair is damp. Was it so bad you needed a shower?"

"A man always needs to be presentable," Great-Grandpa butted in.

Great-Grandma welcomed me.

Rodrigo yelled at Jorge, who sang louder in another room. The blend of sounds became too much. I leaned on the wall and touched my temple, lightheaded. I'd never been to a family dinner this rowdy.

"*¿Estas bien?*" *Abuela* asked, peering at my face.

Abuelo placed an arm around her. "He's okay," he said, pulling her with a smile tugging at the corner of his lips.

I noticed Great-Grandpa watching me, and I straightened up. Someone, please save me!

After dinner, we decided that I'll be staying with *Abuelo.*

I plopped down on the spare room's bed in his house, never having felt so uncomfortable among relatives before. It was horrible to invent stories about myself instead of telling the truth. Even with

Abuelo, I felt like a stranger around the dining table. *Abuela's* warm family reminded me of the time my parents were alive. I wanted to enter that circle, but *Abuelo,* consumed by jealousy, kept me out.

He totally hates me. I recalled how he used every opportunity during dinner to gain *Abuela*'s full attention. It didn't surprise me at all when he suggested I stay with him after *Abuela* opened the topic about me lodging at her house for a short stay.

"You cannot charge him," she told him.

"No problem," he replied, giving me a glance sharp enough to pierce my brain.

I raised my phone, plugged the earphone in, and blasted 'You Can Win If You Want,' my favorite Modern Talking song.

I need to find a way back to my time. Fast. I can't stay here. With that, I let the music drown my thoughts.

I woke up the next morning curled up from the cold, the early light streaming through the white, sheer curtain. For a second, I perked up, thinking everything had been a dream, until I saw unfamiliar furniture surrounding me.

Lying on top of the blanket, still in yesterday's clothes, I puffed out a heavy breath. The earphones were still in my ears. No music, though. A quick check of my phone told me it was dead. I took out the charger and found a wall plug. As I looked around the room, a shiver ran through me. Does *Abuelo* not heat the house?

The clicking of shoes on the stony stairs caught my attention, as did *Abuela*'s startled gasp that followed. I glanced at the little clock on the bedside table. Seven-fifteen. I grabbed a blanket from the bed and draped it over me before stepping out of the room. *Abuela* was standing outside the bathroom door with her hand to her lips, her eyes wide. And there stood *Abuelo* facing her, his dripping-wet hair pushed back, wearing only a towel around his waist, his work-hardened body revealed.

And *Abuela* was ogling him.

I understand why some people liked to roll their eyes. I don't, but this was pure cliché.

"What?" he asked, shrugging—teasing her.

"Why are you still here?" she asked, regaining her composure. "You're usually already in the *campo* by this time." She bent to grab the fallen broom.

I tiptoed back a few steps to hide myself from sight, but not too far—I wanted to know how this developed.

"I'm not leaving until you promise to leave with me," *Abuelo* said.

"You know I will not work there. You'd better remember that if you plan to marry me."

"*No eres, mi novia.*"

That was a surprise. She wasn't his girlfriend yet? But, then again, her reaction when I caught her in my—in *Abuelo*'s bedroom, should have given me the clue.

"Okay, so I'm just a person you're paying to keep this house clean and cook your meals. You don't have to care," she said, with no trace of hurt in her voice. She was used to being turned down by him.

"I care. That's why I want you out with me and not alone here with Leonardo."

I sucked in a breath and puffed my cheeks. *Abuelo* spits my name like poison. Wow, he really hates me.

Abuela laughed. "Are you jealous?"

"So, what if I am?"

Way to go, *Abuelo!*

"I didn't take you to be the jealous type," she said after a brief silence, her voice balanced on a nervous tremor.

"Me neither," he said. "That's why you should come out with me and don't come here again, at least not while he's here."

She released a loud sigh. "You have nothing to be jealous of. He's our grandson."

"Our what?"

"N-nothing," she squeaked.

I chuckled and stepped back to my room.

"You know, I'm only letting him stay because of you," Alonso said.

I closed my door and walked to the window, from where I gazed up toward Benimantell, the village on one of the hills surrounding Beniardá. They had a bird's-eye view and saw every activity here.

The next time I left my room, the air smelled like detergent and every surface shone. *Abuela* hummed as she poked her head out of the kitchen and waved me over.

"I got things for you," she said.

I whipped my head left and right. "Where's *Abuelo*?"

"Oh, he left for the *campo*."

You still can't hold your ground, *Abuelo*. I almost chuckled, remembering all the occasions in my time when he gave in to whatever *Abuela* wanted.

A few minutes later, as I ate the welcome breakfast she served me, I wondered what would happen today? Will I ever find my way back to my time, or am I stuck here forever with my grandparents who are younger than me? Ugh, I hate this. I hate thinking about problems. Getting bored because of lockdown was preferable compared to this. *Abuela* glanced at me as I hesitated over my food. I'd better eat. I'll need strength for whatever lies ahead.

Chapter 9

LEONARDO

My forehead creased as I looked at my reflection in the tall mirror by the main door.

"You need to blend in," *Abuela* said earlier as she dropped a small box of clothes beside me after feeding me Spanish tortilla, *pan,* and a fresh squeeze of oranges. "You need more weight!" She served a ladle of fried bacon on top of the tortilla. I swear, no matter what decade, she dedicated herself to the same mission: feeding me.

I grunted and looked away from the white button-down shirt tucked inside loose blue trousers. *Abuela* insisted on it, which was okay because she was right—I needed to blend in—but the shirt's top button, closed all the way up, was killing me. So uncomfortable. And she didn't go before she "tamed" my unruly hair, which involved a lot of combing and hair gel—lots of it! I ended up smelling like *Abuelo,* while looking like an Elvis Presley fanatic.

Blend in, Leonardo. She's right. But there was only so much blending I could do. Rodrigo's clothes were not my thing. *Abuelo* had better taste, but I doubt he'll lend anything to me. I unbuttoned my shirt to my chest, then grabbed my jacket and put it on.

I pocketed my phone, the charger, and the keys, which *Abuela* ordered me to hide from *Abuelo.* Right, first, befriend *Abuelo,* then get in touch with Celestina and find out how I got here. So far, she was the only person I knew who might be able to help me go back. If I discover the answer I need, it might reveal my path back.

I don't want to ask Isabela where I can find Celestina because I'm sure she will tease me. So, using the excuse of looking for a job, I casually mentioned Celestina's name. However, people who heard, warned me about associating with her.

"There's nothing wrong with her, but it's still better to stay away," they said, instead of giving me her address or hiring me.

In the future, I co-owned a travel agency, before it closed because of Covid and reduced tourism. I often surprised new acquaintances when they found out that I owned a business.

"You don't give the vibe of someone who runs a successful business," they said.

I refused the managerial position and pushed all of it to my business partner because I thrive on guiding people. Besides Spanish, I'm good with languages. I am fluent in French—my father's language—plus English, Swedish, and German. I was also a beginner in a couple of other languages, like Japanese, Korean, and, strangely enough, Russian. All because I had nothing else to do during lockdown but study. Learning more languages was the only fun thing to do. But such skills are useless for time-traveling sixty-four years into the past, especially in a village where most people couldn't care less if I spoke a hundred languages.

The next tune on my phone had me laughing at its irony. '*If Tomorrow Never Comes'* by Ronan Keating. I know tomorrow will come, but not in my time. Not yet anyway.

I kicked the ground where I'd found the bottle with the note. The note! Maybe it's the key to returning. Why didn't I think of it? Everything happened after I kissed it. A buzz ran through me as I looked around, turning the yellow leaves on the ground in my search for any sign of it.

Damn, why did I have to kiss it? Was kissing it really the cause? Maybe just holding it could have triggered the whole thing, or was it because I broke the bottle?

My brain hurt. Shit. I turned off the music, grabbed a stick, and poked the ground.

"What are you looking for?"

"Nothing," I replied, jerking around, using the stick to stop me from losing my balance. "Hey, Miss Purrball. *Buenas días.*"

"You know my name," she said in a whisper as her gaze raked over me, assessing me head to toe and sending shivers down my spine. She lingered on my lips for longer than necessary, then made hard eye contact, and I couldn't hold back a smile. "My name is Celestina."

My cheeks pinched as my grin grew wider. "Okay, Ce-les-ti-na." I bent to better meet her gaze. She was so much taller than *Abuela,* who only went up to my shoulder. Her cheeks turned crimson with either rage or annoyance—perhaps a combination of both. But I was happy to see her, saving me from searching for her. "You need something from me, Miss Purrball?"

Her knuckles whitened as she clenched her fist. "I'm going to the *campo* soon, but can I meet you in the *embalse* in the afternoon?" She looked around, her gaze furtive, before focusing back on me. "I really need to speak to you. Alone."

I inched closer while she kept retreating, until her back was against the wall bordering the road down to Font Vella. "Alone? *With me?* Here?"

If someone asked what I was doing in that moment, I, who never ran out of words, wouldn't be able to answer. I had no idea what I was doing. I shouldn't get too deeply involved with people from the village. It was bad enough that I'd let *Abuela* know the truth, which could change God knows what in the future. I couldn't take another risk by hitting on Celestina, *Abuela's* future best friend.

But it was too hard to hold back.

I grew up seeing and hearing about Celestina. She was like a mysterious myth to me. I met my first girlfriend when I was seventeen. However, no matter how many relationships I ended up in later, Celestina had always been at the back of my mind. This mystery was now in front of me, within my reach. Without thinking, I grasped a handful of curls, right at her cheek. She let out an audible gasp as I let the strands slip through my fingers, the action soft and addictive.

"Leonardo, are you here?"

I snapped straight, the spell broken by *Abuela*'s gentle voice.

Celestina lay both hands on my chest and pushed me. "I'll see you in the *embalse!*" she said and ran off, leaving me wondering what time we were to meet at.

"Was that Celestina?" *Abuela* asked.

I shoved my hands into my jacket pockets. "Yep."

"When did the two of you become close?"

"We're not."

"Uh, huh." She gave me an I-don't-believe-you look, and I knew I needed to confess.

"It's nothing. I'm here looking for a clue how to get back to the future, and she asked to meet me in the *embalse.*"

She glanced in the direction Celestina took. "Why?"

"I don't know. She said she wanted to speak to me. Alone."

Abuela laughed a little.

"*¿Qué?*" I asked, feeling defensive all of a sudden.

"Oh, nothing. She will probably ask you again to get back into that bottle of hers."

The bottle! Right. It wasn't just the note. There was the bottle too. Since I couldn't find the note, maybe the bottle was the answer? "*Abuela,* you're brilliant!"

"*Yo sé,*" she replied, looking proud. "And this brilliant person wants to know if you can drive."

"I can. *¿Por qué?*"

Her brows arched as she smiled. "Because I need a driver to bring me to Benidorm." She dangled the keys in front of me. "Interested?"

"Of course!" I reached out for the keys, only to stop. "But *Abuelo* might hunt me down."

"Don't worry!" she said with a strange glow on her face. "We already worked that out."

It was my turn to study her, and then it clicked. "Are the two of you a couple now?"

"*Sí!*" she squealed, flapping her hands, and it was hard for me to see the grandmother I'd left behind. In her place now was a love-struck young woman. "We haven't told my parents yet. We'll do it tomorrow at dinner. Tonight, the three of us need to talk."

My heart constricted. "Sabel, please tell me you didn't tell him." She looked away. "How could you? No one else is supposed to know."

"On the bright side, thanks to that, he won't hate you anymore. And we're together. Isn't that good?"

"It's not supposed to happen this way!" She flinched. "He should admit his feelings for you because he realized he can't live without you. Tell me, did he tell you he loves you?"

She fiddled with the keys and mashed the orange and yellow leaves under her foot. "But he was going to drive you off to the city. You don't know anyone there."

"Who cares about me?"

"I do! I care about you."

I took a deep breath. "I can take care of myself."

She held my hand. "I know, Leo, but I can't help worrying. Especially because I know it will be hard for you to adjust in this place."

"Thank you, Sabel, but we could have tried another option, you know."

"What's done is done," she said, shrugging.

She's right. I can only hope I still have a future to return to. If I vanished in this era for triggering things and created some butterfly effect, who will save me then?

"Are you okay?" she asked. "You look pale."

Yes, that's what thinking does to me. "I'm alright. Let's go?"

Thank goodness she agrees.

I was such a fool when I agreed to drive *Abuela* to Benidorm. It only occurred to me when we were driving down the long winding road after Benimantell that I didn't have a valid driving license.

"Sabel, why don't you drive?"

She stared at me with horror as I slowed a bit, looking for somewhere to pull over. "I can't drive. Why do you think I asked you?"

I sighed and sped up again. "Let's hope we don't meet a patrol then, because we're sure to get in trouble."

"Why?"

"They'll think my driving license is fake, that's why."

She furrowed her brows. "Is it?"

"No, of course not. But it's many years into the future."

Her face lit up. "Can I see it?"

"You're missing the point!"

She pouted and looked out of the window. "Relax, there's practically no road patrols all the way to Benidorm *centro*."

True. In the eleven years since getting my driver's license, I had hardly ever been stopped. "By the way, where's the seat belts?"

"I don't know any car with them. Why?"

"It makes driving safer!"

"No one uses them. Even the police don't use them."

I stare at her in disbelief but thought it better not to argue the point. "What are you going to buy in the city?" I asked instead.

She cheered up at that, and chatted about fabrics and sewing materials all the way to our destination. Unlike the busy city of the future, this Benidorm looked more like the countryside. The new, colorful sidewalk by the beach, and tall skyscrapers, weren't anywhere to be seen. And, I dare say, it looked more charming. I could stay in this era. The simple life and unhurried pace of its people had a relaxing effect on me. But it was only a matter of time before the skyscrapers would pop up like mushrooms. 1956 was three years after Pedro Zaragoza, the mayor who made Benidorm famous, or infamous, for being the first city in Spain to allow bikinis on the beach. He authorized it despite the outrage of those who deemed it immoral. But the mayor was courageous enough to face the Spanish dictator who banned it in the first place.

I stepped out of the car, looked at the cross on the top of the hill, and chuckled.

Abuela stood beside me. "What's so funny about the cross?"

"Nothing," I said. "So, where to first?"

She remained quiet, still looking up the hill.

"Sabel?"

She glanced at me. "Did you do something to that cross in the future?"

After losing my parents, my annoyance with God for not keeping them alive got the better of me. I rode my bike all the way up there and peed on it. Yeah, sue me.

I looked at her and shook my head. "Nothing."

She squinted. "I don't believe you."

I shrugged, biting back a smile. "I've got nothing to tell. Now, let's go. I still have an appointment with Celestina."

"I'm not moving until I hear it."

"Sabel, you're behaving like a brat."

She crossed her arms and grinned. "I don't care."

I gave up. I don't think I can ruin the future more than I already have by recounting some minor details such as this. So, I told her.

Her mouth hung open before she covered her face. "*Ay, Dios mio.*"

"See, I told you, it's nothing."

She smiled, slapped my back, and walked. "Good job, *mi nieto.*"

I stared at her. "*¿Qué?*"

She looked back at me. "I said good job. I never liked it being up there. Now, let's go. We have much to do."

Chapter 10

LEONARDO

"The Sweet Rose," I said, reading the sign in front of the last sewing shop Isabela brought me to. Another thing that will be a big part of *Abuela*'s future. The son of the shop will be my grandfather on my father's side. My French grandfather will marry my Filipina grandmother and give birth to my father. My grandfather will soon take over the shop and expand it. One branch will be in Valencia, where he and Alonso met and became the best of friends. They will both play matchmaker for my parents.

Abuela looked at me, holding all her shopping bags. "Is that how you pronounce it? I did not know how until now. Hmm." She nodded. "The Sweet Rose."

I bit my bottom lip, holding a smile. Her charming Spanish accent made it sound like 'de eswit rost'

We entered the shop and, once again, I couldn't help but smile when they told her the total price. *Abuela* bought a mountain of fabric, yet the price in pesetas was ridiculously low if I were to convert it to euros. My grandparents sure had it nice. The amount of stress was nothing compared to where I came from.

"If only there was internet."

"What's that?" she asked, dumping more shopping items in my arms. "Is it something you want to buy? I can get it for you, as thanks for driving and helping me."

I let out an awkward laugh as two girls waved and smiled at me. They continued past us when they saw *Abuela's* frowning face. "Did you just warn them away?" I asked her.

She raised an eyebrow. "Yes, because anything you do here can change the future. You told me that yourself."

I snorted. "Like you're the one to talk?"

"What's that?"

"Nothing."

This time, she didn't pry and got back on topic. "*Bien.* Should we get that internet? I don't think I heard of it before. What is it?"

"It's a future thing."

She blinked. Her lips formed into an 'O,' and a wave of dread rushed over me. "What are you waiting for? Tell me. What kind of future thing is it?"

I shook my head and walked out of the shop. She rushed to walk beside me. "Leo, tell me!"

"You just said a minute ago that anything I do here can change the future."

"But this is different."

"*Abuela!*" I blurted out of frustration, aware that people were looking at me like I was a madman. Yeah, I get it. I'd think the same if I was in their shoes. A man in his late-twenties calling a young woman "Grandmother." I needed to stop mentioning future things.

Unfazed by the stares, she grabbed my hand. "Leo what's—"

"No!"

That stopped her in her tracks, and my heart went out to her.

"*Oye*, I'm sorry. Please, just accept, for now, I want to tell you, but I think it's best not to know about some things. Not yet, anyway."

To my relief, she responded with a gentle nod, then piled a couple more bags into my already laden arms. Phew! That was a close one. Be more careful what you say in the future, Leonardo.

A heavy sigh left me as I flopped onto the bed. I'd trade guiding fifty people or dealing with a dozen angry customers over soothing *Abuela*'s curiosity. It was relentless, and I felt drained. However, it was my fault for saying too much, so often.

I lay there for a few minutes, savoring the silence before turning on my side and catching sight of the time. Three-thirty. I sprang up, my heart in my mouth. My appointment with Celestina had slipped out of my mind. Was she already there? Or still there? I didn't even know what time she finished working on the field. It was a long walk down to the reservoir, and I didn't know what part of it we were meant to meet. There were too many ways to go.

As I rubbed my head, I remembered that, for once, people here weren't treating me like an alien. Celestina seemed to like it too. I smoothed my hair back and got up from the bed. Instead of wasting time wondering what and where, I needed to get going.

After choosing the most probable road from the center of the village, I walked until I arrived at the field of almonds and olive trees. The long, winding road down to the reservoir was different too.

I made my way down, humming GTR's '*When The Heart Rules The Mind.*' It was one of my favorites from the 80s—one of the great songs left behind by the moving tide of time. I'd found the four-CD boxset in a garage sale after breaking up with my second girlfriend. The collection contained 70s and 80s songs, which made me stalk YouTube for more. Now, I had more than a thousand songs in my oldie playlist. I missed them. Good thing I copied the CDs and downloaded all the MP3s into my phone.

The track changed from GTR to Thunder's '*Love Walked In*' as I moved to the short path leading to the reservoir. I exhaled with relief on seeing Celestina sitting on top of a stone. She looked back, right as the singer screamed about love walking through his door. I froze. Her wild curls shone under the afternoon sun, which glistened off the tears streaming down her cheeks.

I ripped the earphones away and rushed up beside her.

"*Buenas tardes,*" she said with a smile. She patted her cheeks dry but her long eyelashes were wet and the corners of her eyes were red, as was the tip of her nose.

You didn't need a sharp mind to know what was going on. She didn't want to talk about what happened so I smiled and greeted her back. I glanced at the basket beside her, its contents covered by checkered fabric.

"You brought something for me?" I asked.

She nodded, the action timid. "*Galletas de almendras.*"

I chuckled. "I wonder why I feel so calm whenever you're around. You're like a tranquilizer."

Her gaze met mine. "*Que*?" Her silky voice sounded like it was part of the wind.

She was far from the Celestina I'd imagined. Fierce and intimidating, full of secret surprise, which described all the women who became my girlfriends. All of whom broke up with me, with the longest lasted five months.

The Celestina in front of me was quiet, gentle-spoken, mysterious, but easy to read. Strong in a fragile kind of way that would break a man's self-control.

"You make everything around you so cozy and tranquil," I murmured, inching my hand toward her hair. The urge to caress it was so strong but I brushed away the desire and lifted the basket's covering instead. As I checked out the contents, I couldn't help sneak a peek at her out of the corner of my eye. She pushed her hand over her hair while glancing back with a shyness that made my heart melt. When our eyes met, she blushed.

Basking in the moment, I felt courageous enough to not look away. She held my gaze for what felt like an eternity before averting her eyes. It was a powerful moment, and I was drawn toward her like never before with any other woman. So much so, I had to fight every urge to kiss her right there and then.

"I-I also brought coffee," she said, and bent to a bag on the other side of the stone. "And milk."

She fretted over the bag for a long moment before I couldn't stand seeing her struggle. I stepped behind her and attempted to take the bag from her. When my fingers brushed hers, she let go without warning. On reflex, I caught it just as it dropped. I felt cool for a second before I lost my footing and we both fell toward the hard stone. Reacting again on reflex, I threw out my left hand to protect her head, still keeping a grip on the bag. The sound of something cracking filled my head as we hit the ground, and an intense pain shot through my arm and into my brain. I don't know how I suppressed a scream but I did, placing the bag down and looking at Celestina beneath me.

"Your hand, it's—"

"Don't worry, I'm fine," I said, while my mind shouted, *this isn't the time to play cool!* The aching of my hand under her head pulsed like a razor-sharp heartbeat. I remained in our position, inhaling her sweet chocolate scent and relishing her softness like a pervert.

"*No, no, no estas bien*," she said, shaking her head. "I heard it when we fell."

She met my gaze and seemed to have realized something. For a second, I thought she had me figured out. She raised her head, her face so close I could kiss her with little to no effort, and I had a feeling she wouldn't mind, but I looked away. Maybe it was cowardice, or fear of feeling attached to her. She belonged in the past, while I needed to get back to my own time. Falling for her was unacceptable. I moved away, and she gasped. I turned to look—my left hand was bleeding, the skin lacerated, and it had swelled to double its original size.

"I'm so sorry, I broke your hand!"

"Relax, it's okay."

"No, it's not."

"I'm all right. I can still move it."

"You're bleeding," she whispered, just loud enough for me to hear. As she focused on the crimson droplets spilling onto the cold stones, I had a feeling she was seeing something else.

I held her soft cheek with my good hand and forced her to look at me. "Celestina, I'm not dying. Look at me!" I commanded, my voice hard. She blinked a rapid sequence and reality seemed to crash back around her. "See? I'm okay," I said in a much softer tone.

She blinked again. "The bag?" I pointed it out to her, and she looked relieved. "Thank you. I brought some coffee cups, and Mom would be furious if I broke them."

"You're welcome to blame it on me."

She let out a small laugh, and I was stunned. Her entire face lit up when she smiled. Dangerous.

"*¿Qué?*" she asked, pulling out a thermos flask.

"Don't smile when someone else is around."

"*¿Cómo?*"

I leaned in. "You look too cute when you smile." She responded with a deep blush, and I felt disgusted with myself for teasing her.

It's a mystery how I endured the pain pulsing from my hand as I drank coffee and ate almond biscuits through a calm façade. But I did. Still, as much as I loved sitting with Celestina, listening to nature around us, I had to break the silence. Who knows, maybe *Abuela* was right. Maybe she wanted me to return to her bottle?

I glanced at her bag. "Is the heart bottle in there?"

She choked and gave me an apologetic smile. “I left it at home.”

“I see.” I sipped my coffee. “If you don’t mind me asking, did you really see me come out of that bottle?”

Her eyes widened. “I wasn’t lying. I saw it. You came out like a light made of liquid and slowly materialized in front of me.” Her usual timid expression was now masked with determination. “It’s a gift from *Papá*. I inserted a piece of paper with a message inside, but it disappeared just before you came out.” She cupped her coffee and looked nowhere. “I asked to meet you here because I wanted to say sorry for the way I acted.”

“You could have just told me anytime. You didn’t have to go through this trouble.” My hand could have been spared but I would rather cut my tongue out than say that to her.

She rubbed her cup and fidgeted as she looked toward the crystal-blue water. I remember it being more greenish in my time.

A bitter laugh came from her. “I can’t handle facing people. I guess I was pretty desperate to change that, and my life in general. I made myself believe in magic.” Her fidgeting quickened. “*Papá* said he could travel through time, and visit parallels worlds, so I assume another stranger—”

I touched her shoulder with my left hand, forgetting my injury, and grunted at the resulting pain. “Celestina, what did you say about your father?”

“I know. No one will believe me, but I don’t think he was lying to me. *Papá* could travel through time, and to other worlds.”

“Celestina, can I meet him? Please, help me. I need to talk to your father.” She lowered her head. “Celestina?”

She looked up. Her eyes glistening. “I wish I could see him too.”

"Your father doesn't live with you?" She shook her head. I straightened up, shooing the negative thoughts away. "Did your parents divorce?

"No. The last time I saw him, he was bleeding out from a gunshot."

My face went cold as my heart sank. For a second, I thought I might have found a solution. "He didn't make it?"

"I don't know. I..."—her voice broke—"I'm sorry. I don't feel like talking about it."

I put my cup down, making sure it wouldn't fall, and slipped my good arm around her.

"What are you doing?" she asked.

"Comforting you," I replied.

She pushed away but I eased her back, keeping her forehead pressed to me until she started sniffling. Not long after, it turned into a wail. "I miss him. I...really, really m-miss him," she said between sobs.

"I know," I whispered, kissing her hair, her emotional outpouring getting to me. I know how it feels. I miss them too. My parents. If only I could— I sat stock still, shocked at the possibilities. I can. I can change the future. How many times did I wish to go back in time and change what happened? I'm now back in time, long before the accident. It's everyone's wish come true, and I'm moping around? No, this isn't me. I've only been here for two days. I'm sure I'll discover other ways to get back. In the meantime, I need to change the future without ruining it, and hopefully without letting Celestina walk into my heart.

Chapter 11

LEONARDO

Celestina took the coffee cup from me. "*Vale. Está bien.* Let me do this by myself." She glanced at my injured hand. "Give me your hand." A command which I gladly obeyed.

She wrapped it with the teacloth.

"Thanks." I straightened up and flashed her my widest and sweetest smile, the one people said reminded them of Ronald Miller from the film '*Can't Buy Me Love*.' But instead of making her blush, like I aimed for, she stifled a laugh. "What?"

"You look cute."

My face fell. "You can't call a man cute."

"But that smile made you look cute. There's nothing wrong with calling you that." She dipped the cups in the water and used the checkered fabric from the basket to dry them. "Besides, you called me cute too."

I stood up and leaned close to her ear. "That's because you are cute." I gave her a crooked smile, raised one eyebrow, and got what I wanted, her face flushing as she dried a cup at a furious pace. "Any more scrubbing and you'll create a hole in that cup."

She collected everything in a hurry and pushed them into her bag, then went for the basket, but I grabbed it before her and pulled it up out of her reach.

"Give it back! I must get home now. It's going to get dark soon."

I looked at the time on my wristwatch—another gift from *Abuela*. Ten-minutes before five. "Wow, your mother's strict. You've got a really early curfew."

She looked hurt. I swallowed a ball of regret at poking something I shouldn't have. She slung her bag over her shoulder and stuck her hand out to me. "The basket."

I kept it up. "No, I'll walk you home."

"No!" she shouted, surprising me with the force of her rejection.

"*¿Por qué no?*"

"*Mamá* will be angry if I bring a man."

"You're lying, aren't you?"

She looked down.

"Unless you give me a good reason, I'll do what I want, and that is walking you back." I walked toward the main road. When I looked back, she was still standing in the same spot. I raised my left hand. "I'll also need help with this one."

She looked resigned as she caught up and walked beside me, her shoulders drooped. I swallowed another ball of guilt. "Fine. I won't enter. How about I just leave you close to your house?"

"My mother doesn't care about me," she said, which caught me off-guard. I stopped, but she walked past me. "You see, a sick man raped her, and I'm the result." She kicked a harmless branch across the main road. "You're right. I lied about her getting angry." She whirled around to face me. Her skirt swirled and fluttered back in place. "There's no way she would be angry because she doesn't care about me. After all, how could you love a person who reminds you of the most horrible moment of your life, right?"

I froze, unable to find the power to respond. Something heavy and bitter replaced the light, fluffy air I tried to fill myself with most of the time. My parents spoiled me with love. Knowing there are parents who would shove their child aside and let them grow without love hurt me in places I couldn't pinpoint. If Celestina's mom didn't want her, she should have stopped her pregnancy before it was too late. It was cruel of her to give birth to an innocent child and blame her for her father's crime.

Celestina laughed, but it sounded like a small cry—the loneliest sound I've ever heard in my life.

"You better not be pitying me," she said, "or I'll beat you with this bag."

My teeth hurt as I unclenched my jaw. I put on my usual carefree smile to hide how her story broke my heart. "Pity? How could I? You are what you are because of what you went through, and if circumstances were different, I might not have met you."

Her eyes softened. "That's true." She took a deep breath, then sprinted up the main road. "Hurry up! We still need to bandage that hand properly.

I jogged to her side and put my arm around her shoulder. She pushed me off, and I faked a groan, laughing when she went into a frenzy of apologies while fretting over my hand. Unlike *Abuela*, who would have smacked me for misbehaving, Celestina gave me a stern look that compelled me to apologize.

My apology was honest. What I felt wasn't simple pity. It was deeper—more intense. Friends once told me about encountering someone for the first time and feeling like they'd known each other for a lifetime. Sure, I'd heard so much about Celestina since childhood but I wasn't ready to dwell on this feeling roiling about inside me.

"Come in," Celestina said, keeping the front door of her house open for me.

She led me through a narrow hallway into the wide double-door-frame living room. The ceiling leaped to a high vault, and I noted a sprawling staircase leading up to the next level.

"I'll just start the fire first and help you with your hand right after." She switched the light on and motioned to the gray-blue sofa bed. "*Siéntate.*"

I nodded and sat on it. Unlike *Abuela*'s warm home, this house felt cold and unwelcoming. I could almost trace the shadow of sadness oozing from every corner. The walls were a dull, uninviting beige—a sharp contrast to the warm furniture. It didn't help that the few paintings were drab, uninspired works that blended in with the wall and added nothing to the atmosphere. There were no photographs or other personal touches, leaving the place feeling empty and lonely. It lacked the life and cheerfulness one would expect from a family home.

Celestina crouched in front of the fireplace, scowling at the wood and cursed it under her breath for not burning. She tried a few more times, feeding it with crumpled newspapers, but then her shoulders dropped. In clear frustration, she shot up, muttering to herself as she stomped to another room. From the sound of drawers opening and closing and cooking utensils being moved about, it was the kitchen. When she trotted back to the fireplace, she was carrying a bottle of liquid.

I pulled out my phone and filmed her as she poured a good amount of it over the sticks. Her gleeful determination made me smile. She held the match up, as if to threaten the firewood before she lit it, then she struck it, tossed it, and flames erupted.

"Take that!" she said, a triumphant smile lighting her face up.

My hand shook but I kept myself from laughing. When she turned to me, her victorious smile vanished, replaced by embarrassment. She went bright red and covered her face with her open hand.

"I completely forgot you were here," she said as she crouched down.

The flickering light created a welcome warm vibe around the room. I stopped filming, and would have walked up to her and done something I'd regret if she hadn't stood and turned away.

"Wait here. I'll go get the first-aid kit."

Fifteen minutes later, Celestina cleaned my hand and wrapped it in a bandage.

"*¡Ya está!*" she said, locking the tip of the bandage in place.

A little too much bandage, maybe, but I'm not complaining. "*Gracias.*"

"*De nada.*" She packed everything back in the medicine box. "It's been so long since I used this on someone else."

"On someone else?" I asked.

Big mistake.

"*Si*, I hurt myself a lot, so I got plenty of practice with myself."

There was that sting inside me again but I did my best to keep it from my eyes.

"I also helped *Papá* a lot because he often had minor cuts and bruises on him when he was home with us."

At the mention of her father, a thought came to me: "Don't you hate him?"

"*¿Quién?*"

"Your father. If it weren't for him, your mother wouldn't hate you. But each time you talk about him, it is with so much fondness." You even cried because you missed him so badly.

"Ah." She nodded. "That's because *Papá* isn't my real father."

"Oh. A kind stepfather then?"

She shook her head. "He's my father, but not the father who raped my mother."

Now I was confused. "Your *papá is* your biological father, right?" She nodded. "Meaning you have his blood. But he's not the man who raped your mom, leading to her giving birth to you? Am I saying this right?"

"*Sí.*"

"Good, because, the way I hear it, I sound like a nutcase."

She smiled, then explained about parallels—about the same person living multiple lives, which meant she and I also exist in another place, doing something else at this same moment. "Or more or less talking about the same thing as us right now."

Okay, that's freaky.

She went back to her *papá*, explaining that the man she loved as her father, who she dearly called *Papá,* was the man who had the ability to jump through parallels, while the one who committed the crime against her mother was in prison.

With that, she took the first-aid box and left the room, leaving me with my mind twisted from all the incredible information. But I couldn't say that to her face—not when I'm here in the mid-fifties after arriving all the way from 2020.

The front door opened and closed, and I readied myself for what was to come. A minute later, a woman in her mid-thirties, who I felt sure was Celestina's mother, entered the room. She dropped her shoulder bag and hat to the floor. Aside from her long straight hair, she looked like an older version of Celestina. She changed her muddy shoes into slippers and walked across the room.

I got up from the sofa before she noticed me.

She stepped back, frowning as she touched the wall beside her. "*¿Quién eres tú?*"

Her reaction was a bit excessive. After all, she wasn't the only one living in this house. She kept watching me as she grabbed one of the wine bottles standing on the small round table.

"Please calm down. I'm Celestina's friend."

She looked hard at me, then recognition registered, her eyes widening "*¡Eres tú!*"

I nodded, thinking she must have heard about me already. News of strangers living among them traveled fast in tight communities like Beniardá. "I arrived in the *villa* yesterday and befriended your daughter."

"You'd better come up with a better lie before I smash this on your head," she said, holding the bottle up. "I know you don't belong here."

"*Mamá,* he's telling the truth," Celestina said, walking to my side and holding up my hurt hand. "He helped when I had an accident in the *embalse.*"

Her mom looked at my hand, huffed, and set the wine bottle back in place. She strode across the room and left us alone.

Celestina let go of my hand and followed her mother as far as the doorway. "*Mamá,* are you hungry? I prepared dinner earlier. I'll warm it up. Let's eat—"

"I already ate," she snapped, her voice cold. Then the door closed. The sound of a shower soon followed.

Celestina took a couple of deep breaths before turning to me. "Looks like I'll be eating alone tonight." She either expected the rejection and was used to it or was able to hide her pain. "Do you want to join me?" she asked, gathering up her mother's stuff.

I figured she was only saying it to be polite, and I should head back because I was sure Alonso and Isabela were already waiting for me. However, what I should do and what I want to do are two different things—what I want always wins.

"Sure," I said and smiled at her surprised face. "It's my chance to taste more of your cooking."

That timid smile reappeared as she stashed her mother's things under the wine table. "It's nothing great. I'm heating the paella from lunch."

"*¿Con pollo y conejo?*" I asked with an edge of desperation, wanted her to confirm that she had chicken and rabbit meat in the paella.

"No, es mejillones y gambas," she answered.

I cringed inside at the thought of eating prawns and mussels, regretting my decision to accept the invitation. Damn it, I can't just leave now. No, I'll have to grin and bear it.

Chapter 12

SWEET TORTURE

Celestina glanced at Leonardo as he waited while she heated the food. He's a cutie. She'd invited him to eat at the dining table but he'd insisted that the kitchen was better.

"It smells of baked bread and chocolate. It smells like you." He looked at her in a way she couldn't explain. Almost like he was peering straight into her soul, and she had nothing to hide. With him, there was no need to hide. He seemed like a playful person but, occasionally, when he thought she wasn't aware, she caught him looking at her with a serious and fiery gaze that made her feel soft and warm all over.

A strange sensation swirled inside her as she divided the meal between them. She'd invited him only because she wanted to distract him from what he'd witnessed. It was the usual scenario at home. She never lost hope but years of rejection from her mother had made her numb. It felt normal, an everyday thing she sometimes forgot wasn't normal for others. Leonardo's presence reminded her of that fact, which made her want to hate him, but she couldn't, not after he let her cry on his chest.

She took two glasses and a bottle of wine, then stopped before setting them down. Leonardo looked up.

"Something wrong?"

It was the first time in years she was eating with someone. The last time was with *Papá,* and he had prepared the food.

"Sorry, I forgot to ask what you wanted to drink."

He looked at the glasses and the wine in her hands. "You're holding them. Unless you want to drink all that, I'm fine with water."

As he smiled, heat crept up her neck. Why did she become so flustered with him? She didn't like how he used every chance he got to tease her, yet she enjoyed it at the same time. Being with him felt like sweet torture.

"I think that's good enough," he said.

She followed his gaze and gasped. She'd filled his glass to the brim. Her face felt like it was on fire as she apologized and reached for it. "I'll just pour you a new—"

"It's all right." He placed his hand on top of hers before bringing the glass to his lips.

She swallowed as he sipped the wine without breaking eye contact with her. It felt like a ritual she couldn't escape, his gaze and the heat of his hand hypnotizing her. The warmth traveled from her fingers straight to her heart, which hammered—something she'd probably mistake for hyperventilating if she was alone, but she knew what was happening inside her. The little human interaction she'd had never left her feeling like that. It had to be Leonardo.

"It tastes better with your hand on it," he said, breaking the silence between them.

She smiled, pulled her hand away, and went to her chair at the other side of the table. It was only then she noticed his tiny grimace as he took the fork and poked the mussels. He then switched his attention to the prawn, twisting the fork through its neck and holding the table knife like a murderer as he stabbed the poor sea creature. It was already dead but she felt bad for it.

"Ouch!" she cried when she bit into the shell of her mussel. She ran to the sink and spat the bits out. The metallic taste of her blood from her tongue accompanied the pain.

Leonardo's chair scraped back and he rushed to her side. "What happened?" he asked, then saw the shell fragments. "Why did you try to eat it?"

She scowled at him.

He backed off a bit. "What?"

She spit the last tiny bits out and pressed a finger to his chest. His gaze followed, and she retracted like he'd burned her.

"It's your..." She did her best to sound normal but her voice still quivered. "It's all your fault."

"Me? How is it my fault?"

"You distracted me," she said, her voice sounding squeaky in her head.

One corner of his mouth curved into a lopsided smile. He advanced until her back pressed against the sink, then lowered his face. He was too close but smelled so good.

"How did I do that?"

She opened her mouth to reply but stopped at the sound of heavy footsteps coming down the stairs. Her mother showed up in the kitchen doorway seconds later, wearing her long nightdress and a deep frown.

"*¿Qué está pasando aquí?*" Her gaze locked on Leonardo. "What is he still doing here?"

Celestina gripped the sink hard. "I invited him to stay for dinner."

He turned to face her mother. "She cut her tongue, *Señora.*"

Her mother shot her a sharp glare, and she was sure she would be beaten by now if he wasn't in the room with them.

"Keep it down, I need to sleep!" her mother snapped, then stomped back up the stairs.

Celestina rinsed her mouth with tap water and face Leonardo again.

They stared at each other for a while, then he walked to the doorway, rumpled his hair, and stood like her mother. "You..." He squeezed his baritone voice, and she bit the inside of her cheek to stop herself from laughing at his exaggerated gestures. "You keep it down, because I need my beauty sleep." He then tossed his non-existent long hair behind his shoulder and stomped back to her side. "Feeling better?" he asked, touching her shoulder.

"Much better." She smiled up at him, his expression switching from silly to serious. There it was again, the look he gave that made her feel like the only girl in the world. She opened her mouth, expecting him to do something—something to stop the fire burning inside her. He leaned down, so close, his warm breath brushed her skin. His scent made her lightheaded, but like all the other times today, he leaned back and left her disappointed.

"We should eat before the food gets cold," he said, turning her toward the table.

"Yes," she said under her breath, "we wouldn't want that."

Celestina glanced at the wall clock. Eight p.m. They were done with dinner but she didn't want to stand. Maybe she was over-analyzing it but it seemed like Leonardo felt the same. Now she only wanted to spend the rest of the night with him. She'd even told him most of her life story. Which was strange. She never considered herself a person who would open up to someone. But Leonardo made it easy. Probably because he exuded the same air as her *papá*—that he doesn't truly belong—like he could vanish the next second if he wished.

They spoke of many things but she had yet to hear his story. He revealed just enough for her to know what he was like, without knowing who he was.

It could be the wine but the aching shyness she'd felt on and off, including that embarrassing war with the fireplace, didn't seem to matter anymore. She wanted to at least ask him the question she'd been dying to ask right after accepting he wasn't some magical genie.

"Leo," she said, using the short version for the first time. The pleased smile on his face told her he liked it.

"Yes?" he drawled, pushing the plate aside before pouring a little more wine into his glass. He wasn't as solid as Alonso, and was more on the beautiful side than handsome. A masculine beauty she couldn't describe.

She looked him straight in the eye. "What are you?"

He threw his head back, and she expected him to laugh, but he covered his mouth and straightened up. "Are you drunk? You're not going to ask me to use magic and get back into your bottle, are you?"

"Of course not." She drank the rest of her wine, then shrugged. "I just want to know where you're from." He sighed, and a buzz of excitement bubbled in her at a thought. "Are you like *Papá*? When I think about it now, that's probably why you weren't surprised when I told you about him. Because you can also jump through time."

"It may not be obvious but I was surprised," he said, not addressing her question, again.

But she wasn't about to give up. "I know little about how *Papá* jumped from one time to another, or to other parallels, but he told me he first experienced it when he was fifteen. He found a portal that connected him to the future. But once he was there, he didn't know how to get back because the portal was gone. Later, he found out that he could use items with spirits."

"Spirits?"

She nodded.

His face contorted into a frown. "How can you tell when an item has a spirit?"

"He said they're things people treasured. It's not simple but, with enough mind power, the items can take you places. He wished to leap through time so bad, he was willing to die for it."

Leonardo crossed and uncrossed his arms, then shoved his hands in his trouser pockets, balancing the chair on its two back legs.

She couldn't read him as well as he could her but it seemed clear that he was weighing his thoughts.

"Celestina, would you believe me if I said I came from the future?"

"If you say it's the truth, then I will believe you. I saw *Papá* appear out of thin air many times, so it isn't much different from how you showed up."

"I come from the year twenty-twenty. Please don't tell anyone else."

Sparks of joy exploded in her heart at the thought that he'd shared a secret with her. Their own secret.

"Sabel and Alonso also know."

"Right, of course." Of course, she wouldn't be the only one. Not even the second. Her shoulders dropped, then the names registered. "Who's Sabel?"

"Isabela. I call her Sabel because of Alonso."

She nodded, understanding why, but that didn't stop her from feeling envious. As she gathered the glasses from the table, she plucked up the courage and asked him to call her by her nickname. She wanted to feel special. He looked without saying anything.

"Of course, you don't have to, if you're not comfortable. I know it's a bit intimate." She regretted the word the moment it left her lips, and turned to go.

"What's your nickname?" he asked, gripping her wrist.

"*Papá* called me Celest."

"Wouldn't *Tina* be a normal nickname?"

"Yes, but *Papá* was not normal."

He nodded to himself. "Celest sounds like Celestial. It suits you." His smile warmed her heart. Still holding her wrist, he got to his feet and leaned over. "Goodnight, Celest." He kissed her cheek and walked to the doorway.

She touched her cheek, then rushed out and caught up with him in the entryway as he was putting his jacket on. "Leo, wait." He stopped and seemed to stiffen, and she wondered what was wrong. "You can't go home now. It's too dark. I don't have a flashlight to lend you." She took a steadying breath. "There's a room beside me. Use it for tonight."

He turned to face her. "You're really clueless, aren't you?"

Her eyes widened. "What?"

"Aren't you worried about what might happen if I stay?"

Her mother came to mind, and she nodded with a wry chuckle. "Right, *Mamá* wouldn't accept—"

"Not her." He stepped closer, his gaze not moving from her face. Next, he grabbed her shoulder. Tight, but not painful. "I'm talking about you. Aren't you worried that I'll do something to you during my stay?"

Yes, do something! That surprised her. She met his fiery gaze with equal passion. "Are you going to?"

He raised both brows. "I might."

"Might what?"

"Do something."

"Like what?"

He lowered his face. "Aren't you going to stop me?" His breaths matched her shallow ones.

"What if I don't want to?"

He let go of her and rubbed his head with his uninjured fingers. "You really want me to...lose my cool?" He opened the door and stepped outside. "Don't worry about the flashlight. I got this." He pulled out the flat thing he'd held earlier while she'd tended the fire.

She hadn't asked him what it was, and lost interest after he revealed where he came from. He tapped around it, and it glowed. Not enough to light the road, but after a few more taps, a bright light popped out.

"See!" He smiled, but she became angry. She had challenged him, pushed him to his limit, even gave him excuses, but he still wanted to escape.

"Cobarde."

"What did you—"

"I said you're a coward."

He opened his mouth but she didn't wait for him to speak. She grabbed him by the collar and pulled him down to her. If he wouldn't make the first move, she'd do it. But she might have done it a little too forceful because, instead of a kiss, their foreheads collided. He groaned, clutching his head.

Too embarrassed, she hurried back inside the house and locked the door. She wilted to the floor, shook by hot and cold flushes, her body trembling as she let out a silent scream against the palm of her hand.

Chapter 13

LEONARDO

I'd been trying to stop the smile but the more I pushed what happened aside, the more it squeezed itself into my mind, taunting me, showing me over and over Celestina's failed attempt at kissing me. The amusement was followed by dread.

If she'd succeeded, I don't think I could have held myself back. How would I handle the consequences that followed? If only I had a way to check what changed in the future, then I could... Wait, could what? Kiss Celestina?

I stopped walking and leaned against the streetlight. Ugh, I'm twenty-nine. I've had a lot of experience with women, but here I am acting like a damn teenager with his first love. Hold on, it's not far-fetched to say I'm having my first love, in a sense. Even if Celestina is a lot younger now, she's still the same woman I've been crushing on since I was a boy.

The pole was cool against my forehead. Maybe if I knocked my head hard while wishing to return to the future, it would happen. I wanted it so bad, but was I willing to die to get it?

Another groan. I never realized it until now but lying to yourself is one of the hardest things to do. No matter what, you know your lies—they'll eat you from the inside. However, what could I do? Make her my girl?

I wanted to cry. Maybe Celestina was right—I'm a coward.

"¿Estás bien, hijo?"

"Huh?" I said, feeling like Marty Mcfly from *Back to The Future*, except I'm not as funny as Micheal J. Fox. I'm babbling inside my head now, feeling like an idiot. I turned and backed away from the pole when I saw my great-grandmother Juliana looking at me the same way I felt about myself.

Un idiota.

"*Si, Señora,* I'm okay."

"*¿Estás seguro?*" She studied me, then looked at my injured hand as she waited for me to reply to her question of whether I was sure I was okay. "Come with me. I've cooked *gambas al ajillo* for dinner."

Like that will make my hand better. If the thought of banging my head didn't make me cry, this invitation brought tears to my eyes. Why does everyone around me want to feed me seafood? Do I look like someone who loves what he hates?

I took a step back. *"Gracias, Señora* Juliana, *pero—"*

"No pero, you're obviously moved to tears. Don't be shy, come." She took my arm and, with an iron grip, pulled me with her. I couldn't break free. She babbled away, ignoring my reluctance. "Isabela took some of it for Alonso. She will for sure eat with him. Alonso loves seafood, so I always prepare extra portions. There's a lot left."

So, it's because of *Abuelo.* He's the reason my family torments me with seafood?

Damn you, *Abuelo*!

I should be energized after eating two meals in one night but I'm drained instead. Great-Grandma was worse than *Abuela.* She almost threw the food at me, and so much of it. Like *Abuela,* she kept pointing out that I have no muscles.

I have muscles! I'm not skinny—I'm fit! But in a place where people do physical labor everyday, I guess I'm not built enough for them.

As I made my way back to *Abuelo's* house, I shivered. No more seafood. Any more and I'll have nightmares.

I didn't bother using the key—the lights were on inside. After knocking, I opened the door when *Abuela* told me to come in, to find the two of them flirting with each other in the living room, over apple pie and *cafe con leche.* It was an odd feeling seeing them behave with each other the same way I remembered, but looking a lot younger. Younger than me.

"Goodnight, *Abuela*—I mean, Sabel."

"See?" she said to *Abuelo*, puffing her already puffed curls. I was halfway up the stairs when she called me back. "Don't be in such a hurry, Leo. Come back here. I told you earlier, didn't I? We need to talk."

Grumbling, I made my way back, sat beside *Abuela,* and waited for one of them to speak. But more than a minute passed, or maybe five? I had a strong urge to take out my phone to set a timer because we were just sitting there like three idiots.

"Are we just going to sit like this? Staring at each other?" *Abuela* asked, breaking the awkward silence. She looked at *Abuelo.* "Don't you have anything to say to your grandkid?"

I bet my twenty-six-year-old *abuelo* felt as uncomfortable as me, or probably worse. He shifted in his seat, cleared his throat, and met my eyes. "*Hola.*"

Cringe. "Good night," I replied and got to my feet.

"*¿Qué?*" *Abuela* grabbed my arm and pulled me down to my seat. I landed hard. "Is that all the two of you are going to say to each other? Alonso, didn't you want to confirm what I told you?"

I rubbed the side of my neck, suspecting a strained muscle.

"You, don't you want to talk to your grandfather properly?"

Abuelo flinched. Yeah, I felt just as awkward about all this. But stubborn as she was, *Abuela* would have none of it.

"Okay," she said, "let's start with the names."

"We already know each other," *Abuelo* and I both said.

She grinned. "Now you're behaving like family. Now, Alonso, let Leo stay here until all this..."—she waved her hand in an arc—"this thing gets sorted out." She turned to me. "Don't you think it was kind of him to let you stay?"

I snorted. "He obviously doesn't want me to. He just volunteered because you offered to let me stay in your spare room."

"That's not true. Is it, Al?"

He didn't reply.

I let out a mocking laugh. "*Abuela,* in case you didn't notice, he practically wanted to murder me for hugging you."

"I didn't know who you were then!" he said, glaring at me. "I still have my doubts, but I prefer to keep my enemies close. And I don't like to see strangers hugging Bella."

I got to my feet again. "Oh, yeah? What right do you have? It's not like you had any relationship with her back then."

Abuela, who seemed to panic, pulled me back down. "Leo, that's no way to speak with your *abuelo.*"

"You should be grateful I'm letting you stay," he said, ignoring her.

"No one asked you."

He shrugged. "If you really hate it here, then get out."

"Fine, I will!" I jumped up and put an arm around Isabela. "I can always temporarily stay with *Abuela.*"

"You wouldn't dare." He got up and stared at Isabela, who didn't know who to look at.

"Argh, *¡callate*! Both of you, shut up." She removed my hand from her shoulder and walked out of the room. "Leonardo, you are staying here. We'll talk again when the two of you can behave like adults."

We listened to the clicking of her shoes on the way out and stared at each other when she slammed the door behind her.

"You got her pissed," I said, smiling.

"No, you did." He chuckled and sat down. "So, is it true?"

"What?"

"You know, that you're from the future and you're my..."

"Grandson? Yeah, that's true."

He nodded, studied my face for a few seconds, then turned to the glass cabinet door beside him. "I'm not sure if I should believe you, but if it's true, why are you disclosing it so easily? Aren't you afraid of changing the future?"

"I want to change it."

"Is that so? Why?"

"It's not something I can explain right now," I said, doing my best not to show how much it worried me. "I'm tired. I'm heading to bed."

"Hmm. *Buenas noches.*" He squinted at his blurry reflection.

I hurried out before he could come up with more questions. To be honest, I wasn't ready to confess everything about the future. Alonso might be a quiet man but he was a hopeless romantic, and I'm sure it was only a matter of time before he asked about his relationship with Isabela.

I lay in bed that night, my mind going back to Celestina without my permission. Her lonely figure as she waited for me—her shaking shoulders under my hand—and how she dealt with the fireplace like a child, yet seduced me in the entryway of her home like a real woman. The thought of touching her lips was enough to set my body on fire. Before I knew it, my hand had made its way down.

Stop it! Stop thinking about her and go to sleep!

I brought my hand out of the bedding and closed my eyes but it only made her face clearer. Her untamed tight curls, which seemed out of place compared to other women her age. Her beautiful, gentle smile. Her gaze, both mature and curious, like an inexperienced girl.

"Celest," I whispered and slipped my hand back down, visualizing her beautiful mouth, and those eyes, drawing me right in...capturing me—all of me—until I achieved an explosive release. "Oh, no, now I've done it. Damn it."

Horrified, I stepped out of my room, carrying another pair of pajamas, and went to the bathroom to get cleaned and changed, shame spreading through me. I did it almost without noticing. It was like I was in a trance. How am I going to face her now?

Wait, do I really have to face her? I should be busy finding ways to get back to my time. Still, a big part of me would like to stay—to live a simple life. No internet or any modern comfort but I think I could be happy here.

Abuelo was in the living room when I stepped out of the bathroom. He held a balloon glass with brown alcohol in it. His natural bad-ass style, even when alone, outshone me.

"What's the matter? Pee your pants?" He looked at the crumpled pajamas under my arm.

Like you've never done it. A stupid image of *Abuela* in lingerie, like those models in men's magazines, popped into my head, and I had a sudden urge to punch *Abuelo* if he had ever done it. But, then again, he would probably knock me down if he knew what I'd just thought about. Besides, I wasn't the one to talk. I just did it with Celestina in my head. Ugh.

"Sweat," I said. "A lot."

"*¿Quieres cerveza?*"

The thought of cold beer on this chilly night was torture. I shook my head. "That's okay, *Abuelo,* I'm not hot anymore after washing up."

He got up and took out another balloon glass, half-filled it with brandy, and stretched it toward me. I didn't want to drink but his expression told me he wasn't taking no for an answer. Carrying the pajamas, I entered the room and took the glass from him. He waited for me to sip, ignoring my grimace as he sat back in his comfortable chair.

"Don't call me *Abuelo* again. I understand how you see me if you're really from the future but there's no way I'll accept the reference. Just call me Alonso. Also, Bella may be okay being called *Abuela* but you have to stop it. Everyone will make fun of us if they hear it."

"Oh, don't worry, I call her Sabel in public."

His eyes narrowed. "What did you call her?"

"Sabel."

"Call her Isabela." He poured more brandy into my glass, almost filling it, knowing well I didn't like it. I'm sure it showed on my face earlier. He lifted his glass. "*Salud.*"

"*Salud,*" I said, my voice weak, clinking my glass with him. Damn, I thought after knowing that I'm no threat to his relationship with *Abuela,* he'd chill out. But I was wrong. He still hates my guts.

I woke up the next day with a hangover. And the banging on the door wasn't helping. I turned on my side and covered my ears with my pillow, determined to go back to my dreamland.

The knocking got harder. "Leo, get up and let's go," Alonso said.

I tapped my phone and groaned to see the time was barely six in the morning. What is going on? I threw the pillow aside and flipped the bedding away.

"What is it?" I asked when I opened the door.

"Aren't you coming with me? Let's go."

He looked more like a cowboy, in old denim jeans and shirt, topped with a brown leather jacket. Far from his dress style when we first met. "Where are we going at this inhuman hour?"

"*El campo.*"

"The field? Are you even human? Did you sleep?" We drank brandy late into the night—I remember seeing the clock close to midnight when I wobbled up to my room. While I could only make out bits and pieces of our conversation, I recall him saying I'd need to work in the field with him if I wanted enough income for my plan. I don't remember the plan.

"Come on. Hurry up."

"No way, I want to sleep. Besides, I can't work with this hand."

He considered it and nodded. And, for a second, I thought he agreed. "You can assist me using your right hand. Now, get ready. Act your age. You're older than me."

I groaned. I'm also not made for farm work. "You're a cold man, *Abuelo.*"

He glared at me. "Call me that one more time and you'll be picking a tooth off the floor."

I pressed my lips together and made a zipping motion. "Got it.

He clapped my shoulder and gave me half a smile. Ah, there's my *Abuelo*.

"Get ready. Bella's downstairs making breakfast."

Chapter 14

All They Wanted

Like every morning, Celestina woke up, cleaned the house, ate her breakfast alone, and went after her mother to the field. Except for her embarrassing memories of Leonardo last night, it seemed as if everything would be the same as usual. But her eyes widened when she saw the man beside Alonso. He had his back to her but she couldn't be mistaken.

"Leonardo?"

Even though she was far from him, he turned and looked at her, and smiled. She flashed him a graceless smile, her face burning as people around gawked at her. These people usually stayed out of her and her mom's way. Now, she clenched her fists and gritted her teeth, wanting to yell at them. Instead, she hardened her expression and pretended they didn't exist as she made her way to her mother.

Later that night, right after dinner, Celestina heard a knock on the door. Her mother, as usual, ate before her, and was now in the living room. She went to the sink and rinsed the plates, waiting to see if her mother would open the door. The visitor knocked again.

She dried her hands and walked by the living room door, seeing that her mother had dozed off on the sofa. With no choice, she opened the door and gaped when she saw Leonardo standing two meters away, looking up at the moonlit sky. The sight of him was surreal. He truly did belong somewhere else. No matter what he did or how he tried to blend in, he carried an air of the future.

He turned, the action slow, and their gazes locked in a tender moment. The memory of colliding with him flashed through her mind, and it seemed he was thinking of it too. His smile teased her, and heat surged into her cheeks. But then his smile vanished and he looked down, and she heard him taking a couple of deep breaths, his chest rising and falling.

"Do you want to come in?" she asked, growing impatient, then cringing at the thought of her mother in the living room. If he agreed, they had to sneak into the kitchen and be quiet. Her mother worked hard today, and she wanted her to rest. Preferably in bed, but she knew better than to wake her. She'd made the mistake of doing that a couple of times before when she was a kid, and they were some of the more painful moments of her life. Her mother would insult her, comparing her to her 'stupid father,' who made a hell out of her life. Those words hurt more than any physical pain she received over the years. Physical pain heals but emotional and mental wounds scarred her for life.

"No, I don't think that's a smart idea," Leonardo said. "And it seems you agree," he added when he noticed her sigh. "We can't spend time alone."

"Why?"

"You know why."

She did. He probably felt the strange, comfortable but uncomfortable tension when they were alone. She looked up, her heart pounding faster as he drew closer, his warmth radiating from his skin, his eyes full of passion as they searched her face. He caressed her bottom lip with his thumb, soft and light, sending sparks through her body, like lightning. She wanted him to kiss her more than anything in the world. And in that moment, she was sure, if he asked, she would be his.

But then he stopped. "Celest, we need to ignore each other from now on."

She held tight to the doorframe, the oxygen drained from her lungs. Tears welled, then slipped over and ran down her cheeks. She brushed them away. "I—"

"Let go of Celestina," her mother demanded, and Leonardo snapped away, his eyes almost bulging. "Celestina, if you want to talk to him, get out and close the door. If not, close the door and finish the dishes."

"*Sí, Mamá.*"

Trembling inside, she glanced at Leonardo, not missing his grimace, or the muscles of his jaw twitching. He was in as much pain as her but there was nothing she could do about it. She closed the door without another word.

When she turned, she caught a look she had never seen before from her mother at the sight of her crying, but a second later it vanished.

"I'm going to bed," her mother said, ignoring her when she said goodnight.

She dried her eyes and finished washing the dishes before heading to bed, where she poured all her sadness into her pillow.

After a couple of weeks, Celestina noticed that Leonardo no longer had the bandage around his hand. And Alonso's group seemed to have adopted him. By now, everyone in the village knew him, liked him, and, most of all, knew that he shared a home with Alonso. He'd also befriended Isabela. She both admired and envied him. He had achieved in less than a month what she couldn't accomplish her whole life.

The moody weather didn't seem to have affected Isabela as she bantered with Leonardo and ruffled his hair. Usually, when a girl and a guy behaved like them, people would assume it was only a matter of time before they came together. But everyone already knew that Isabela and Alonso were in a romantic relationship. Besides, anyone with eyes could see that Isabela and Leonardo behaved like a mother and son. Odd, because of how young she was compared to him. Yet, somehow, it suited them. And it didn't stop her from wishing she, too, could touch him.

She noticed him a lot around Font Vella, muttering to himself and acting as if he was searching for something. Once, she even heard him say the words she'd written for her bottle before he appeared.

Often, when he saw her, he looked as if he wanted to speak to her but change his mind right away.

"What are you dawdling around for?" her mother asked.

Leonardo looked up, and their gazes met. Time seemed to stand still for a second before it broke when her mother shouted at her.

Embarrassed, she turned from him and walked away. She had grown accustomed to the heartbreak, as she'd done with all the pain she'd experienced in her life. In the days that followed, she ignored him, tilting her chin and looking away whenever their gazes met. Even so, she felt like a fool for wishing he would look at her as she passed him. It was tough because she couldn't lie to herself. She missed talking to him, and longed to see his thoughtful smile, which appeared only when they were alone. Most, though, she missed how his gaze traced her face, like she was the most precious person in his life.

"Men like that are like Ángel," her mother said. "They will never stay."

It was the first time she heard her mother say her *papá's* name. It had to be him because she would never utter the name of that man in prison. Also, despite the irritated tone of her mother's voice, it contained a hint of yearning and pain.

She clenched her fingers around the tool she was working with, wanting to ask her about him, but the time for *siesta* had finished. When the day ended, the question still floated around her head. Her mother hadn't said another word, and for each passing minute, her curiosity grew. But her courage didn't match it. She lived with her mother but knew nothing about her. *Mamá* wouldn't let her into her world. No matter how many times she tried knocking, a coldness she was accustomed to remained. Until Leonardo came along.

On the way back from the field, she felt like a toddler trotting behind her mother. Hearing her say *Papá's* name for the first time made her observe her as a person. Her mother lost her parents when she was five and grew up with her aunt, who stopped her from aborting her pregnancy when she was raped at fourteen. Her chest burned with pity for her mother.

How hard it must have been for her mother carrying her until until giving birth. If not for her, her *mamá* might have a complete family now.

Celestina was two years old when her mother's aunt passed away. It was around that time when her *papá* showed up. Back then, she was oblivious to the world, but her *papá* taught her to love. Not only to love him, but her mother too.

When she recalled the way her mother said '*Ángel,*' she quickened her step to catch up with her. The woman only reached above her chin, and standing side by side like this at thirty-four and nineteen, they could be mistaken as sisters. But the burden of being a single teenage mom showed. She looked more haggard than other women her age.

When her mother looked at her, Celestina forgot what she wanted to say. But her heart wouldn't relent and, without thinking, she pulled her mother into her arms. Nearby workers stared but she didn't care. "*Te quiero, Mamá,*" she whispered.

Her mother stiffened, then softened, her mouth opening, as if she wanted to say something. She raised her arms and, for a moment, Celestina thought she would embrace her back and say 'I love you too,' but, instead, her mother pushed her so hard she stumbled and fell to the ground. The few people who were not aware of them, now also watched, worried. Some made a move toward her but stopped when her mother glared at them, then at her.

"I don't need your concern," she said to her. "If you want me to have a better life, go and disappear."

With these words slicing fresh wounds into her heart, Celestina kept a blank face and attempted to stand up as if she wasn't affected. Even if only for show, she wanted everyone to think that her mother's voice didn't cut her. But her knees buckled when she was almost standing straight, her legs numb from the shock. A strong arm held her steady, and her heart thumped on seeing Leonardo's face.

His grip was firm but gentle; however, his expression showed his ire as he looked at her mother down his nose—an arrogance she didn't know he was capable of. He looked so much like Alonso, and if she wasn't in such a distressed state, she would have pointed it out to him. Maybe even teased him, calling him Alonso's brother. But it wasn't the time, not when he looked so angry.

"Do you have any idea how Celestina feels?" he asked her mother.

She lifted her hand to him. "Leo, stop."

He ignored her. "You can't vent your hate and anger for your tragic past toward her. She never asked you to give birth to her. She's innocent and guiltless."

Celestina looked around at everyone pretending not to notice, but she knew their full focus was on them now. Isabela's too, but with unjudging eyes. She grabbed Leonardo's arm. "Leo, stop. Please!"

"All she wanted was your love," he continued. "But, instead, you tell her to disappear?"

In that moment, a warm feeling spread through her, erasing her pain.

Leonardo truly cares about her.

A spark of guilt flashed in her mother's face, looking as if something trapped inside was struggling to come out but couldn't.

"Why don't *you* disappear instead?" Leonardo shouted.

Her blood turned cold, and she pulled away from him and slapped him so hard her palm stung. Without wanting it, her eyes flooded, and she opened her mouth to reprimand him but the hurt in his eyes as he mouthed "*Perdón*" while reaching to dry her tears was enough to make her back away.

Unable to deal with her jumbled emotions, she ran after her mother. They walked in silence all the way home, and when they arrived, her mother went straight to her room.

Celestina stood outside the bedroom and listened. Her mother was muttering as drawers were opened and shut. She caught "Where is it?" a few times, then a long moment of silence followed by loud sobs. It was too much, and the only thing she could do was sit there with her back against the wall and cry silent tears with her mother.

Chapter 15

TE AMA

Celestina stayed outside her mother's room late into the night, listening to sobs of despair inside. At some point she fell asleep, only to be woken when her *mamá* opened the door and asked her to come into the room. The bed was too small for two but *Mamá* still lay beside her. The revulsion in her face wasn't there as their arms touched. Celestina wasn't sure, because she was far too sleepy, but she thought her mother hugged her before she fell asleep, whispering, "I will make things up to you, *lo prometo.*"

When she opened her eyes, she stiffened on realizing she was in her mother's bed, with tears welling as the blurry memory returned to her. She pulled the cover over her face and inhaled the comforting scent of her mother, until her nose ached and became runny. *Mamá* had forbidden her from entering her bedroom when she was a child, so she'd never set foot inside. Once, when she was seven, she snuck in and took her key from her purse. She wanted to get out before her *mamá* became sober, but she caught her and beat her so much it terrified her. The woman had turned into a demon, using a belt.

In the middle of the thrashing, Celestina became numb to the stinging pain on her skin but her heart broke to pieces as her mother shouted "I hate you. You're a reminder of the most horrible time of my life. I would never have given birth to a rapist's daughter if they had given me the choice!"

She never attempted to do anything that might anger her mother after that, except for hiding the heart bottle her *papá* left her. There were times during puberty when she wanted to hate her mother, but no matter how much she was hurting inside, her love for her never went away. Last night was a dream come true. She would never want them to go back.

Before she left, she took one more look at the room. There was nothing special about it. It looked like hers, with a wardrobe at the foot of the bed near the door, and a vanity mirror on top of a small table, but she smiled when she saw a frame among the make-up set, which seemed untouched for years. A photo of *Papá*. She knew because only her *papá* could smile the way he did. And there was no way *Mamá* would put a photo of that detestable man, who forced his seed into her, anywhere in their house. She glanced at the table clock and nearly jumped out of her skin on seeing the time.

"Eleven?" she shrieked. She arranged the bed before running down the stairs, expecting to find her furious mother in the kitchen, but what awaited her was silence. The dishes were washed in the tray, and something was covered on the table.

Her heart flipped when the front door opened and closed. She turned, expecting her drunk mother to appear and reprimand her, but what greeted her was a sober woman, her dark, straight hair curled around the edges, her face cheered by light make-up.

"*¿Mamá?*" She was about to tell her she looked good but bit it back, preparing for a yell. But her mother just sighed and removed her jacket. Instead of tossing it aside and leaving her to clean it up, she hung it on the stand, then went about placing the groceries she'd bought in the cabinet and fridge. Celestina remained standing by the kitchen door, still unable to wrap her mind around the change.

Her mother removed the cover from the food on the table. *"Queres desayuno o no?"*

She looked at the *tostada con tomate, aceite, y jamón* and her mouth watered. *"¡Sí, Mamá!"* she said, with a vigorous nod. No way she wasn't eating what her mother made for her for the first time. She hurried to take a seat and bit into the toast. While she had eaten it on many occasions, today, toasted bread with tomato and ham never tasted so good. The corners of her eyes stung, and her heart ached with happiness.

Her mother set a glass of orange juice beside her. "I'll make you something better next time." She left the kitchen before Celestina could invite her to join. By the time she was done, her mother was nowhere to be found.

Curious about her whereabouts, she knocked on her bedroom door and dared open it. It wasn't locked. She entered and saw something lying on the bed. A bunch of tulips made of colorful fabric. It had to be her mother's handiwork. A piece of paper lay on top of an envelope in front of the flowers. Her mother's handwriting:

Para ti

She swallowed, lifted the envelope, and noticed the dark smear of dried blood. A cold chill shot down her spine. It was the envelope her *papá* left for her mother.

What is going on? She wants me to have this?

Her nerves were all over the place as she opened it. It contained a letter and a photo of the three of them—taken when she was five, and one of the best days of her life. Her *papá* drove her and her mother to Alicante. They went shopping, ate in a restaurant, and walked the *Paseo de la Explanada.* She loved it so much. Not only because it was near the beach but the *Explanada* itself was magical. The mosaic paving, mimicking the waves of the Mediterranean, was almost half a mile long, flanked by four rows of palm trees and flowers. That joy reflected in her young face in the photo, taken by a freelance photographer. Her mother didn't want the image taken, saying the price was too high, but her *papá* put his arm around them both as the photographer took the shot.

She put the photo down and flipped the letter open.

Maria Josefa, mi amor...

With her bottom lip between her teeth, she read again and again the way her *papá* addressed her mother. Each time she read it, a piece of her broken heart glued itself back into place.

By the time she was done reading, her soul felt complete. She kissed the paper. *"Te quiero, Papá."*

"*Y él también te ama.*"

She turned to the door and her mother stepped forward.

"He loved you, too. Very much." She stepped forward again. "And I loved him, too," she whispered, her bottom lip trembling. "I never got to say it to him. I was blinded by hate. I ignored you both." Tears flooded her eyes. "*Hija, perdóname.*"

Celestina rushed to her and embraced her. Her mother hugged her back, and both of them cried together for the first time in their lives.

Chapter 16

LEONARDO

December 7th, 1956

Farm work wasn't as hard as I'd first thought. It took a lot of energy but I wouldn't say it was difficult. Like any job, once you got the hang of it, it became simple enough. That, or it was in my roots. My hand healed during the two months of working in the field, and I even developed my muscles. And my appetite grew, too, though I still backed away from seafood, which I suspect became the talk of the village because everyone who invited me for dinner made a point of saying they wouldn't be having seafood.

Life felt good, and was fun, but it darkened whenever I thought of Celestina. She was avoiding me. I guess what I did to her mother really hurt her. On the bright side, their relationship seemed better, and a rumor was going around that Maria Josefa had stopped drinking.

Keeping my distance from Celestina made it hard to think, though. No matter how I viewed it, she or her bottle are my only key to getting home. But do I really want to return? As mad as it sounds,

I could stay and watch my mother grow, and maybe even befriend her like Alonso and Isabela. I groaned. Get a grip, you idiot!

Friday afternoon, I was hanging out with Alonso and the guys by the spring, trying to catch nonexistent fish, when Celestina marched up to me and handed—or thrust—a bag of fresh-baked cookies at my chest.

"As an apology for feeding you something you hated, and for the slap, and for ignoring you for a long time. Also, thank you."

She raced off before I could say anything. That woman likes to run.

Adalberto, Hernan, Gonzalo, Luisano, and Pedro Miguel jumped me, each of them grabbing a cookie from the bag.

Arturo, the one in the group most similar to Alonso's personality, also took one but didn't step away. "Are you close to Celestina?"

"*Hombre,* that's Leo's gift!" Juan Martin cut in. "You shouldn't take it for yourself!" Juan Martin was the mischievous and cheerful best friend of Alonso. When he shoved his hand into the bag, Alonso whacked him on the head. "Yeow! That hurts!"

Alonso gave him a bored look. "If you want to reprimand someone else, set an example yourself."

We all laughed. I took the chance to hide the remaining cookies before they were all taken. By now, everyone in the village treated me as one of them. I'd grown fond of them and had become the odd member of Alonso's gang. There was only one person I couldn't stand—Celestina's mother. She glowered at me every chance she got. I'm sure it wasn't because I hurt Celestina's feelings when I told her we couldn't keep spending time alone together. No, it was because I stopped her from bullying her daughter.

My feelings for Celestina have cooled quite a bit since then, though she still haunts my dreams, and I feel like a fool for making love to my hand with her in mind. Ah, okay, maybe things haven't cooled so much, but I have it under control. Now that she has approached me again, I plan to have a deep conversation with her about her father. But, first, I need to be able to look at her and think about something other than putting an engagement ring on her finger. Damn, is it my age? It's like I'm desperate to have a girlfriend.

"Hey, guys, who wants to visit Benidorm tomorrow?" Juan Martin asked, hanging upside down from a tree branch.

"I'm in," I said. It had been a while since I'd shopped for clothes. I'd been switching between three jackets, two jeans, and five shirts, and had already returned the clothes to Rodrigo. As expected, he didn't know his sister had given them to me.

Adalberto clapped. "That's a good idea. Let's spend the whole day in town to celebrate. We have only eighteen days left until Christmas."

"That's not a bad idea." Luisano nodded to himself. "Maybe I'll find a girlfriend this time." He grabbed a stick and poked Juan Martin, who swayed, begging him to stop between hysterical laughter. Pedro Miguel joined the poking, and poor Juan Martin turned purple. The laughter spread to everyone, including me.

"I'll go if I can bring my girlfriend," Arturo said.

"Dolores is busy tomorrow," Luisano responded.

Arturo's shoulders dropped. "Luisano, can't you just do the work for her?"

"And let you and my sister have fun? *¡Nunca!*" He poked Juan Martin with more enthusiasm.

"*¡Basta, basta!*" Juan Martin cried before flipping off the branch and dropping to the ground.

Gonzalo tossed a stick to him, then picked another up before joining him. Soon, we all had our own sticks and a messy sword fight ensued all the way home, with the gang of us giggling like adolescent boys.

Although the group decided to go together, it came down to only four of us: Me, Alonso, Isabela, and Celestina, who I hadn't expected.

"I found her looking for you," Isabela said. "So, I invited her too. It's fine, right?"

"*Está bien,*" Alonso and I replied at the same time. The two girls looked at each other with unspoken understanding before getting into Alonso's car.

Celestina sat beside me in the backseat, as enchanting as ever in her long, green checkered swing dress, her small waist accentuated beneath a black belt, and her curls somewhat tamed under a wide green headband.

I'd dressed myself in a light-green shirt, blue jeans, and a blue bubble jacket, but didn't bother to gel my hair. It's tiring. Alonso, being a rockabilly, had, dressing in a white T-shirt tucked into black jeans, and topped with his black leather jacket. Too light for winter, in my opinion, but he complemented Isabela's black and white polka dots.

Celestina lifted her hand to rearrange the bow of her headband, and I couldn't help following her fingers as she lowered it around the curls at the neckline of her dress. She then brought her hands to her lap and clasped them together.

Control!

Isabela's cheerful voice as she chatted with Alonso about their Christmas plans faded away as I placed my fingers on Celestina's neck. She stiffened before softening, then turned to face me, her gaze searching my face.

"There are strands...in your hair. I mean, at your neck." I faked a cough. "I mean, some hair strands are under your neckline."

A tender smile graced her lips as she leaned her head to the side—an invitation I couldn't resist. I tweaked her soft locks free, then cradled the back of her neck with my hand. She parted her lips—so inviting—and I closed the gap between us. Her sweet breath was warm on my cheek, and our lips had almost touched when Isabela popped her head between the seats. I pulled away and pressed myself to the door.

"What about you two?" she asked. "What are your plans?"

Celestina glanced at me. "I don't know. I haven't talked to *Mamá* about it yet."

"Ah." Isabela nodded and looked at me. "What about you, Leo? My parents said you're more than welcome to celebrate with us."

"You can also have the house for yourself," Alonso said, catching my eye in the rear-view mirror. I realized then that he'd been watching us.

"You want him to be alone at Christmas?" Isabela snapped, oblivious to what he was insinuating. "What kind of grandfather—"

I cleared my throat to interrupt her. Alonso pretended not to hear anything, and I shook my head. When it came to Isabela, I could never rely on him to back me up. *Abuelo* never scolded her. No wonder *Abuela* always behaved as she wanted. He spoiled her rotten.

Isabela gave him a wicked smile and changed the topic but the knowing glint in Celestina's eyes when she glanced at me told me she wasn't buying our act. I had a feeling she'd got what was happening between the three of us. Damn, the woman was so sharp, and I could see why *Abuela* called her mysterious. Once she was out of her mother's sight, the sad girl stepped aside to become a complex character.

When Alonso parked, Isabela wondered where we should head first. Celestina surprised me when she hooked her arm on mine the moment I stepped out of the car.

"I'll go with Leo, so he won't be a third wheel."

"Leo would never be a third wheel between me and Alonso. We're like family."

Smooth, *Abuela*, smooth, but you already got us busted!

"But I bet you want to have the chance to go on a date, don't you?" Celestina said.

Alonso said nothing but I saw the respectful look he gave Celestina when Isabela agreed. I knew little about how their story went, except Alonso was supposed to confess his love on their date before the Christmas of 1956. Maybe this is the day? I decided not to interfere. The essential thing was Mom being born. Who knows, maybe I'll fade away like Marty McFly if they don't solidify their romance. I studied my hand.

Nope, no transparency. Yet.

After we agreed on where to meet once we were done, Alonso pulled Isabela away, and Celestina dragged me off. Maybe a little too eager. Weird. Did her personality change? What happened to my timid Celest?

Mine? the annoying part of my brain asked. I shoved it away and looked at her as she walked like there was no tomorrow, noticing her red cheeks.

"What's so funny?" she asked, turning at my chuckle, still pulling me along through a crowd outside a store. They'd pasted *70% Rebajas* on the giant window and were playing a Christmas song inside.

I stopped when she turned down a narrow, isolated road. She had no choice but to do the same, unable to budge me. "Where are you going?"

"S-someplace."

I studied her face. "Where?"

Her cheeks went red and she looked down, her long lashes fluttering as she blinked.

Hmm, this is...interesting.

She looked up, then leaned in, until our lips touch. The soft, fluffy feeling on my lips felt like warm chocolate during a snowstorm. So satisfying. No, wait, I shouldn't. Ah, who cares?

Recovering from the surprise attack, all my fears vanished as I clasped my hands around her waist and kissed her back with a passion that surprised even me.

She pulled away, panting. "Are you trying to kill me?"

"No. Since you're so eager to kiss me, I kissed you back." I imprisoned her between my arms and a wall. Being in this position, I could understand at last why almost every 90s' romcom I'd ever seen contains this scene. "I wouldn't want you calling me *cobarde* again."

She lowered her face, blinking those lashes again. "Sorry."

I raked my fingers through my hair and forced myself to stand upright. This woman had a talent for driving me up the wall. What was going to happen to my future now? Would it even matter with her around? "Everything's messed up."

"Why? Because I figured out that Isabela and Alonso are your parents?"

I laughed at that. "That's impossible, Miss Purrball, *Abuela* was fifty-four by then."

"*Abuela.* I see." She grimaced. "I just kissed someone old enough to be my grandchild."

"In case you forgot, I'm twenty-nine, and you're missing my point, Purrball."

"Can you stop calling me that?"

"Purrball."

"Stop."

I grinned. "Purrball."

"*¡Basta ya!*"

"And if I don't have enough yet?" She looked lost. I laughed. "Anyway, the thing is, kissing you—being here with you now—shouldn't be a part of the story."

"What's it supposed to be, then? I marry some random man and have babies with him while dreaming of having a life with you?"

I cupped her face. "Celest, I'm not the man for you. In the future, you..." Disappear. Why hadn't I thought of that? I've been so occupied with so many things since I arrived in this time, I forgot the stories *Abuela* told me about her.

"She vanished into thin air right in front of my eyes." The memory from so long ago flashed in my mind. *"I'm sure it was because of her favorite heart bottle. That bottle was a curse."*

The heart bottle. Could that really be the answer?

"In the future, I...what?" she asked, holding my hand to her cheek.

I lowered my hand and flipped it to hold hers in mine. "Celest, did your father ever bring you on his time-related travels?"

She shook her head. "He never did."

"Did you experience it yourself?" I wished she would say 'yes' because, if she could travel through time like her father, maybe history wasn't messed up. Maybe I'm meant to be here. Maybe she disappeared to be with me in the future. Dreams and hope swam in my mind but shattered like fragile glass when she shook her head.

"I only heard about his adventures, but I have never done it." Her eyes looked sad, her expression glum. "If I could, then maybe he wouldn't have to die. I could have traveled with him and lived a happier life."

The pain in her voice made me forget my worries. I pulled her close and guided her out to the main street. “Come and help me buy some new clothes. I need to look good if I’m going to spend Christmas with you. Don’t you think?”

Her face lit up, and a prickle of guilt stabbed me. We’ll talk about the bottle another time.

Chapter 17

HIS FUTURE

"Mira su pelo."

Celestina didn't look at the three girls, one of whom had commented on Leonardo's hair. They were close to where the two of them stood.

"He probably rushed to get here for the sale," another girl said. The three of them giggled. "But, even with that crazy hair, don't you think he's handsome?"

"He is," the third girl answered.

Hey, that's my boyfriend! Celestina wanted to say, but aside from how embarrassing that would be, she didn't feel qualified to even think about it. Sure, there were undeniable sparks between her and Leonardo, and he'd kissed her back to the point of breathlessness, but that didn't mean they were in a relationship.

Or are we? She glanced at him and caught him spacing out again. He spent more time doing that than looking at the jeans he was holding. She nudged him. "Are you having a hard time choosing?"

"Huh? Ah, *si... si.*"

She wanted to believe that he was spacing out because of their kiss, but she knew better than to lie to herself. Besides, if he was thinking about her, he wouldn't have such a blank expression. Ever since entering the shop, his cheerfulness had vanished. That worried her.

It took about half an hour before they finished shopping. Leonardo paid the cashier but just stared at her hand when she handed him the bags.

"Gracias," she said to the clerk and took the bags herself.

"Oh, ah, thank you!" Leonardo said, smiling at the clerk, whose responding smile was nothing short of awkward.

Celestina dragged him out of the store and kept going until they were away from the entrance. "What's wrong? You were spacing out in there."

He gave her an aching smile, and her insides twisted. She reached for him, just as he had when she was having a painful time at the *embalse.* With his head on her shoulder, she rubbed his back. "What's wrong?"

He straightened. "It's nothing. Just something I remembered."

She didn't want to feel jealous but she did. "Is it a girlfriend you left behind? The one who gave you that flat flashlight you always carry with you?"

His brows furrowed. "I don't carry a flashlight."

"Yes, you do. You used it the first night we ate dinner. You keep looking at it."

"Ah. No, this is a phone." He pulled the object out of his pocket.

"A phone?"

She took it from his hand, and nearly dropped it when its smooth face glowed. "This thing is a phone?"

"Shhh!" He glanced around, then attempted to take it back but she backed away. It reacted each time she touched the surface. "I'll show you how it works later. Give it back."

Though reluctant to part with it, she did as he asked, glad to see him looking better. "Is that thing from her?"

"No, I bought it myself." He smiled. His usual smile—light and carefree.

"Then what happened to you in there?"

He looked around, guided her to the closest bench by the roadside, and sat with her. "I lost my parents when I was thirteen. It was the day we went shopping together for new jeans. Now, each time I look for new jeans, I'm filled with a bittersweet feeling. More bitter than sweet because it never fails to remind me of that day."

Her shoulder dropped. "Oh, how did it happen?"

"I killed them."

A chill washed over her, and her mind refused to picture him murdering someone, not least his parents. But, then again, maybe he was even more abused than her? What horrible things could his parents have done for him to take such extreme action? She shifted away from him but stopped. No, it must have been out of his control. If he murdered them, he wouldn't look so miserable. There is no anger in his voice—only regret.

"How did it happen?" She inched closer and noticed the corner of his mouth curve up. It vanished as he watched the traffic crawling by them. Then his gaze focused on a family crossing the road.

"I carelessly stepped into the road without looking at the traffic. Everything happened so fast. I heard Mom scream my name. The speeding car screeched to a stop but couldn't avoid us. Mom shoved me out of the way. I hit my head hard on the pavement, while the car threw her up, like a rag doll. The last thing I remember was Dad rushing over to us." He leaned back and looked up, his Adam's apple bobbing as he swallowed. Her heart went out to him, moved by how he looked and sounded like a lost young boy.

"Dad died trying to save my lifeless mother. He carried her, crying for her to wake up as he walked toward me, failing to see another car speeding from the opposite direction." Tears glistened in his eyes. "Celest, I watched both of my parents get smashed by speeding cars, and I couldn't do anything. It was my fault. Me. I caused the accident. I killed them."

She wiped the tears streaming down her cheeks. "No, you didn't kill them, Leo."

"I did!"

She dropped the bags, got up, and stood in front of him. Sniffling, she lay both hands on his cheeks and made him look at her. "You did not take their lives, Leo." She emphasized each word. "It was an accident."

Thirteen-year-old Leonardo looked back at her, shaking his head like a stubborn child. "I'm the reason it happened. I should have been the one on that road." His eyes cleared then, as if what he'd said had only just occurred to him. He jumped to his feet. "That's right, I should have been the dead one. Not them. I should!"

She trembled, having no idea how to help this broken man or what to say to make him snap out of making himself the bad guy. "Listen, Leo, they loved you. They loved you so much, they didn't think twice before giving their lives for you." No one loved me. That made her both envious and sad as she pulled him into a tight hug.

"They would never want you to die or punish yourself. They did what they did because they loved you."

He clung to her, his shoulders shuddering through his silent sobs. Passersby stared at them with concern but they saw no one. Nothing else mattered as they sheltered in each other's arms.

Isabela waved at Celestina and Leonardo from the corner of *El Bar Rojo*, where they'd agreed to meet. She had sipped from the same cocktail for thirty minutes and forbade Alonso from getting another glass of beer before the two arrived.

"Sorry we're late," Celestina said, letting go of Leonardo's hand. The two of them seemed elsewhere, and she didn't like how they were acting.

Leonardo looked from her to Alonso. "What's wrong?"

Even under the soft light of the bar, his eyes looked puffy. The same with Celestina's. She was dying with curiosity but it wasn't the right moment to pry. Alonso was playing with his empty glass, rolling the bottom in circles. She sighed. "He's sulking because I wouldn't let him get another glass of beer."

"Why?" Leonardo asked after exchanging glances with Celestina.

"He's driving us back. It won't be safe if he's drunk. The road to Beniardá isn't for drivers who have had too much to drink."

Leonardo pulled a chair for Celestina before taking one for himself. "If you're worried, I can drive. That way he can enjoy another beer."

Alonso lightened up. "I like you, kid!" He slapped Leonardo's shoulder.

"If I'm a kid, then you're a baby," Leonardo said. "I'm older."

"Oh, yeah?"

Leonardo put an arm on the table and grinned. "Yeah!"

Alonso pushed his glass to the center of the table. "Let's drink and see who remains sane."

"You're on!" Leonardo grabbed the empty glass and waved it to the waiter.

"Stop!" Isabela gripped his arm and tried to lower it. No luck. "You can't both get drunk! Who will drive?"

"Right." Leonardo lowered his hand and looked at Alonso. "Sorry, I surrender."

As the waiter approached, Celestina spoke up but nobody caught it.

"What's that, Celestina?" Isabela asked.

Celestina lifted her chin. "I can drive."

Everyone stared at her.

"Alright!" Leonardo said. "Looks like we're back in the challenge, Alonso."

"And you will lose."

"Let's see about that!" And the two of them gave their orders to the waiter.

While the men argued about the best *tapas*, Isabela turned to Celestina. "You can drive?" No one had seen her drive in their village.

If someone had, it would have reached her. "When did you get your license?"

"Five months ago." She smiled at the waiter before ordering a soft drink and salted peanuts.

Isabela got the feeling she would poke Celestina too much if she pointed out that everyone knew her mother wouldn't let her drive. So, why get it? She ordered one more drink, then scolded Alonso and Leonardo for debating every tiny little thing. They never did so when their friends were around—only when she was present. She glanced at Celestina. Hmm, Celestina, too, it seems.

She shook her head. "I swear, they only look like men—"

"But are kids deep inside," Celestina continued.

She laughed. "Exactly!"

Two hours later, the four of them made their way out of *El Bar Rojo.* The two men were walking in zigzags, still competing over who was drunker.

"You are both drunk!" Isabela said.

"Aw, *Abuela* is angry," Leonardo said, putting his arm around her.

"I'm not your *abuela!"* She snapped a look at Celestina, who didn't seem to care what Leonardo called her. That bothered her a bit, too. From what she could see, Celestina liked Leonardo. If she saw Alonso hugging another woman, even if he was drunk, she would become angry. But, then again, ever since grade school, until they graduated, Celestina barely showed any expressions of interest. Except now, with Leonardo.

"Of course you are *Abuela*!" Leonardo insisted. "Just younger and cuter."

Alonso pulled him off her. "Get off my girl."

"Oh, yeah? But I'm her darling *nieto.*"

"But I'm her man!" Alonso said, putting an arm around her.

She loved that Alonso wanted to monopolize her but felt bad for Leonardo. She was way too young to be a grandmother. But the blood bond between them must have been strong, because she felt responsible for Leonardo despite him being older.

Celestina let out a small laugh and offered to assist Leonardo. He accepted it, leaned on her shoulder and whispered something, which made her blush, her cheeks growing redder after he whispered something else.

Isabela had nothing against her—she had been curious about her for a long time—but knowing that Leonardo was from the future made it different. If she had to play the villain to stop whatever developed between the two, she would. If they had feelings for each other, it was doomed to fail. It would only hurt them.

After much struggle, the two women managed to bring their men back to the car, where they maneuvered them onto the backseat. Alonso smiled at her when she searched his pockets, but she ignored his teasing and pulled the keys out. The thought of letting Celestina drive shook her more.

"You can really do this, right?" she asked again before handing the keys to her.

"I can. I can show you my license if you want."

She waved her hand in dismissal. "No, need." They had no choice now. The guys were already snoring in their seats and she couldn't drive. She only needed to trust Celestina now.

Chapter 18

A DIFFERENT FUTURE

It was nine p.m. when Celestina parked Alonso's car in his garage. Isabela got out and staggered to the back passenger door, which she pulled open. Seeing her boyfriend and future grandson's peaceful, sleeping faces made her want to slap them black and blue. If one of them had been sober, she wouldn't feel like she had just gone through a speed race without protection. Celestina could drive, all right, but she had never been so frightened of the winding road from La Nucia to Beniardá.

She jolted when Celestina tapped her shoulder and gave her Alonso's keys.

I'm never letting you have my grandchild!

Celestina may look like a mild-mannered girl, but she was a madwoman deep inside.

She shook her boyfriend. "Al. Alonso, wake up." He moaned, pushed Leonardo off his shoulder, and started snoring. Pissed, she reached in and shook him harder. "*¡Levántate!*"

His eyes shot open and he looked around. "I'm home?"

"Yes, you're home," she said.

Celestina was at Leonardo's side, trying wake him. "Leo, we're here," she almost whispered.

Isabela couldn't believe she was looking at the same woman who drove like there was no tomorrow, cutting road curves at high speed without consideration for the nervous disposition of her front-seat passenger. The thought of what might have happened if they'd swerved off the road and over one of the countless cliffs made her tremble. Celestina was the definition of 'you can't judge a book by its cover.'

Scary. She regretted bumping into her before they'd left for Benidorm. However, her compassionate side kicked in at the thought of her not having anyone to go anywhere with. It was Christmas season, and she'd been to Benidorm, Alicante, and other cities close by with friends, but Celestina hadn't. Therefore she thought that was their a chance to get to know each other.

After Leonardo first had dinner with her family, she'd waited to get closer to Celestina. They'd known of each other since childhood, and though she often greeted her, she'd never made a specific move to befriend her.

"Leo," Celestina said again, giving his shoulder a soft shake. Unlike Alonso, who sat up and stepped out of the car, Leonardo lifted his arms, wrapped them around her, and pulled her down on top of him. Then he kissed her.

"Good morning, Miss Purrball," he said.

Alonso snickered, while Celestina, who Isabela expected to bolt out of there from embarrassment, stayed, looking a bit flustered as she smiled down at Leonardo. "It's nighttime, crybaby."

"Who are you calling a crybaby? Maybe I should—"

"And please let go of me. I really don't feel comfortable being in this position in front of Alonso and Isabela."

His eyes opened wider and he sat up and looked around, his cheeks reddening when he made eye contact with them. However, instead of easing her off him, he hugged her waist. "Hey, you enjoying the show?"

"Leo!" Celestina tried, without success, to break free.

"I have my own!" Alonso said, putting an arm around Isabela. Her heart danced at his display of affection. He tossed the garage key to Leonardo, who caught it mid-air. "I'll leave the rest to you." He turned to Isabela. "Bella, *¿vamos?*"

"Hmm?" She looked at him, calmer now, getting over the rush from feeling her life slipping away from her.

"I'll bring you home."

"Okay," she said, but hesitated on seeing the sweet scene developing between Celestina and Leonardo. "But we should invite Celestina to come with us."

"Leonardo will take care of that."

Leonardo stepped out of the car. "Alonso's right, don't mind us."

"*Pero—*"

"No, let's go," Alonso said, his voice a harsh whisper.

She looked at him and swallowed the rest of her protest, not liking that he was angry.

Alonso wasn't the talkative type. His silence was nothing new for Isabela but the short walk from his home to her house was stifling. Over the years, they'd had their fair share of arguments. Yet, for the first time, she, who was known for her braveness in standing up to Beniardá's rebel, hesitated to look him in the face and confront him. It almost scared her to see what expression he had.

Ever since he'd become an orphan, the people around saw him wear three looks: disgust, anger, and indifference. Sometimes, he smiled a bit with friends, but that was about it. He was a man before she came of age but, privately, she always saw his playful, mischievous look that everyone had forgotten. It was the thing about him that assured her—gave her courage and made her feel special.

When they reach her door, she kept her eyes down. "Goodnight—"

"Are you really not going to explain what's going on?"

"I have no idea what you're talking about." When she looked up, her heart constricted. She had never seen him look sad before, but he did now. His shoulders hung low and his usual confidence was nowhere in sight.

"Are you interested in being with Leonardo?"

"What?" Her stomach flipped the moment his words became clear. "I am not!"

"You seem unable to take your eyes off him. You also seem disturbed by all the attention he's giving Celestina."

"Al, are you hearing yourself? How can you even think that? He's our grandchild."

"That's what he said, but we have no proof of that."

She looked him up and down, biting back the urge to laugh. "Have you seen yourself in the mirror and looked at that young boy?"

"He's a man, Bella. Even if he doesn't look like it, he's older than me."

"Still, I see him as nothing more than a boy. He could be ten years old or fifty, and I'd still treat him like a child."

Relief washed over his face, then his eyes darkened as doubt crept in.

Isabela studied him. Wow, she was seeing so much now. She would probably dance with joy had this happened for another reason. "Al, I assure you that, ever since I was old enough to love a man, I have never felt it for anyone but you."

He straightened up with a fake, indifferent expression, which she read as proud. With his confident tone returned, he almost looked taller. "Then why are you behaving like that toward him? It's almost like you don't want him to be with anyone."

"Because I don't want him to be with anyone. It's bad enough that we know the truth. The villagers and your friends accept him, but Celestina seems to know the truth. Worse, there seems to be something between them."

"Bella, that's their business. They're adults like us."

"Yes, but Leonardo came from the future."

"Yeah, so he told us."

"Celestina lives here in the present."

"Bella, what are you trying to say?"

She sighed. "If he starts to influence anyone here, won't the future change?"

"Of course. Simply showing up here and interacting with you and me already did that. We ended up together because of him. I was afraid of losing you to him, and realized I had to admit my feelings for you to prevent that. So, yes, I think a lot of things have already changed from his future."

"*His* future? You mean *the* future."

It didn't leave much of an impact on her when Leonardo kept stopping her from prying about the future, but hearing it from Alonso made her feel the full weight of it.

"No, I meant *his* future," Alonso said. "I'm sure if he truly came from the future, that future has a different story of you and me. He needs to be born from our daughter first, which means you and I got together another way."

"I get it. I think. No, I actually don't, just stop." She raised her hand, not knowing what part of her body she wanted to touch. Her heart thumped so hard it shook her eardrums. Her head ached, too, and she felt sick to her stomach. "I may have ruined my grandchild's future."

"No, you didn't."

"How can you say that? You just said *his* future. The story has changed completely. What will happen to him?"

"Nothing."

"What?"

He crossed his arms and leaned against the wall. She hated how calm he seemed but felt too rattled to point it out.

After a long moment, he eased away from the wall and held his arms out. "Nothing will change because that time already exists. Nothing will change it."

Her mind came to a complete halt. He might as well have invented a new language, because she understood nothing of what he'd said. From the way he looked at her, her confusion must have shown on her face.

"Think about it, Bella. He existed with everyone in the future. With the older you and me. Do you think the time he came from ceased to exist because he's here? The future he comes from is the future of those from our time, but that future is his past. The past always exists."

She shook her head, still not getting where he was going. It was obvious that time existed for everyone, but...

"So," he said, holding both hands up, palms facing him, "if things suddenly changed for the people in the future, wouldn't it be strange? If you can travel in time, I will still exist here, missing you. If you kill me, my past won't be erased. I will still be there, but you'll create a future without me in it."

The thought of the future without Alonso made her want to cry, but everything he said floated around her, refusing to stick to her brain. Also, she realized for the first time just how complex his mind was. His intelligence awed her, making her fall for him even more.

"What I'm trying to say is," he continued, "I don't think you have to worry so much. I think there are multiple futures. The one where Leonardo came to meet us..."—he spread his arms and hugged her—"and the future where you and I are heading after meeting him." He kissed her on the cheek, then on her lips. "Sweet dreams, Bella *mia*."

"Buenas noches."

Leonardo locked the garage and turned to Celestina. "What's wrong?"

She looked up at him, his energy sweeping her away. Not that she minded. Spending time with him, no matter where they were, was her favorite thing to do. But now that she thought about it, she felt unsatisfied.

"Maybe I'm greedy?"

"Why do you say that?" He pocketed the keys and held her hand. She looked at it but he didn't seem to notice, easing her along with him. "I'll bring you home. Is this because of your mom again? Just blame everything on me if she scolds you for being out late. She can't possibly hate me more."

She shook her head, still looking at their hands, wanting to ask him, needing to be sure if they both felt the same. However, what if they didn't feel the same? Maybe she was only a passing fancy for him. Could she accept that? And, as he said, they came from different times. Would going into a relationship together be a bad idea? But she had spent a good amount of her childhood and teenage years worrying. Maybe now was the time to address the issue head-on.

"Leo, are you in love with me?"

The moment she said the words, his face changed. For the first time, she found her answer by looking at him. Her whole body relaxed, and a warmth spread from her heart. She saw it in his expression: the longing, the sweet way his lips curved up, and the gentleness she now understood was only reserved for her. Anyone at this moment could read that he was saying '*Yo te amo*' with the way he gazed at her.

But then he looked away. "I'm not sure I should feel that."

"Right," she said, wanting to appear sad and make him feel bad for not admitting what she knew he felt for her. But the bounce in her step gave her away; however, if he noticed, he didn't show it.

"By the way, great driving."

She stopped and glared at him. "*¿Qué?* How can you say that when you and Alonso were busy sleeping in the backseat?"

His brows arched above a breezy grin. "Simple. I looked at Isabela's face. She was white as a sheet."

Oh, no, it wasn't my intention to scare her. "I was trying to impress her with my driving skills."

His hearty laugh reverberated through the surrounding trees. Good thing they were far from the *centro.* If not, people might look out and gossip about them being so loud at night.

They walked on, until the village lights no longer illuminated their path and darkness took over the road. Leonardo took out his phone and used it as a flashlight.

"What a strange phone," she said. One day, when he became her man, she wanted to take time to study it. "What else can you do with it?"

"Hmm, well, a lot, actually." In the dark, his voice sounded mysterious, tickling her senses.

"What things?"

"You can browse the internet and interact with people on social media."

"Sounds exciting. What are they?"

"Never mind," he said. She couldn't see his face, but the smile in his voice was clear. "Well, you can also send letters with it. It's called email and texting."

"Really? How do you get the envelope inside?"

His sudden burst of laughter made her twitch, and she let go of his hand, not impressed with his reaction. He apologized right way, and went on to explain the digital world to her—about the internet that let people read information at the push of a button, and much more than books and libraries could give. It allowed you to watch movies and music videos in color, and other stuff like home videos.

Why anyone would want to share their private videos with strangers they've never seen was beyond her, and she chose not to question it.

"But why are you telling me all this? Aren't you worried it will drastically change your future?"

"Not really, because you'll—"

There it was again. The abrupt stop when it came to her future. She sighed. "I get it. You don't want to tell me about my future. I hope I didn't get murdered."

"No, you did not. At least, as far as I know."

A strange sadness in his voice gripped her hard. He knew her truth. She hooked his arm in hers. "I did, didn't I? I got killed."

"No. Trust me, you didn't." He eased away from her. "But please don't ask more."

"Fine." She took his hand, and he stiffened for a second before relaxing as she laced her fingers through his. It felt so right and natural holding him. It didn't matter what he knew. She was satisfied to have this time with him. "Okay, tell me more about that phone." She dreaded the sight of her house coming into view.

"You can also take a photograph with it."

That one got her full attention. She remembered him holding it up toward her on several occasions, and, in normal circumstances she would have been wary of him. But it was Leonardo. She knew how he felt. Instead of worrying, she savored the thought of him secretly taking her photo.

"Maybe we can take a picture together?" she said, squeezing his hand, taking a bit of his confidence.

He stopped walking and looked at her for a long moment. "That would be nice."

The way he said it felt bittersweet, his voice raspy. Again, she needed to push aside the urge to make him confess what he really knew, and his true feelings.

Chapter 19

LEONARDO

I turned off my phone flashlight when we got to Celestina's house. The outdoor light was bright, so I opened the camera app and turned on the shutter sound for her before setting a ten-second timer, then waved her closer. "Celest, *ven acá*."

When she stepped over to me, I pointed at the screen.

"Hmm?" She peered at it just as the countdown ended.

My lips were on her cheek when the shutter clicked. As I turned off the timer, her eyes turned from surprise to excitement. I pressed the video button and put the phone into her hand.

"Wow, *magnífico*." She raised the phone, not knowing she was recording, watching herself on the screen with childish fascination. "How do you take the picture?"

"Here. Press this button." I pointed to the picture icon beside the *stop* button.

"That simple?"

I nodded, and she surprised me with a kiss at the same time as she tapped the button. She frowned at the screen.

"Strange, why is there no sound like when you took the photograph?" She pressed the button again and again, unknowingly taking a string of selfies. Silly selfies.

I chuckled, taking the phone from her. "You're adorable," I whispered. She shrank back, blushing. I stopped the recording and showed it to her, and she almost jumped, then moved back to my side.

After the two-minute video was finished, she pouted. "You could have told me."

"But then I wouldn't have this adorable girl on my phone."

She looked away, muttering about forgiving and liking me. "What about the photographs? I want one of you and me."

"I have them too." I opened the gallery, aware of her watching me swipe.

She took the phone when I got to the first photo of us. "Oh my god, I look horrible!"

"No, you're adorable."

"Flattery," she said, her voice soft. Then she scrolled on before I could take my phone back. I reached for it, remembering all the shots I took of her. "Don't you dare. These are my photos. I've got the right to see..." Her voice faded, her eyes watering as she stared at the screen. I stood beside her and looked at the last photo I took back in 2020. Her heart bottle.

"I took a photo before digging it up."

"Oh, it looks so old."

"It's over sixty years from now."

She looked at me, her eyes searching. "You're really from the future."

"You already know that."

"Yes," she agreed, her voice soft. She swiped on again before stopping. I panicked on seeing the black-and-white photo of her, stuttering to explain myself, but she turned and put her hands on my shoulders, rising on her tiptoes to kiss me. Not what I expected. I relaxed and placed my hand on the small of her back, pulling her closer, responding with equal need.

We gasped for air when we both let go. I dropped one more kiss, intending to say 'I love you,' when she stepped back and held my hand.

"Do you want to come inside?"

Despite the bittersweet taste in my mouth, and questions on how I should ask for the bottle, I broke into a smile.

If a woman back in 2020 asked me this question after a date, I would have taken it as an invitation for something more. But I was sure Celestina didn't mean it that way.

"Sure."

Celestina welcomed me to the living room and worked with the fireplace before serving chamomile tea.

"It's better than coffee before bed," she said.

While she arranged the tiny cakes and tea on the table, I looked around the room, wondering what made it feel different from the last time, and then it clicked. It looked more like a home now, with living flowers by the windows and photos adorning the small tables around the place. I looked at the mirror above the fireplace, with the mounted shelf below it dressed with two beautiful fabric flowers. Then my focus locked on the photo in the standing frame between the flowers, showing Celestina as a child with a smiling man and her mother. He held the disgruntled young woman beside him, but something about Maria Josefa told me she wasn't altogether against it.

"Could it be that she actually liked you?" I asked.

She sat beside me, nodding once at the photo, the flickering fire casting dancing shadows across her face. No doubt about it, she was the most attractive woman in my eyes. Something about her beauty made her seem timeless. Maybe it was the way she conducted herself that I never saw from women in my time, or because of her simple feminine charm, like a wildflower, fragile-looking but resilient.

"That day, after you reprimanded her, *Mamá* gave that to me. She read the letter *Papá* left her and gave me that photo. All because of what you said to her."

Love was written on her face, and she did nothing to hide it. No, she wanted me to see it, letting it hang in the air. I grabbed the chamomile drink and downed half of it in one go. "You're breaking my defenses, Celest."

"That's not what I want," she said before sipping her tea.

My focus went to her mouth, to those lips I'd kissed so many times today and still couldn't get enough of. I gulped down the rest of the tea, gripping the cup hard. "What do you want then?"

"I'm trying to make them crumble so you'll set your feelings free." She placed the cup down and faced me with a defiance I'd only seen in the old photographs. A fire ignited inside me.

Damn it. Damn it. Damn it. Damn it! I reached for her and pressed my lips to hers. "Damn you," I whispered, with a temper I never thought I could lose. Once more, I kissed her, with both love and anger for being unable to resist her.

I kissed her neck, trailing my lips down in a slow line, savoring her smooth, warm skin. My hands took on a life of their own. One slid up her shoulder, the other reaching down to her knees to glide up under her skirt. A sweet moan escaped from her, intoxicating the stupid part of me that couldn't seem to stop growing. I eased her back, wanting to hear more. Wanting her.

"Leo...wait."

"You've got an addictive voice, Celest," I whispered. "Let me hear you more." I shifted my weight as I lay her on the sofa.

"I hope you don't mind hearing mine instead?" a woman said.

I jerked around, my fire turning to ice at the sight of Celestina's mother in her nightgown. Celestina squirmed beneath me and I eased off her and sat up straight. I'd forgotten about her mother.

"Good evening, *Señora.*"

She ignored me and looked at Celestina, who pushed and pulled at her crumpled dress.

"*Mamá,* I thought you already went to bed. It's—"

"*Pasado ala una*," Maria Josefa said. We all looked at the wall clock, and she was right, it was past one o'clock. "Have you eaten?"

Celestina looked at me. "We have. Outside."

Maria Josefa looked at me. "I assume you'll be heading back home soon?"

"*Si, Señora,* I'll just finish..." I glanced at the empty cup and almost grimaced as heat surged through my face. Even so, I grabbed it and looked at Celestina. "One more cup?"

She took my cup and held a smile as she rushed to the kitchen. Her mother glared at me. God, she hates me even more now. But instead of annoyance, I felt good because, unlike the first time, she was now acting like a protective parent.

This must be what Cameron James felt in *10 Things I hate About You* when he came to get Bianca for prom and got interrogated by her dad. I groaned inside. Nah, I have it harder. Cameron wasn't caught making out with Bianca. If he had been, he'd be dead.

I was so much inside my brain, I almost didn't notice myself say "Please don't kill me."

"*¿Qué?*"

I gave an awkward laugh. "Nothing, *Señora.*"

"*Señorita,*" she corrected. "I'm not married."

"I'm sorry. I thought you were." A painful look crossed her features. I'm such an idiot. I should have known. Celestina's biological father raped her mother. Sympathy washed over me, then faded when I thought about the pain this woman caused her daughter. I got to my feet. "I don't think I've introduced myself yet. I'm Leonardo." I stretched my hand out but she just looked at it.

"Maria Josefa," she said.

Wow, even her introduction pricked me like a hundred needles. I lowered my hand, toying with a lame response like "Nice to meet you," but she straightened and I knew she was about to speak.

"Do you still meet Ángel?"

I had no idea who she was talking about, but there was an undeniable hope in her voice. Her gaze shifted toward the photo above the fireplace. In my head, I snapped my fingers as realization struck. The something I saw in her expression in the photo was love. She was in love with that man. But I couldn't lie.

"*Lo siento,* I don't know who he is. I've never meet him in my life."

She frowned. "Stop lying! You were with him the day he showed up hurt on my doorstep."

"I'm sorry, but I'm telling you the truth. I really don't know him."

"You're lying! Where is he? What year?" Her eyes widened with anger, then desperation, followed by regret. "*Por favor,* tell him to come back. Tell him... Tell Ángel, I accept."

"*Mamá,* Leo, what's going on?"

We turned to Celestina. She'd only been gone a few minutes but it felt like a full hour. I looked at Maria Josefa, waiting for her to explain, but she just straightened and walked up to her daughter. "May I have this one, *hija?*"

Celestina seemed to have forgotten whatever was on her mind. She lit up at the word her mother used. My heart sank despite how happy she looked as she handed her my drink.

Maria Josefa looked back at me, giving the impression she wanted to say more, but maybe she saw something that made her change her mind. She faced Celestina, who looked like a little girl waiting to get complimented for a job well done, and said goodnight. Then, just before she climbed the staircase, she turned to us. "It's late. Your guest should go home soon."

Celestina still seemed to be on cloud nine when she marched toward the sofa and sat down. "She called me *hija* again. That's the second time." She grabbed a cake and chewed on it, her eyes all dreamy. Gone was the woman I'd kissed. The person in front of me was a child filled with hope for parental love. She looked at me, "Did you hear it, Leo?"

Hurting for her deep inside, I sat beside her and kissed her temple. "Yes, I did."

She snuggled up to me. "You know what?"

"What?"

"I think *Papá* was right,"

"About?"

"You."

I pointed at myself, suppressing a smile. "Me?"

"*Si, Papá* told me when he gave me the heart bottle that it would bring me to places I wanted to be, and I was right there at the place you arrived." I opened my mouth at the reminder of the bottle but she put her fingertips to my lips to stop me. "I know you're not a magical genie, but ever since you showed up, things have gotten better. Stuff's happened I could never have dreamed. Like that photo, and the flowers *Mamá* made for me, and hearing her call me *hija*," She gazed up to me with the happiest smile I'd ever seen. "All these good things happened because you're here with me. So, please stay."

And once again, I lost every nerve to ask for the bottle. I hummed, caressing her soft curls, wondering if she would agree if I asked her to come with me. No. As far as I could tell, at this point, she seemed happy to stay in her time.

Chapter 20
LEONARDO

February 6th, 1957

Four months. It had been four months since I first arrived in the past, and I still had no single clue how to get back. I was now used to living in the 50s, and, if not for my cellphone, I'd question if my future was actually a dream.

The joyful months with Celestina, the fun bickering with Isabela, my friendship with Alonso and his friends, and the nagging of the older folks at the village made me feel at home. Except that Elvis Presley was young and alive. His music played a lot on the radio, and almost every girl worshipped him, while the men admired him, and the older generations hated him. The irony. If only everyone knew the legend he would create.

"But no matter what, you are still the best," Celestina told me last night when I brought up the topic of the singer. The woman really knew how to soothe a man's pride.

"Come in," she said, snapping me out of my thoughts. She opened her bedroom door wide and stepped aside. I felt like I was intruding, like a teenager wanting to see his girlfriend's room. Now that the awkward phase between her and her mother was over, Maria Josefa gave her the freedom to make changes in the house. She'd changed nothing as far as I could see, but said she'd renovated her room and wished to show it to me before Valentine's Day.

With nothing to compare it to, I was unsure of what to say. I even practiced what to say when I got in but none of the words I memorized came out of my mouth. Her room had refreshing white-painted walls. The pastel green at the head of the bed matched the flowery-green bedcovers, and the pastel-gold furniture was a cheerful splash that made the room soothing. I would never have imagined that this was created by the gloomy and nervous girl I'd first met four months before.

She closed the door behind us. "You like it?"

"Not for myself, but this room is as gorgeous as you."

"It's been my dream, you know."

"To have this kind of room?"

"No—I mean, yes, I wanted my room this way. But it's been my dream to design home interiors. I like to imagine what kind of fun the family would have in the rooms I design. I want to decorate the house so it will create warm memories."

I smiled as she gazed into the distance. It seemed logical for her to fantasize about it after dreaming of being loved all her life. I cupped her cheeks and planted a kiss on her lips. "I think it's a wonderful dream."

"Thanks, but do you know what my other dream is, Leo?"

"What?"

"To build a home with you someday. Do you want to marry me?"

I chuckled. Does she realize she just proposed? This woman is way ahead of her time. "Yes, I will. But first you need to be on your knees and offer me a ring."

The realization dawned, her eyes widening and her cheeks flushing a bright shade of red. "I—I didn't m-mean to..." she stammered, covering her face with her hands. "*Dios mio,* how shameful!"

"No, it's adorable." As I took her hand and leaned in to kiss her, I saw something familiar in the large mirror beside the door. I looked back, and there it was, across the room, on the table at the corner, right beside the bed. The heart-shaped bottle.

"Leo, what's wrong?"

"Celest, if I ever found a way to get back to my time, are you willing to come with me?"

She looked at the bottle and understood me, her mouth opening as she lowered her face.

"You will, won't you?"

She looked up and my heart ached. I hated how easy it was to see what was on her mind. "Can't you stay?"

"Celest, I need to return. My grandparents—"

"Alonso and Isabela *son tus abuelos*. They're here. I'm here."

I shook my head. "Yes, Alonso and Isabela are my grandparents, but they aren't *my* grandparents. You get it, right?"

A knock on the door almost made me jump. She looked at the bottle again and nodded at me. "I'll think about it."

I forced a smile and attempted to kiss her again but the knocking continued.

"*¿Hija?* Are you in there?"

"*Si, Mamá.*" She planted a kiss on my lips and turned to open the door.

"I saw a stranger's shoes outside, so I thought I'd say hi," Maria Josefa said and threw a sharp glance toward me. "I thought you finally invited Isabela over."

Now I understood why some of my ex-girlfriends loved rolling their eyes. Seriously, there's no mistaking the man's shoes at the door. There's no way Isabela would have worn loafers, even if it killed her. And they're size eight—way too big for her.

Celestina looked back at me with a close-lipped smile. Her expression seemed to say 'Are you seeing what I can't leave behind?'

I don't know what changed in the history because of my interference, and I wish I'd asked *Abuela* more details about Celestina. About how her family was. Who knows, maybe it wasn't me who triggered this peace between mother and daughter. Maybe it was already predetermined that Maria Josefa would decide to make amends for her horrible treatment of Celestina. I knew I was making excuses but I didn't care about it anymore. I was in too deep, and I wanted it all. I wanted to bring Celestina back with me. The story of her vanishing after the fire could be because she was with me.

Hold on. The fire. When is the fire supposed to happen?

"Leo?"

I blinked a few times as Celestina's beautiful face came into focus. "What?"

"*Mamá* wants to know if you'll stay for lunch."

"You don't need to stay if you've got other plans," Maria Josefa said. She wrapped a possessive arm around her daughter. "Celestina and I will understand."

You're kicking me out? Nice try. "No, I'll gladly accept the invitation, *Señorita* Josefa. *Gracias.*" I gave her a discrete, smug smile before stepping out of the room and descending the stairs before them.

Maria Josefa grumbled something that made Celestina laugh. "*Relájate, Mamá.*"

On my way back to Alonso's house, I smiled at the thought of how Maria Josefa did her best to monopolize my girlfriend. But the smile faded at the thought of how Celestina's relationship with her mother seemed to strengthen each day, and I felt cruel for making her choose whether to stay or come with me. We didn't even know if I could successfully use the bottle, or if it would transport more than one person. Besides, is she really my girlfriend? We kissed and spent so much time together, but I hadn't told her yet how deep my feelings were. Not verbally. I couldn't make our relationship official when we seemed to tread on a thin line between friends and lovers.

A couple walking in the opposite direction greeted me, the girl laughing as the man put an arm around her. I didn't realize that loving a person could be so emotionally tiring. If only there was a way for me to communicate with my grandparents.

"Leo!"

I turned and smiled at Dolores, Arturo's girlfriend. She walked up to me, opened her arms and pressed her cheek to mine.

"Welcome back!" I said. "When did you return?" Arturo had been in a slump the whole of January when she went to La Nucia to stay with her aunt.

"Yesterday," she replied, and I nodded, understanding Arturo's sudden change of mood yesterday. "Come with me. I have a lot of fruits and vegetables. Bring some with you."

I followed her. Giving and sharing produce and baked goods was something Beniarda still did in my time. It surprised me when I first experienced it. At first, I refused it, saying "No thanks" politely, but ended up bringing home a lot when I saw the disappointed face of the old man concerned.

Hmm, I forget his name. I'm sure he lives in this area. Dolores opened the door, and Arturo and Luisano greeted us, both munching some cake. The faces of Arturo now and the old man overlapped as I looked at him, and I couldn't stop myself from bursting out laughing.

"You look so much like your older self!" I said, confusing everyone.

"Are you picking a fight?" he asked, jumping to his feet. Dolores stepped in front of me and called his name, her tone gentle. I had to bite down more laughter as he sat back like a scolded dog.

Dolores dressed and acted so much like her mother. She wasn't ugly but not really a beauty, either, though we all knew she was Arturo's life. And we loved her for her motherly qualities: sweet, gentle, with just enough strictness to stop the boys whenever they stepped out of line. Pair her with Isabela, and the men behaved like children. Although, as funny as it was, when I brought Celestina into the mix, the group became tense. Dolores seemed to shrink behind Arturo, and Isabela became restless. It was so different from what I'd thought, and it was times like these that I felt like punching myself for ignoring *Abuela's* story.

When did she befriend Celestina? When was the fire going to occur? What date did Celestina vanish? I wished I knew all the answers.

I walked back home, carrying a paper bag of baked goods in one arm and fruits and vegetables in the other. Alonso was humming in the kitchen, so I went there and nearly jumped back. The room looked like a murder scene, and the culprit was holding a cleaver knife in front of a giant tomato.

"Isn't that a knife for meats?" I asked, setting the bags on the kitchen counter.

He looked at me. "I use this for everything." He turned to the tomatoes and sliced, not doing a great job of it, the poor vegetables looking miserable as a result.

"Do you want me to help?"

"No! I need to do this myself. I'm practicing so I can surprise Isabela with a romantic dinner." He leaned closer to the cookbook in the corner, touched the page with his finger, and smeared it with tomato juice.

Isabela's going to freak out when she sees it. *Abuela's* voice flashed in my head: *"You know why I banned your abuelo from the kitchen? Because he ruined the pages with the recipe for simple pasta, his hands covered with tomatoes and chorizo! But it was the most wonderful dish I tasted."*

I smiled at him. "I'll go to my room." But he didn't hear me, engrossed in his culinary mission. I walked out and climbed the stairs. After opening the door, another memory returned:

"This cookbook was the reason I ran back into the house when the kitchen caught fire. It was the day after your abuelo cooked for me. Luckily, Celestina came and saved me. We became inseparable afterwards... No, more like I didn't give her a chance to shy away. But then she went away a few days later."

I ran down the stairs and nearly fell on my ass on the last step. "*Abuelo!*" I said, backing away when he turned to me, the cleaver blade facing me.

"What did you call me?"

"*Perdón*. When are you going to make dinner for Isabela?"

"You're not invited."

"I don't want to join, even if you asked me!"

"Then why are you asking?"

"Just tell me. It's important."

He put the knife down and faced me with a hard expression. "Is it something to do with the future?"

"Yeah."

"*Dime.*"

Tell him? How can I tell him about such a life-changing event? I scratched my head. "Just tell me, when are you going to surprise her?"

"No. You tell me what's going to happen that day. Then I'll tell you."

I produced an exaggerated shrug. "Nothing. Isabela will love it."

He turned back to the counter. "Okay, then wait for that day. You'll know it when it comes."

I wanted to scream in frustration, even punch him, but I knew I would be the one ending on the floor. He might even throw me out of the house. It was too cold to sleep outside, and too embarrassing to crash into someone else's house.

"It's because Celestina will come a day later, okay? And what she will do will make her and Isabela friends."

Alonso turned and studied my face. I buried my clenched hand in my pants' pocket, wishing he wouldn't see through me. He nodded. "It will be next week."

"When?"

"On Valentine's."

I sighed with relief. "Thanks." I left him to cut the *chorizo* into tiny pieces, which *Abuela* would tease him about through the years, saying the slices were so fine she didn't know what meat it was until she tasted it.

Before leaving, I glanced at the calendar. Eight days to Valentine's Day. Nine days until the fire.

Chapter 21

LEONARDO

Five days before Valentine's Day, I woke up and headed down to the bathroom. I had to find the cause of the fire and prevent it.

"Good morning, brat!" Isabela said when I stepped into the kitchen.

"Good morning, *bruja!*" I retorted with equal cheerfulness, using my new 'hag' nickname for her. I glanced at the wooden tray in front of her. *Churros,* a thick hot chocolate, and Alonso's quirky addition—a glass of apple juice. His morning was never complete without it. "You're bringing that to him in the field?"

"Estás loco."

A warm feeling wrapped around my heart. I missed my *abuela.* I kissed Isabela's forehead. "I'm crazy because I inherited it from you."

She laughed. "I know that." Then she looked around the clean kitchen. "I don't know what you guys did to sleep late but you sure made me work."

I looked at the clock, surprised to see it was a little after ten. I'd overslept. Because of farm work, I'd grown accustomed to waking at inhuman hours, but, after finding out when the fire would happen, I'd been tossing and turning trying to figure out how to convince

Celestina to go back with me—if that could even happen. I had no guarantee the bottle was the answer but I wanted her to be ready when I got my hands on it.

"Isa, can you think of anything that may cause a fire in your house?"

"*¡Ay, dios mio*! Why are you asking about something so horrible? Do you want me and my family to burn?"

"*¡Claro que no!* I'm just being cautious."

Her mouth hung open for a moment. "Is it something to do with the future?"

I groaned. "Can you and *Abuelo* stop obsessing over it? I want to change it, but not your way."

"You can't blame us. Besides, as Alonso told me, it's impossible for us to disturb your future, because it already exists."

That got me thinking. Somehow, it made sense. I hadn't heard such a theory before.

"*Bueno*, help yourself here," she said. "I'm bringing this up." She lifted the tray and left me.

I was just done pouring a cup of milk into a pot when the clatter of broken glass and plates came from upstairs. With my heart in my mouth, I rushed up and pushed the door open.

"Isabela, what happened?" I took in the food, juice, chocolate, and broken pieces of glass on the floor. She stood in the middle of the mess, stock still. I followed her gazed and saw Alonso, half-naked, kneeling on the bed, holding the ring I had seen on *Abuela's* finger all my life.

The two of them were lost in a staring contest. Worried that I'd disturb them, I backed away without closing the door.

"Are you out of your mind?" she cried as I took the first step down the stairs.

"I will be if you don't answer me soon," Alonso replied. "I've been in this position for ages, waiting for you to come up."

"You scared me!" she yelled.

"I'm sorry. I am. But you need to answer me. Will you marry me?"

The bedroom door closed, so I didn't hear her response, and I didn't waste any more time. I returned the milk to the refrigerator, put my jacket on, dropped my house key and phone in my pocket, then grabbed a couple of *churros* and locked the door behind me before heading up the road to Celestina.

Celestina wasn't home.

I'd adjusted easily to the 50s since technology had never made a major impact on my life growing up with my grandparents. Conveniences like washing machines, microwaves, color TV, or internet weren't a big deal to me. But in moments like this, I wish they at least had a telephone. Then again, even if Celestina had a telephone at home, where would I call from? My cellphone was more or less a dead thing, and I didn't know anyone with a home telephone. As I walked away, a small yellow car stopped in the driveway. A Fiat 500. I stifled a laugh and went to greet them, going straight to Celestina's side because Maria Josefa was already out the moment she stopped the car, wearing a swing dress and flat shoes.

"Buenas días, Señorita Josefa."

She replied with a groan and reached into the car.

Celestina stepped out with a radiant glow on her face. She kissed my cheek. "Have you been here long?"

"Not very long." I held up what was left of the *churros*. "Isabela and Alonso just got engaged, so I kicked myself out. I thought of begging you for chocolate."

She laughed. "Come in then."

I took her shopping bags and followed them into the house. Maybe I can steal Celestina while her mother is distracted and sneak up to her room to check the bottle. I haven't touched it since it broke in my time.

Celestina smiled at me, and my pulse sped up. *Maldita sea*. Okay, fine, I want to be alone with her for the bottle...and more.

I was on my way up the hill to Beniardà *centro* when Maria Josefa called me. She hurried toward me, still wearing the swing dress and flat shoes, her dark hair curled around the edges and tied up in a ponytail. The woman looked far from the drunk I saw the first time I visited her home. She looked like her daughter's older sister now. In another life, I might even go for her. But it was impossible for me to imagine loving anyone other than Celestina now.

"You need something?" I asked, smiling when she reached me.

She took a deep breath. "Can we talk?"

Those words made me anxious but I nodded, knowing I had no choice.

We walked toward the Font Vella in silence. I sat on the long stone bench beside the water and invited her to sit beside me, but froze when she glared at me. What's with her? I got up and gestured for her to sit instead, which she did, and I sat a couple of feet away. She looked like she wanted to bite my head off, so I'd better keep my distance.

"Is this about Celestina?" I asked when she seemed unable to begin. I guessed silence ran in the family. She was so much like Celestina, except for being more fragile and fierier. I stopped myself from chuckling, not wanting her to dislike me even more. I, after all, also have something to speak to her about. Her approaching me saved me the awkwardness of asking. "I just want you to know that I'm serious about her."

"Do you also want to take her away from me?"

"*Señorita*, Celestina will find someone for herself sooner or later. I don't need to take her away. She will leave the nest when she's ready to build her own—"

"Don't play me for a fool, Leonardo." She looked straight into my eyes, her fragility now overtaken by an intimidating firmness. "I know that you're the same as Ángel."

"Ángel?"

"I said don't play me for a fool."

It was impressive how she could express anger without raising her voice. "Who's Ángel? You mentioned him before but, I assure you, I have no idea who he is."

"I know you came from another time."

I stiffened. "Did Celestina tell you?"

"She did not. Now, stop pretending."

"I know you don't belong here." At last, those words from her when she saw me the first time made sense. She knew who I was from the start. "How did you know?"

"I saw you with Ángel," she said, balling her hand. "It was the last time I saw him."

"Your husband?"

"I'm not married."

I cleared my throat. "Right. Your boyfriend?"

She blushed. "He's... He's..."

I exhaled. "Celestina's *papá."*

"*¡Eso es!*" she said, looking relieved.

"Sorry, but I've never seen him in my life." I'd seen enough time-travel—even *Back to The Future* had a scene where the timelines collided but it felt wrong to admit something I hadn't experienced.

"You can deny it as much you want but I saw what I saw." Her body language shifted, her expression becoming more serious. "You came for my daughter. Are you planning to take her back with you?"

"Yes," I replied without hesitation. "I have loved her since my childhood."

She laughed, but the smile vanished when she saw my surprise. "You must have been at least ten years old when Celestina was born, if you're from our time."

"I'm from...my time. The future."

"And you want to bring my daughter there?"

I nodded. Where else?

She pulled out an envelope and handed it to me. "Give that to Ángel."

I held it up. "What? But isn't he dead?"

"You tell me." She got up and turned to go.

This was annoying. It was too early for me to have mother-in-law issues. "Will you let Celestina come with me?"

"Celestina is an adult. She can decide for herself...without my influence."

I pocketed the letter. I'd give it to Celestina when the time was right. "If she wants to go, you won't stop her?"

She studied my face. "I'm not old. I can take care of myself. She can do what makes her happy."

"Thank you," I said, unable to mask the joy in my voice.

"And, Leonardo, I want to plan a surprise for Celestina on her birthday. I know she will love it even more if you join us. I need you to help make it happen."

"I'll help with anything, *Señorita*."

"*Bien, hasta luego*," she said with a friendlier tone, then left. Somehow, I felt a prick of guilt for disliking her so much before. She wasn't a cruel woman, simply hurt and unable to love her daughter because of her tragic experience. Celestina saw all of that and never gave up, and for that, I'm falling for her even more.

I pulled out my phone and browsed through Celestina's photos, wanting to give her the best birthday of her life.

Chapter 22

I'LL MAKE YOU CRY TOMORROW

February 11th, 1957

Celestina woke up smiling, a common occurrence since her *mamá* started treating her like a daughter. But, now, thinking of Leonardo's question, a heavy weight pressed on her chest.

She pulled aside the curtain and let the sun's rays bathe her room. While she did her best not to look, her attention still ended up on the heart bottle. If only there was a way to speak to her *papá,* then maybe she wouldn't feel bad for dragging out her response to Leonardo. She'd spent her childhood expecting her *papá* to return any moment. They'd buried him, sure, but the whole thing felt unreal, more so because her mother never let her see his corpse. There were many moments when she expected him to materialize in front of her. In her mind, it wasn't an impossible thing. After all, if there were two of him, a third and a fourth should also exist.

Her shoulders dropped at the thought that it may not be the father she grew to love. Just as Isabela and Alonso in her time would never be the *abuelos* Leonardo needed.

The sounds of activity in the kitchen wiped her sadness away. She wrenched her focus from the bottle, pulled her robe on over her nightdress, then made her way down to the kitchen in her slippers.

Unlike her, her *mamá* was dressed, wearing a long emerald dress, a black belt, low chunky-heel shoes, and looked ready to face the outside world. Now that the cloud of hate and depression seemed to have left her, she looked her age. Her beauty shone like no other, to the extent that, when men approached her, it annoyed Celestina that she might find someone to replace her *papá*.

"Great timing!" her mother said without turning to see her. *"Zumo de naranja para ti, ¿si?"* She placed the fresh-squeezed orange juice on the table without waiting for an answer.

Celestina smiled. It was a dream come true. She walked up to her mother, who turned to get *cafe con leche* for herself, and hugged her from behind, wrapping her arms around her shoulders. *"Te quiero, Mamá."*

Her mother stiffened a bit before tapping her hand, still reluctant to express her love vocally. But she was more than satisfied to hug her and say those words without being swatted away.

"Come on, *hija, siéntate*," her mother said, chuckling as she motioned toward the seat at the table. "I won't be able to move with you on my back."

She let go, promising herself that she would get her *mamá* to say *"I love you"* one day.

And Leonardo. She smiled at that.

"*Mamá,* would you miss me if I moved away?"

Her mother pursed her lips before getting up from her chair. "Why? Did your boyfriend ask you to move in with him?"

Boyfriend? She loved the sound of it but it wasn't that official, and *Mamá* didn't need that information. Leonardo was antagonized enough by her. If she knew, she might forbid them to meet again.

"No, *Mamá*, not exactly." She stood, and they both grabbed their own plates and glass and brought them to the sink.

Her mother waved her off and rinsed the dishes, then faced her. "Do you have any plans today?"

Her mind wandered to Leonardo. He never failed to drop by every day when they hadn't seen each other in the field, but she had no idea what time he might come. They'd made no specific plan. She shook her head.

"Good. Go get changed and come with me." Her mother walked out of the kitchen and Celestina followed her to the storage room.

"Where are we going?"

Her mother pulled out some tools she used for the field and waved her off. "Go get changed. You'll know when we get there."

'There' was the place where Celestina spent a big part of her life. Her *papá's* grave. She swallowed the lump forming in her throat and opened her arms, ready to hug her mother, but her *mamá* held the pruning shears out to her.

"Start cutting."

When she cleared the weeds at the gravestone, she looked at the inscription and her eyes watered. She hadn't been to her *papa's* grave in months, after she and her mother got closer, but now placed under his name and date of death were words she had never seen before:

A loving father and a caring man, forever in our hearts.

She glanced at her mother, who had the kindest smile, and fell to her knees. Her mother had added it there recently. Old wounds from losing her *papá* opened and, for the first time since losing him, she mourned him wholeheartedly, crying out loud as she hugged the tombstone. Her mother sobbed beside her and touched her shoulder.

"*Mamá*, he's the best father I could ask for. He's..." It became too much as the sobbing took over.

"He's a wonderful man," her mother said, wrapping her in an embrace and soothing her like a child. They cried together for a man they would never see again. "He truly loved you, *hija*. And for that, I fell in love with him because he gave you the love I denied. I'm sorry, *y te quiero mi niña*."

After cleaning her *papá's* grave—pulling the weeds, then trimming and setting new plants—Celestina helped her mother lay out a green checkered picnic blanket. Both looked funny with their tear-stricken faces and puffy eyes, but they smiled as they prepared the picnic. They arranged their *merienda,* which consisted of *tortilla Española* slices of *pan de barra,* and *olivas verde*. Another time, Celestina would have groaned and grumbled from seeing the orange juice after drinking some earlier but the weight on her soul had now lifted and she was happy to take whatever her mother offered.

Her mother's words replayed in her mind. She lowered her head and grinned like a child. *Mi niña.* Her mother not only called her 'my girl,' but also told her she loved her, and apologized for neglecting her. Just when she thought the day couldn't get better, her mother turned to her.

"I invited an extra person to make the group complete."

Celestina looked around, not understanding what she meant.

"Bring out the cake already," her mother said.

"Cake?" she asked, and froze when Leonardo appeared behind a nearby gravestone, a bouquet in one hand and a cake with lit candles in the other. He sang '*cumpleaños feliz*' as he stepped toward her.

"Happy twentieth birthday," he said before planting a light kiss on her slightly parted lips. He tilted his head toward the flickering candles, the flames tiny in the bright daylight. "Blow."

Celestina glanced at her mother, who nodded in support.

She took a deep breath and blew out the candles, then glanced at the gravestone Leonardo had hidden behind. "How long were you there?"

"He arrived shortly after we finished planting the lavenders," her mother said.

She was thankful he'd waited. Although she loved him, she was glad she'd got to cry with her mother for her *papá*.

"Para ti," Leonardo said in the gentlest voice she'd ever heard from him. He laid the flowers on her lap, and the tenderness in his eyes melted the tiny bit of sadness in her heart.

"Thanks, Leo."

And that was it—an awkward silence fell over the three of them. A passing gull's screech, however, sounded so much like laughter—loud and crisp—that they all burst out laughing.

"What are you waiting for?" her mother said to Leonardo. "*Siéntate.*"

He sat beside Celestina, then leaned over and whispered, *"Te amo."*

"Hey, behave!" her mother said, wagging a finger at him.

He straightened. "*¡Sí, Señorita!*"

"*Señora.*"

"What? But you told me not to call you that."

Her mother scoffed and glanced at her *papá's* stone. "That was then. This is now."

More words were exchanged but Celestina's mind floated away as warm sunlight dissipated the chilly breeze. It was a wonderful day, where her *mamá* had greeted her with real love for the first time, with both of them caring for *Papá's* grave, and then with Leonardo showing up. Perfect.

As Celestina stood outside her house with her mother, her heart lifted when Leonardo dropped a quick kiss on her lips.

"Goodnight, Celest." He then took a tentative step toward her mother and gave her a light embrace and peck on the cheek. "Thank you so much for making me a part of this celebration, *Señora.*"

Celestina watched him fret as her mother nodded. He glanced at her, and when his focus wandered down to her lips, her face burned.

He cleared his throat and waved. "I'll come again tomorrow."

"What time?"

"After lunch." He glanced back at her mother and said goodnight again before jogging off.

Her mother laughed before turning back. She followed. "*Mamá, por favor,* stop teasing Leonardo so much."

"What did I do?" She stopped in the middle of the living room.

Celestina shook her head and swatted away the tinge of bitterness from her heart. It was something she'd probably be doing a lot in the years to come whenever she thought of how fun it was to be with her mother. She hugged her. "*Muchas gracias por todo, Mamá.*"

Her mother hugged her back. "Did you have fun?"

Celestina broke away from the embrace and beamed.

"That's good." Her mother reached up and caressed the side of her cheeks, a hint of sadness in her smile. "I feel like an idiot for not making you smile this way for a long time. For not noticing how lucky I am to have you."

Celestina tilted her face away from her mother's touch. "Please stop, *Mamá.* I don't want to cry."

"You're right. It's still your day. I'll make you cry tomorrow."

She laughed, thanked her mother again, and walked toward the bathroom.

"¿Hija?"

She turned. *"¿Sí?"*

"No matter what you decide to do, I'll always support you. No matter where you go, no matter when—I'll always love you. That will never change."

"Good night, *Mamá.*" She walked away with a smile, a final decision in her mind.

Chapter 23

COME WITH ME

After rummaging through her clothes, Celestina gave up and went to look for her mother, who she found in the living room, all comfy with her feet propped up and humming while cutting pieces of fabric for her flower crafts.

"*Mamá,* can I borrow some of *Papá's* clothes?"

"Why?"

"Ah, so we do have his clothes still!"

Her mother glanced up, then looked back down. "I never said that. I only wondered why you're looking for them. You know I burned everything he owned."

"You told me you did but I never saw you do it."

"What makes you think I didn't?"

She flopped down beside her mother and leaned close to her. "Because you loved him too much to let it all go."

"You!" Her mother stared at her for a long moment before releasing a long sigh, shoulders dropping. "Look in the drawers beside my wardrobe. You'll find them there."

"*Gracias, Mamá*!" She kissed her mother's cheek and ran up to the stairs.

"What are you going to do with them?"

"Surprise Leo!" she replied before opening her mother's bedroom door.

After looking through her *papá's* clothes, Celestina settled for his light-blue polo shirt and flannel shorts. She tried them on and burst out laughing at her reflection, holding the shorts up, feeling like a kid playing grown up. Everything hung loose, her waist nowhere in sight. She couldn't understand how those women on the video on Leonardo's cellphone looked good in them.

She crouched, laughing while tears pricked the corners of her eyes—another reminder that they belonged in two different times.

"Is it that funny?" her mother asked as she walked into the bedroom and folded the rest of *Papá's* clothes back into the drawer.

Celestina dried the lone tear that dripped down her cheek and changed back into her clothes. She folded what she had tried on. "*Mamá,* was it always this hard for you?"

Her mother looked at her, her brows furrowed. "This hard? Losing him?"

She shook her head. "Loving him."

"Is this about Leonardo?"

She looked away, then helped place the clothes back. Her mother kept quiet, even when they were done, giving her the chance to brace herself for what she wanted to say next.

"He asked me to go with him."

"Oh." Her mother sat on the bed and patted the spot beside her. "Do you want to go with him?"

She let out a long exhalation and looked at her mother for what felt like ages. It was the hardest decision she'd ever had to make. "I want to, but I also want to stay."

"Because of me?"

She nodded, tears slipping down her cheeks. "I hate how greedy I feel. I want to be with you—here with him—but I know he can't stay because he wants to be with his *abuelos.*"

"Remember what I told you, *hija*. No matter what you decide to do, I'll always support you."

Celestina shook her head. "*No me entiendes, Mamá.* You don't get it. Leo won't simply bring me to another city. We won't see each other again when he returns."

"I understand."

"No, you don't. Leo isn't from here. He isn't—" She looked at her mother's wardrobe. It wasn't her place to reveal the truth about Leonardo without his consent. "He..."

"He's from another time."

Her face and neck went cold. "You knew?"

"*Sí.*"

She realized her mouth was hanging open. "Since when? When did he tell you?"

"Before your birthday." Celestina wilted. "But I recognized him the first time I saw him."

"*¿Qué?*"

"I saw him with your *papá* before."

"*Eso no es posible, Mamá.* He comes from the future. He never met *Papá,* and he can't easily travel across time like *Papá.*"

Her mother sighed, her hands clasped in her lap. "*Sí,* he also told me that he'd never met Ángel. But I'm sure he was the one I saw." She touched Celestina's forearm. "Anyway, aren't you forgetting something important concerning you wanting to go with him but also wanting to stay with me?"

Celestina raced through their conversations but couldn't remember what she'd said before. "What?"

"I don't have family other than you. I can always go with you both. That is if you found a way."

Happiness surged through Celestina as she lunged at her mother, sending the two of them to the floor, aching and laughing.

Leonardo arrived after lunch, as he'd promise. He looked so attractive, wearing a white shirt, open jacket, and faded blue jeans, with his hair styled just as it was when they'd first met—tousled but fitting. In comparison, her curls looked like a demon had chased her, and she was thankful when her mother helped her tidy it.

After putting her red coat on, she lifted her hand to her hair, tied up in a hairband. "Is it bad?"

"It's different than usual." Leonardo leaned over and kissed her. "But you never look bad in anything."

She smiled and grabbed his arm. "Let's go then."

"You're blushing," he whispered.

"I know," she replied, squeezing his arm. She blushed every time she remembered the way he'd looked at her the other day. A look mixed with love, desire, and something she couldn't explain. She glanced back in the house. *"Mamá, ¡me voy!"*

"Have fun!"

"She's not coming to give me a stern warning?" Leonardo asked, grinning.

"Why would she do that?"

"Because I don't plan on bringing you home tonight."

She stopped and looked at him, amazed at how he could switch from serious to goofball in no time. "You're joking."

"Was it obvious?"

"*Sí.*" It wasn't but she hated how her heart beat with excitement at the thought that he was serious, and she hated herself for feeling disappointed at making him admit the joke.

Using Juan Martin's car, they drove to Benidorm. According to Leonardo, the car didn't cost a single peseta. "Alonso's help," he said, and she could only imagine what the two of them told Juan Martin to get him to agree.

He took her window shopping. Along the way, they tried wedding dresses, and secretly took photos with his phone. They had a candlelight dinner and went to Balcón del Mediterráneo, viewing the coast while drinking Agua de Valencia, the most delicious drink she had ever tasted.

"Unbelievable how everything seems familiar and unfamiliar," he said.

"How different is Benidorm in your time?" she asked, and she couldn't help but gasp at the stories he told her about the tourists, the buildings, the population and, most of all, about the tallest hotel in Europe. The height sounded extravagant. But, at the same time, a part of her felt sad knowing that her charming city would change so drastically.

"They also dug up there," he said, pointing at the Balcón del Mediterráneo.

"What?"

He shrugged. "Apparently, a historical castle is beneath it."

"So, the Balcón is ruined?"

"It was hideous the last time I saw it, but they'll put it back again."

"Oh, that's good."

It was about eight in the evening when he invited her to walk. They went down to the balustrade and watched the sunset before moving on to the beach. Even though the sand was cold, they continued barefoot, carrying their shoes. The moon was bright and silent as they walked between the boats. At one stage, Leonardo leaned over and asked for her hand. She gave it without question, thinking he wanted to hold it as they walked, but she stopped in her tracks when he placed something in her palm.

She looked down at a silver, heart-shaped locket, with an elegant flower decoration on its front. "This is—"

"I was originally going to give it to you for your birthday," he said. "But I thought it would be better when we were alone."

She flipped the locket over and her chest tightened. The moonlight wasn't strong enough to read the engraving.

"Allow me," he said. "My heart is yours, always."

She swallowed, then hugged him. "Thanks, Leo, I'll treasure it."

"You haven't opened it yet."

She let go and hurried to the closest streetlight. When she unclasped the lock and opened it, she gasped on seeing a painted portrait of her and Leonardo. "How?"

He smiled and kissed her. "Happy birthday, and advanced Happy Valentine's."

She looked around, a bit embarrassed but proud of how openly he was showing his affection. Then her shoulders slumped. "I haven't prepared any gift for you."

He took the locket from her and placed the chain around her neck. "Your smile is enough," he whispered.

She looked down at the locket, clasping it. "I bet you've used that line with all your girlfriends."

He turned her around. "I haven't. It's the first time I've ever said it to a girl, and I'm glad it's to my first love."

"Yeah, right."

"It's true."

She stared at him, and he told her how he had always had a crush on her. Ever since he was a child after seeing her old photograph in Isabela's album. And, just like that, the magic of the night faded. She had been doing her best to get on Isabela's good side—ever since the four of them went to Benidorm before Christmas—but, even now, months later, she had made no progress. Maybe she wasn't meant to be friends with her in this lifetime. She was stealing her grandchild, after all.

The sky was darkening, with thick clouds covering the moon, like sadness creeping in on her wonderful time. To not ruin the mood altogether, she turned to Leonardo and asked what they should do next.

He arched his eyebrows and shrugged. "What about you? What do you want to do?"

She could think of nothing until she remembered the most important thing. "Leo, I want to go."

"Oh, okay. No problem. It's probably best to get home before the weather turns bad." He nodded toward the clouds. "That looks like a rain. Driving on wet roads at night isn't—"

"Leo,"—she placed both hands on his cheeks and made him look at her—"what I meant is that I want to go. With you."

His expression softened. "Go with me?

She nodded.

"To the future?"

She nodded again.

"Are you sure?"

"*Si*, I am."

Chapter 24

LEONARDO

You know how in films the dramatic music plays in the background the moment something big happens? Like some wonderful love songs that make everything extra epic? They're real. The moment I heard Celestina's words, the surrounding sounds muted and Jason Donovan's *Too Many Broken Hearts* blared in my head. Yeah, it's cheesy but I grabbed her and spun her around.

It probably wasn't something someone nearing his thirties should do but she laughed and danced along with me, to the music only I heard.

"You're not allowed to take it back," I told her the moment the two of us dropped in the sand.

"*Por supuesto que no.*" She sat up and smiled at me. "Of course not. I can't imagine a world without you."

"And I will not accept a life without you." I reached for her head and pulled her in for a kiss. "I actually planned to kidnap you if you didn't agree." She playfully pushed away from me, then her expression turned serious. I sat up. "What's the matter?"

"Well, there's a condition for me to come with you."

"What's that?"

"I want *Mamá* with me."

I could already imagine so many scenarios and plenty of reasons to refuse to have Maria Josefa tagging along but there was no way I could say *no* knowing it would bring Celestina happiness. "I see no reason why she can't come with us."

She pounced on me, her smile the brightest I'd ever seen. *"Te amo."*

"I love you too," I said, tucking a loose hair behind her ear, but before I felt her lips, a drop of rain hit my face.

We both looked up and more drops fell on us. Laughing like two kids in a summer shower, we put our shoes on and made a run for it.

It was pouring by the time we got to the car, and we were soaking wet and chattering from the cold. I couldn't stand the thought of abusing Juan Martin's kindness by wetting his seats, and I doubted the car's heater would be enough to dry us or the seats. The long, winding, often steep roads would also be hard to drive on now that it was dark and wet.

"Let's go to a hotel."

Celestina looked at me, horrified.

"We need to get out of our wet clothes as soon as possible." I slipped my arm around her and put on my brave face, fighting the chill seeping into my skin. "We can take two rooms, okay?"

She nodded at that and let me take her to the closest hotel. Benidorm had so few hotels but we found a warm welcome in the one we chose. When I asked for two rooms, however, the cost made me swallow. I would have laughed at the prices back in my own time but it was no joke now that I lived in this time and had to work hard for every peseta.

Celestina stood beside me, shivering, looking pale, and I was sure it wasn't just from the cold. "Just for her, please," I told the receptionist, but Celestina stepped up to the counter.

"No, we'll take two rooms." She pulled money from her purse. I smiled, loving how modern she was. But the way the receptionist looked at me hurt.

"No, no, you need it more. I don't—"

"Sorry, but we only have one room available," the woman said.

"We will take that," Celestina said, accepting the key. I paid for the both of us.

We said our thanks to the bellhop who guided us to our room and flip the light switch inside the entrance. The decor was plain white, with one painting of an olive farm hanging above the night table between the two single beds. An open, empty wardrobe stood at the wall across the room, the bathroom door beside it.

I turned to Celestina. "I thought you didn't want me to be in the same room with you?"

"I don't have a choice. I didn't want to even think about what would happen if you stayed in those clothes." She tossed her purse and the room key onto one of the single beds. "I'll take a shower first."

She went to the bathroom before I could respond. Despite the chill, my imagination ran wild as the sound of the shower filtered out. My mind pictured her under the water, soaping herself, and I groaned, searching for anything to distract myself. I found nothing.

Before I took my jacket off, I put my phone on my bed. Then I took two hangers from the wardrobe and hung my jacket and shirt up. I was done taking my pants off when Celestina opened the bathroom door, wearing the hotel robe.

I never lacked confidence, having no problem standing naked in front of my exes, but when Celestina blushed when I caught her looking me up and down, I had to bite back the urge to cover myself like a victimized teenage girl.

"I-I didn't want to stay in wet clothes for too long," I said.

She nodded, left the bathroom door open and headed to her purse. I almost ran to the bathroom and got straight into the shower. The warm water felt like heaven as it ran over me.

When I was done, I dried myself with a soft towel and put the waiting robe on. They had no hair dryer, so I let my wet hair drip and cling to my face. When I entered the room, Celestina was fiddling with my phone.

"You won't be able to open it, as it only recognizes my fingerprint."

Her embarrassment was replaced by amazement. "It recognizes you?"

I nodded and sat beside her, smiling when she took a deep breath. What idiot wouldn't fantasize about easing her down there and then? Not this idiot. But the reason I agreed to take two rooms was to ensure it didn't happen. I reached for my phone and pressed my finger to the screen, then went to *Settings* and disabled the security lock.

"You move so quick!" she said, impressed.

"Training," I replied, my ego inflating as she eyed me with admiration.

"Do you mind teaching me?"

"No, not at all."

For the next half hour, I showed her around the phone, or at least the apps that weren't dependent on the internet. She was a quick learner, and by the time my hair dried, she was doing it for herself, going through my collection of music videos. After a while, she sighed, looking gloomier than the weather outside.

"Something wrong?" I asked.

She looked at my phone for a long moment, and I wondered if she wanted it for herself.

"I wanted to dress like the women in those videos," she said. "But when I tried, I looked ridiculous."

I put the phone on the bedside table and touched her cheeks. "I'm sure you didn't."

"I did! It looked ugly and didn't suit me at all. How am I supposed to fit in when I get to your time?"

"You will fit in. And trust me, no matter what clothes you wear, no one will bat an eyelid. A jewel suits anything."

She leaned into my hand, still on her cheek, and kissed it. A spark of electricity surged in all directions inside me, and I pressed my legs together to stop the animal from growing, but it was impossible when she looked at me with her seductive eyes.

"Thank you," she said.

I looked away. "You should stop doing that."

She tugged at my arm. "Stop doing what?"

"That," I said, looking into her eyes. "If you keep pushing me, I might overstep my boundaries, and we both don't want that to happen."

She arched an eyebrow. "What if I want you to overstep it? What will you do?"

She'd barely finished speaking when I covered her lips with mine. I tried tasting her at first, then I kissed her longer—harder. When she moaned against my mouth, I let go of every brake I'd been holding, easing my tongue between her lips until she opened up and tried to match my rhythm with her clumsy effort.

I eased her robe open and covered her bare skin with my kisses, moving from her chin, down her neck and across her shoulder, soon getting carried away in the heat of the moment.

"Leo," she whispered, her fingers in my hair, urging me to go further. So I did. I explored every inch of her body with my tongue and fingertips, relishing her shudders beneath me, and almost crying with joy as she came undone. Just being there for her, as her moans reverberated through the room, was like being in paradise.

As she lay on the bed, dazed, she spotted my arousal pushing against the robe. "Are you not going to enter me? Or is there something I should do first?"

I chuckled. The question was both innocent and alluring.

She must have seen how much I wanted her, because she covered her flushed cheeks the moment our gazes met. I removed her hands and climbed on top of her. "You don't have to do anything you don't want." I kissed her below her ear. "Do you want me to...enter?" I whispered as a gentle warmth flooded my entire being.

"I do..." she said, her voice so soft, and it was all I wanted to hear. I inched my way into her, letting her warmth envelope me until I reached halfway in. She was gripping me so tight it was hard to move. Then her tears drop, and felt like an asshole.

Celestina was a virgin. Of course she was. It never occurred to me, since I was never anyone's first before now. I lay against her and apologized, hating to see her in pain. "*Lo siento, mi cielo.*"

I was softening when she looked up and laced her fingers behind my neck. "Leo, push. Kiss me, please, and claim everything I want to give you."

"It may hurt a bit."

She smiled and kissed me. And just like that, I hardened. My desire for her overflowed as I eased into her with gentle, almost imperceptible thrusts, until we were fully connected. My heart filled with love, her addictive voice in my ear as she dug her fingernails into my back.

"*Te amo,* Celest."

Chapter 25

CHANGES

Celestina blinked away the tears threatening to spill—this time from happiness, not pain—feeling complete and satisfied beyond words. "Leo?"

"Hmm?" He pulled her closer. The single bed they shared was a tad too small for them but their tangled arms and legs as they lay in the dark felt good. Like medicine against the dull ache between her legs.

"Do you know how to go back now?"

"No, but I have an idea," he whispered. "We may need to break the heart bottle."

She pinched him and he yelped. "There's no way that will solve your problem!"

"But that's how it happened to me. I opened the rusted cap of the bottle, took out the paper that said '*I wish to have someone who will love me for me,*' and kissed it—"

"You kissed it?" she exclaimed and buried her face against his chest. She'd written it thinking of her mother.

"*Si*, I kissed it because I got the feeling a charming Purrball wrote it out of loneliness."

She pinched him again. "Be serious!"

"I am."

The smile in his voice was clear, though his tone had a serious edge.

"After I kissed the paper, it stung me. Out of surprise, I let go of the bottle. It broke and a light beamed up, enveloped me, and sent me here to the past. Wait, I think someone pushed me."

She imagined breaking the bottle she treasured so much and shook her head. "I can't break it. It's *Papá's* last gift."

"I know, *mi cielo*, I know." He kissed her forehead. "We will find another way."

"Okay," she said, snuggling into him and falling asleep to his humming of a beautiful melody.

When she woke up after a few hours, she found herself alone in the room. She got out of bed and knocked on the bathroom door. "Leo?"

No answer.

She opened it and saw that her clothes were gone. When she looked in the wardrobe, Leonardo's clothes were also missing. Her heart hammered but she composed herself before jumping to any conclusions. The dimmed light of dawn streaming through the sheer curtain lit her way back to the bed. She switched on the table lamp and her heart lifted on seeing a note waiting for her.

Buenas días, mi cielo. I couldn't sleep, so I went out to get our clothes ironed so they would be dry. In my robe. ;)

See you later, if you're reading this. - Leo

Her mouth fell open and she laughed as she imagined the workers' reactions. Wait, even her undergarments? She pressed her face into her pillow at the thought of him carrying her underwear. The pillow smelled of the hotel's shampoo she and Leonardo had used. She peeked at the table and sat up when she saw his phone.

He never let it out of his sight, but he'd left it with her. She picked up the device and stared at the black screen, which flashed seven fifty-five for a few seconds before going dark.

What a weird thing.

When she touched the screen, the time flashed again. A couple more touches brought the main menu up. She looked around the room, feeling like a little girl doing something forbidden. It wasn't difficult to recall everything Leonardo had taught her about it, and soon she was scrolling through the contents. She smiled and giggled at the candid shots he'd taken of her, and felt renewed embarrassment at the video of her talking to the fireplace during his first visit. After swiping through their recent photos and some from the future, she stopped at one she didn't remember taking.

It was black and white, of herself wearing her favorite dress. Her untamed hair hung loose, and she was with a girl who wore a cheery smile while hugging her arm and leaning on her shoulder.

"Isabela," she whispered, joy rising from her heart. So, we are going to be friends.

"*My first love.*" Leonardo's voice from the other day echoed in her mind and she stifled a squeal, but then an intruding thought dampened her mood. Was what happening between her and Leonardo really okay?

Will Isabela still befriend me now that I have stolen his heart?

She moved on to the music videos and watched with a bittersweet smile when she recognized the melody Leonardo hummed as she drifted to sleep. *Love Walked In* by a group called Thunder. She could dedicate it to Leonardo instead of herself. He was the one who appeared out of nowhere and gave her what she wanted. She was in so much pain but he'd helped her. And, now, she wanted to have him beside her, always. She sighed with a heavy heart. Isabela might hate me for it, but I can no longer be without him, not after he walked right into my heart.

After the video ended, she browsed through his music files until she came to a title: *Do That To Me One More Time* by Captain and Tennille. Thinking it was a kinky song he didn't want her to hear, she played the song and, instead of her plan to tease him when he returned, she ended up wanting to dance with him.

She took the bedsheet from his bed and swayed across the floor, closing her eyes when the soothing flute dominated the room. In her mind, Leonardo whispered sweet words in her ears, but then the song stopped and restarted, and she snapped out of it when someone embraced her from behind, guiding her to the lyrics of the song.

Leonardo. She hadn't seen him come in.

Her legs went weak and her heart swelled as his warm breath caressed her ear.

"I can never get enough of you," he whispered, then sent delightful shivers through her body with each touch of his lips as he trailed kisses down her neck to her shoulders. As the flute once again took over the melody, he spun her around and moved with a sensuality that made her heart race. He caressed her back before exploring the contours of her hips and curling his fingers around her thigh. A delightful flutter ran through her when he pulled her closer. She came to a halt, yearning for nothing but to lie in bed with him. However, he kept up the gentle swaying, pressing himself against her, his mouth at her ear. "Don't stop dancing with me, *mi cielo.*"

He teased her with light kisses, making her crave him more and more. She'd enjoyed last night's experience but this felt different—much more special. Powerful emotions filled her as he whispered his love and continued to dance with her long after the music had ended.

His hand touched her waist and, with a gentle tug, he drew the robe open. He ran his long fingers up her body as they shimmied and swayed to the rhythm of their own silent music. She embraced him as they tumbled back onto the bed, and let him fill her body and mind until they were exhausted.

"You're going to be my downfall, *mi cielo,*" he said before rolling off her, chuckling when she pinched his side.

She traced her fingertips across his chest. "Then I'll fall with you, Leo *mio*, no matter how far."

Celestina filled the silence in the car on the way home by humming *Love Walked In,* but stopped and squirmed in her seat on seeing the unreadable smile on Leonardo's lips. Does he think I'm childish? She'd never thought about the almost ten years' difference between them but, sometimes, he made it obvious. It made her feel strange. Like an enjoyable frustration.

"Songs are very different in twenty-twenty," he said, taking a corner from La Nucia toward Beniardà, "Most of the songs and videos you find in my phone are from the nineteen-eighties to early two-thousands."

"Why? Is music horrible during twenty-twenty?"

"I don't know." His smile had a bitter turn. "I never stopped to listen because, for a long time, I've been stuck in a loop. The music I listened to reminded me of my childhood. Some because they were famous, and others because my parents loved them. I guess, in a way, I wanted to keep them alive. Even by ignoring what music came after their death."

She rubbed his arm. No matter how old people become, they'll always long for their parents' love. "How about now? Do you still feel stuck?"

He tilted his head to his right. "Yes."

"Oh."

He glanced at her and smiled. "Stuck with you, that is."

She removed her hand from his arm and covered her mouth as she looked out of the window, sure she had a foolish smile.

They were close to Benimantell, the town before Beniardá, when she broke their comfortable silence. "Leo, when did you start falling for me?" Please say when you saw my photo.

"When I saw you waiting for me in the *embalse,* and when you had that fight with your fireplace."

Her heart warmed at the memory, but then disappointment took over. She wanted him to talk about the photo so she could ask him when it was taken, in a casual manner, without sounding obsessed. While she wanted to go with him when the time came, it didn't stop her from dreaming of being Isabela's friend and, well, get her blessing for their relationship.

"But it all started with a childhood crush when I first saw your photograph in *Abuela's* album. After meeting you, that turned into curiosity until, well, you made me fall for you."

Her heart hammered, not only from his beautiful smile but because he'd just given her what she wanted. She opened her mouth as they approached the main road crossing Benimantell but Leonardo pointed out his window.

"Look, it's Juan Martin." He pulled over and stopped beside the car's owner, who stood with two young women.

Leonardo opened his door but Juan Martin stopped him. "I'll get in the back with the ladies." He gestured for the two women to join him in the backseat, sandwiching himself between them.

They exchanged greetings and Leonardo pulled out onto the road. Juan Martin popped his head between their seats. "How did the date go?"

"Great," Leonardo replied and pushed Juan Martin's face with the back of his hand. "And move your mug. You're making my girlfriend uncomfortable."

"Girlfriend!" the girl behind his seat said. She leaned forward and looked at Celestina. "So, the rumor about the two of you in a relationship was true?"

Celestina nodded.

"Wow," the other girl behind cried. "We always thought you were a bit scary. Some boys were even scared of approaching you. I guess you were simply waiting for someone from outside the village."

"I never told them to stay away," Celestina said.

"Then Leonardo must have the charm you're looking for?"

Leonardo chuckled. "Yes, a weird charm!"

The atmosphere lightened and everyone, except Celestina, joked around for a while.

"Hey, did you fall for Leonardo because he's such a goof?" the girl behind Leonardo asked.

Celestina turned to her. "No. He saw me for who I am."

"Of course," she said with an awkward laugh as she sat back.

The tense atmosphere fell over the interior again, which Leonardo broke with a single word: "Purrball."

Juan Martin chuckled. "You're seriously thinking about cats now?"

"Is that a cat's name?" one of the girls asked him. While he explained how Leonardo sometimes mumbled *purrball* whenever he saw a stray, Leonardo glanced at Celestina and gave her a half-smile.

Her heart warmed as she smiled back and looked out to Beniardá down the hill.

The communication remained light the rest of the way, with the girls excluding her from their in-jokes. She felt exhausted by the time she and Leonardo said goodbye to their three passengers.

"Are you alright?" he asked when they walked hand in hand toward her house.

"I'm sorry."

"For what?"

She squeezed his hand. "I don't know but it's really difficult for me to be casual around other people."

"They poked a bit too far."

Even though she knew it was to comfort her, his response was satisfying. She leaned on his shoulder but a chill ran down her spine when she saw her mother waiting for them at the door. The anger on Maria Josefa's face was something she hadn't seen for a while.

She straightened and pulled away from Leonardo but he gripped her hand. "I think you should just go for now," she whispered, wanting him out of there.

He kissed her forehead. "Hey, stop trembling."

She couldn't help it. And while she didn't care if her mother beat her again, she didn't want him to see it—to witness the cruelty she'd almost forgot.

"It's going to be alright," he said before putting a protective arm around her.

Relief showed its face for a moment until her mother grabbed her. For a second, she thought she would throw her to the ground but, to her surprise, she positioned herself between the two of them, her chin high.

"Where have you taken my daughter? Do you have any idea how worried I was?"

"Relax, *Señora*," Leonardo said, laughing. "I won't take your daughter away without permission."

Her mother ignored him and turned to face her. "Where have you been all night?"

"We got soaked by the rain, and Leo and I couldn't possibly take a chance on a wet road at night, so we spent the night in a hotel."

A knowing look reflected in her mother's eyes but she didn't press further. She turned to Leonardo, then back to her. "In exchange for making me worry so much, the two of you won't be spending any time together for the rest of today and tomorrow."

"But tomorrow is Valentine's Day. I should spend it with my boyfriend, should I not?"

"That's why it's called punishment."

Leonardo reached out to kiss her but her mother pulled her away. "Inside now."

She smiled when Leonardo blew her a kiss, making a mental note to confront him about the photo after her mother calmed down. Then she wondered if she should bear her mother's anger and escape tomorrow to spend Valentine's with her man.

Chapter 26

FIRE

Isabela let out a sigh when everyone except her youngest brother left. Rodrigo was busy preparing for his first date, and from the look Leonardo gave when she mentioned it yesterday, it wasn't part of her brother's future. After her long talk with Alonso, she'd calmed down about the future stuff. Besides, no matter how much she disliked the idea of her grandson dating someone her age, and from her time, she couldn't do anything about it.

Leonardo and Celestina's relationship seemed like an unstoppable curse. Even at a distance, she could feel their attraction for each other.

Does she know about my grandson?

The concept of the future appeared all messed up in her mind, but as she looked at the engagement ring on her finger, her anxiety eased. All that mattered now was the man she loved was hers.

The front door opened to reveal Jorge and Alonso.

"Alonso, *¿Qué es eso?*" Jorge asked, his voice echoing down the hallway.

"Al!" she called, stepping out of the living room. She grabbed Jorge by his collar and pushed him away, mouthing "Go inside." He responded by sticking his tongue out as he left.

She looked back to Alonso, and the calm air around him sparked a slight panic inside her. They'd been dating for months now and were even engaged. She had loved him for almost a lifetime but time stood still when he gave her that gentle smile.

"Come in," she said, her focus on the wrapped gift in his hand. It was their first Valentine's together, and she struggled not to grab it from him. His first gift other than the house key.

He noticed, but waited until she closed the door before pulling her close. When she looked up at him, he kissed her cheek, her forehead, and her lips. "Happy Valentine's." He handed her the gift.

Is it a book? She held her bottom lip between her teeth as she unwrapped it. Her jaw dropped. Her first thought was to beat him with it. "This is my book! You're such a cheat!"

He gave her a tight-lipped smile. "You want to see the actual gift?"

She couldn't hold back a smile. "Of course I do."

"Then come to my house tonight." He turned and stepped out of the house without waiting for her reply, leaving her puzzled, excited, and a bit annoyed.

"Did he finally dump you?" Jorge asked, munching the cake she'd just finished baking. "I knew he was too good for you."

"I'm going to strangle you, you little brat!" she yelled, then chased him around the house.

Alonso's smile faded when he walked into the house and found Leonardo sulking in the corner of the living room. He looked gloomier than the cloudy sky. "What are you doing here?"

Leonardo looked up and leaned back on the sofa. "Should I be someplace else?"

Now, of all days, he was sure he would be with Celestina. "Didn't you save for a date?"

"Huh? Oh, that? I used it for a hotel room two days ago."

"And that's why you're here? You got nothing more to spend?" He pinched the bridge of his nose. "Hey, you can invite her for a date that costs you nothing." He needs Leonardo out so that he can have the place with Isabela.

"*Señora* Josefa won't let her out. She's punishing us for spending a whole night away."

"I see. But, tonight, I want you out."

"Why?"

"My dinner with Bella."

Leonardo's eyes widened, his mouth forming an 'Oh.' "Is it okay with you if I ask *Señora* Juliana to let me sleep in the guestroom?"

Alonso stared at him for a moment. "Of course. As long as I can be alone with Bella."

What was going? Why wasn't Leonardo protesting when he was desperate to know when he would cook for Isabela? It was as if he knows something will happen to her.

The day after Valentine's, light streamed through the curtain of Celestina's room. Seeing Leonardo being sent away by her mother without letting them speak to each other felt more horrible than being physically hurt. But despite the torment, she couldn't help but love her mother more.

She'd spent Valentine's Day trying to placate her *mamá's* anger, only to realize she wasn't upset.

"I only wanted you to know that every action has consequences," her mother said after they'd had dinner. "You're an adult now. You're free to do what you want. But, please let me worry for you, even if I'm too late." Then she brought out a surprise gift for her. "And happy Valentine's Day. I want you to spend it with me first, instead of a man who will soon steal you from me."

Celestina looked at the heart bottle, the locket from Leonardo, and the silver ring with a small pink and blue fabric flower from her mother. This filled her with love and happiness but it was also scary. Spending so much of her childhood in loneliness and sadness made the joy in her heart seem like an illusion—a fantasy that could vanish anytime.

She stepped out of her room, took a shower, then had breakfast with her mother. While she had nothing much to gift Leonardo, she wanted to at least greet him. Now, she understood why he said that it would be much easier if they had a phone at a time like this, because then they could send messages to each other anytime. It sounded like science fiction but she really liked the idea.

"Me voy, Mamá," she said, kissing her on the cheek.

"You should wait until he comes here. You should not chase after him."

"You already chased him away. Besides, there's no rule saying that men are the only ones who should come and visit." She kissed her opposite cheek and left her to grumble on her own.

She was a few meters from Alonso's home when she saw him step out wearing his working clothes—alone. Perfect.

It means Leo's alone.

She opened the tin box, peeked at the heart-shaped chocolate cookies she'd made for Leonardo, and marched up to the front door. No response after the first knock, so she waited a minute before knocking again. It took a few more before the sound of steps descending the stairs filtered out.

"I'm there now," a woman called before the door opened.

"Celestina, *buenas dias,*" Isabela said in greeting. She looked down at the tin box. "You're looking for Leo?"

She nodded.

"Oh, he's—"

"Isabela, look!" Celestina pointed at the smoke coming from the kitchen.

"Fire? The kitchen is on fire!" Isabela turned to run inside but Celestina grabbed her wrist.

"Let's go call for help!"

"You do it! My cookbook is in there!" She pulled her arm free and ran inside.

"Isabela, wait!"

"Celest? What are you doing here?"

She turned to see Leonardo stuffing a *magdalena* into his mouth, and looking cute with it as he licked his fingers. But she couldn't dwell on that with smoke billowing from the house. She thrust the chocolates at him. "That's for you."

"Thanks?"

She moved inside but stopped, turning back. "Go get help!"

He frowned. "What's going on?"

"Can't you smell the smoke? The kitchen is on fire! Your stupid *abuela* went in to get a cookbook. Seriously, a cookbook?"

"Damn it!" He gulped down the rest of the cake. "Celest, you get help. I'll take care—"

"Go!" she yelled, running inside.

Left with no choice, he shouted for help while she took a deep breath, preparing to rush into the heat. The sound of water gushing came from outside. Seconds later, she was hit from behind by a wall of water, its chill taking her breath away.

"Celest, it's dangerous to rush in this way!" he shouted, yet he was dry as a bone. He grabbed her elbow. "I have to get more water! Come outside with me—this is too dangerous!"

"No!" she cried over the sound of cracking glass. The fire was getting stronger. "I have to save Isabela."

Angry flames licked the walls, scorching anything they reached. She could hardly see through the black smoke but still moved away from Leonardo and toward the kitchen.

"Celest!"

She ignored him. "Isabela!" She received a cough in response. Covering her nose and enduring the heat, she dashed into the room and found her on the floor, her eyes closing as she hugged a book. "Why did you return for a book?"

"A-Alonso's first m-meal is in here."

Celestina wrapped her arm around Isabela and prepared to help her up. In that instant, a searing pain shot through the back of her neck and into her head, and her nostrils pinched at the smell of burning plastic. Then her sleeve caught fire but there was no time to stop and react to the pain. She gasped as more of her clothing caught fire, and she had to cough hard against the smoke she'd inhaled.

"Celestina, g-go save...yourself," Isabela cried between coughs.

She batted at the flames on her arm. "No, I won't leave my future best friend to die in a fire."

"*Gracias, amiga.*"

"Come on, do your best." She dragged her toward the kitchen door. It was only a few steps away but it felt like forever as she tried to reach it. They were dry, and the fire was growing. The smell of burnt hair and plastic was so strong, and, like Isabela, she couldn't stop coughing. Her chest hurt, her eyes stung, and she was desperate for a gulp of fresh air.

They were almost at the door when Leonardo showed up, dripping wet and carrying two buckets of water. He poured everything over them, and their bodies sizzled as steam rose from every part of them.

"My book!" Isabela cried.

"Shut up!" Leonardo shouted, and pulled them both out.

"It holds important memories of your *abuelo!*"

"I'm sure he won't cry if the book burned, but he will be devastated if you got hurt saving it!"

Isabela lowered her head, continuing to cough. Leonardo turned to Celestina, and she prepared to be scolded as well but, instead, he touched her hand. "Let's get you treated, Celest."

More people came, as well as Alonso, but he was unhelpful, only coming to his senses when he was sure Isabela had regained her breath.

The kitchen looked like a disaster, with the locals continuing to throw buckets of water into it.

Sick of Alonso and *Señora* Juliana reprimanding Isabela for going back for a cookbook, Celestina and Leonardo stepped out of the house.

Instead of bringing her home, he brought her to Dolores's house.

"Bringing you straight home would be a disaster," he said.

She nodded, knowing that her mother would throw a fit. The last thing she wanted was her *mamá* worrying too.

Dolores had heard what happened and needed little explaining. She loaned her a new set of dry clothes and served her a warm *cafe con leche,* then handed ointment for burns to Leonardo. "I'll leave you two here. Just call if you need anything else."

"*Gracias,* Dolores."

"*No hay de qué,*" she replied, giving her a warm, motherly smile.

Leonardo applied the ointment to her arm and the back of her neck, ignoring how she flinched from each touch.

"Did you know this would happen?" she asked.

He wrapped the burn on her arm before answering. "I heard about the fire in my time," he said and moved on to cover the wound on her neck. "But I got too comfortable, thinking it wouldn't happen because, unlike in the future where Alonso prepared the meal at Isabela's house, in this time he invited her to his home. I should have known it might still happen."

Celestina only noticed it then. Leonardo was far from calm. He was shaking, and seemed to be on the verge of tears. "Leo, it's all right. No one got hurt."

"You got hurt."

"I'm fine now."

"Still, you got hurt. I was scared. I imagined seeing you in the fire and I thought my heart would stop beating." He hugged her, his touch gentle. "This incident will trigger the friendship between you and Isabela, but I wanted so desperately to stop the fire. I'm sorry."

She hugged him back. While she should be angry at his selfishness, all she felt was love. A sadistic side of her even thought of tormenting him but he'd suffered enough. "I won't die, okay? I'm fine now."

He straightened, and the shivering Leonardo returned to the serious, bewitching man who claimed her lips. "You're right, you won't die. I won't let you."

Chapter 27

LEONARDO

The night I brought Celestina back from the fire, I wanted to tell her mother what happened but she stopped me. As a result, I got banned from seeing her for another week, while Isabela, that brat, seemed to relish in my misery, even showing off her newfound friendship with my girlfriend.

"All she needs for now is a friend. Soon she'll forget you."

"More of that and I'll forget you are *Abuela*!" I wanted to say, but mentally smacked myself to keep my mouth shut. "Come on, Isabela, *por favor*. At least help us meet in secret. I need to speak to her."

"You can always tell me. I'll pass it on."

"No."

"Then write her a letter and I'll deliver it."

I eyed her under my brows. "You'll read it first."

She clicked her tongue. "Have it your way." With that, she ran off to join Celestina and her mother.

"That witch." I looked at Alonso beside me, giving me daggers. I had to speak to Celestina.

"*Señora,* please wait!" I called out, leaving Alonso and the group that evening. Maria Josefa, and Isabela, who had her arm wrapped around Celestina's elbow, stopped to look at me. I swallowed, ignoring the urge to glance at my girlfriend instead of giving all my focus to her mother. Just thinking that she was my girlfriend made me want to jump like an idiot.

Image, Leonardo. Take care of your image. I kept my focus on Maria Josefa.

"*Señora,* I understand that you're angry that I didn't immediately bring Celestina home after the fire, or because I couldn't stop her, but please understand that, if I could, I would have traded places with her. Everything happened so fast."

Maria Josefa glanced at Isabela. "You didn't tell him that he's free to visit anytime?"

I looked at Isabela. "What?"

Isabela looked away, as did Alonso and the group. "I have to go. I think I forgot to make Alonso's meal. See you later." She turned on her heel and ran to Alonso, who put a protective arm around her.

I sighed and turned my attention to Celestina and her mother. "Isabela hasn't said a thing to me."

Celestina laughed. "She has a tendency to be a bit naughty."

I glanced at my young grandparents, and the small annoyance in my heart vanished. "Yeah, but what was she supposed to tell me?"

"I'll see you both later," Maria Josefa said. She took the farm tools from Celestina's hand and left us.

"Both?" I asked Celestina.

She smiled and kissed my cheek. "Both."

"But... Oh, I should wash up and change." I sniffed my sweaty underarm. "I stink."

She pulled my arm. "Before that, there's someplace we need to go."

A few minutes later, we stood in front of her *papá's* grave. Celestina glanced at me and motioned to his stone.

Am I supposed to know what to do next? And I did. The answer came to me when she took my hand.

I cleared my throat and pictured the man in the frame over the fireplace. "Ángel, thank you for loving Celest. I know you treasured her dearly, and I promise that I'll protect her in your place now and love her for both of us."

Her coy, satisfied smile told me I'd done the right thing. It felt right. I cupped her cheeks, kissed her lips, and held one of her hands, and right there and then everything clicked. While I didn't plan this but it felt so right to go down on one knee.

"Celest, I don't have a ring but I have this." I pointed to my heart while looking at her glazed eyes "This first beat for a girl when I saw your photo, and I want to offer it to you until its last beat. Will you marry me?"

"Yes," she answered with sobs and hiccups. "Yes, I want to be with you forever."

I sucked my lips behind my clenched fist. It might seem unmanly if I cried. It's also too embarrassing to shout 'Yes!' So, I stayed in that position and only moved when she knelt facing me and hugged me tight. When her embrace loosened, we exchanged soft kisses and wordless communication.

"Let's go. I don't want to give your mother more reason to dislike me."

"That won't happen."

"¿Sí?"

She nodded with finality. *"Sí."*

We walked back hand in hand and were welcomed by Maria Josefa's delicious cooking. Thank goodness it wasn't seafood. The dinner was fun, filled with laughter and teasing. As the night deepened, the topic also grew more serious.

"So, when are we supposed to leave this place?" Maria Josefa asked as we sipped our coffee. "Travel to the future," she clarified when I looked at her.

"I don't know yet. All I know is that I ended up here when the bottle broke. However, Celest doesn't want me to break it now." I glanced at her.

"It's *Papá's* last gift for me."

Maria Josefa frowned, and for a second I thought she was going to scold Celestina, but then she looked at me. "Didn't Ángel teach you?"

I sighed. Of course, this could be one of those non-chronological events I've seen in time-travel films, but I didn't want to give her false hopes. "*Señora,* I've been saying this to you each time—I really haven't met him."

She shook her head. "Impossible. I'm sure you're the man who took him after he handed that letter to me. Both of you vanished, and you were the one holding the bottle."

Celestina looked at me, her brows furrowed. "Bottle? My bottle?"

"I haven't held it since twenty-twenty, and it broke." I jacked my shoulders up. "You saw the photo on my phone, right? It was the first time I saw it."

She didn't seem to hear me as she looked at her mother. "Vanished with *Papá*? Didn't *Papá* die in front of you?"

"He did. He collapsed in front of me in the yard but..."—she glanced at me—"but he showed up and took him away."

"Then...who's in the grave?"

My body stiffened. Celestina looked like she was about to cry, with anger and sadness whirling around her face. It was my first time seeing it, and it scared me. My chair felt like it vanished as she shot me and her mother a sharp look.

Desperation gripped me, and I grasped for calmness before I spoke. "Celest, I'm telling you honestly, I have never met your *papá* in person."

Maria Josefa, looking just as desperate to get away from the burning gaze of her daughter, seemed determined to throw all the heat toward me. "Then who was that man who looked so much like you? He was holding a bottle too."

"Who is lying in the *cementerio* if *Papá* was taken?"

Maria Josefa fiddled with her finger. She lowered her head, took a couple of deep breaths, and faced her daughter. "No one. We buried an empty coffin."

Celestina inhaled, and it seemed like she'd stopped breathing as her face turned several shades darker. Large droplets fell from her reddened eyes.

Maria Josefa and I were on our feet at once but Celestina raised her hand to stop us.

"*Hija*, please understand. It was the only way I knew how to get over my grief. If he was alive, he would have returned." She turned to me. "Right?"

I wanted to disappear. But I also wanted to grab her and shake her as hard as I could. Maybe then she'd get it into her head that there was no way I could have met her man. Not in this life.

"He died, didn't he?" Maria Josefa continued. "That's why he hasn't shown himself to me—to us." She glanced at Celestina, who gave me an expectant look.

I wanted to cry. "Look, I swear on my life, I never met him. If I'm meant to, then I haven't yet."

Maria Josefa muttered to herself, now also in tears, while Celestina dried her eyes and got up from her seat. I made a move to follow her but she shook her head. "Leo, I believe you but I really need to be alone right now."

She left without another word. Maria Josefa's sobs filled the room, her large tears dropping into the coffee in her hand.

The only time my chest felt this heavy was when I lost my parents. What the hell is going on? I wish I knew how to solve everything and prove that I'm telling the truth.

I dragged my feet toward Maria Josefa, turned her seat, and hunkered in front her. "*Señora*."

She looked at me and cried even more. "He used to sit like that in front of me, too, whenever I cried, but I never told him, not even once, how much he comforted me. *Por favor*, tell me he's alive."

I gritted my teeth. Her stubbornness pissed me off but a part of me understood her. If I saw a person take my parents away while they were dying, and someone looking like that person appeared years later, I might have had a tough time believing they weren't the same person. I took her hand. "I'm really sorry but I haven't met Ángel. If I had, I'd be more than happy to tell you and Celestina, but I haven't."

She took a deep breath, dried her face, and drank the rest of her tear-flavored coffee before straightening in her seat. "I'm sorry for causing you trouble."

"I only want you to understand that I'm not lying." I stood up, feeling lighter but still filled with worries as I looked toward the stairs.

"Don't worry, I'll speak to her," she said. She glanced at the clock and motioned toward my seat. "*Sentarse, por favor*. We need to talk about your return."

She gave me more coffee, and, for the first time, we had a long talk. I explained everything I'd already told Celestina, and while I talked, an idea took form in my head. "What if it was the piece of paper in the bottle?"

"What? How could a piece of paper send you back in time?"

"Celestina said it vanished the moment she put it in the bottle, and I appeared. I was sucked into the broken bottle right after I kissed her note."

"You kissed my daughter's note?" she asked, her mouth curling in disgust.

It wasn't like that, but I can't explain it. "The thing is, it happened after that."

"Okay, then we should ask Celestina to write it."

Silence lay heavy between us. Is she thinking about the same thing as me? Celestina's crying face and the way she acted before heading to her room.

"Lo siento," she said. "I did something unnecessary. But you really don't need to worry. It may not be obvious but she loves me the most. She'll forgive you if I tell her so."

Is she bragging about Celestina's love for her? I pushed the annoyance away and nodded, then glanced at the clock. Eight. "I had better get going."

"Buenas noches."

"Good night, *Señora*." I leaned down and pressed my cheek against hers. When I glanced up the stairs one more time, my heart lifted on seeing Celestina peeking out of her door before retreating out of view.

Adorable.

Alonso grilled me for answers when I got home, and while I didn't want to, he succeeding in making me confess every little detail about the future, including tragic situations involving Isabela and her family.

"Why all of a sudden?" I would not have been surprised if he'd acted like this after the fire. But now? "Did something happen to Isabela?"

"No, but Rodrigo is in the hospital."

Oh, was that today? I flinched at the menacing way he looked at me.

"You knew, didn't you?"

"He only broke an arm. There won't be any permanent damage."

"Everyone rushed there except for Bella. She's distraught. I hate seeing her in pain, so you better tell me everything you know. Now."

I looked him in the eye and knew he would accept nothing but the truth, so I told him. And right before he left to be with Isabela, I told him about my parents. "It will happen in nineteen-ninety-eight." I was unable to look at my *abuelo*, the man who will grow old without his daughter.

He laid his hand on my shoulder. "Leo, I'm not a parent yet but I'll do everything in my power to prevent that tragedy. However, if something happens to my daughter because she saves you, there's no way Bella and I would hate you for it. Remember that. If you have doubts, be a man and confront us in the future."

Minutes after he left, I stood in the corridor blinking the tears away from the ache and happiness in my chest. I truly was a blessed idiot for having such wonderful people around me. Even if they kept feeding me seafood.

Chapter 28

TRAVEL LOOP

February 19th, 1957

If it was up to her, Celestina would have walked out of the door and looked for Leonardo the moment her mother left the room. It was strange for her not to be asleep close to midnight, but here she was wide awake and thinking of everything that had happened.

The truth was, her mother didn't need to 'have a talk' with her. Her dark past was haunting her—she didn't consider her daughter's feelings then, and had to deal with that all her life, but it still hurt. She understood her mother. Grief would have swallowed her if she saw Leonardo dying in front of her, then disappearing with someone, but she could never imagine holding a funeral for him—not when she knew he wasn't there.

That thought created a hollow feeling, which she did her best to bury. It won't happen. As soon as daytime comes, she'd look for Leonardo and try what her mother suggested. She pouted, a small, selfish part of her jealous at the thought of her boyfriend and her mother alone and brainstorming together. Her petite, young *mamá* could have easily been her boyfriend's lover. She froze as she pictured them together.

"No, no!" she shouted into her pillow, then beat it with her fist.

She curled, uncurled, twisted and turned, and squealed as the memory of Leonardo sitting on his heels flashed in her mind.

After a few more minutes of silent squeals, she reached for the locket. She opened it and smiled at the portraits, her heart going into overdrive as she gazed at Leonardo's face. But then she had to bite her bottom lip to stifle an ugly shriek from escaping. Her emotions were all over the place where he was concerned, and she had no idea what to do with herself. In the end, she fell asleep hugging the locket but woke up panicking that she might have broken it.

After breakfast, her mother got serious when she said they should try her idea that day. Celestina drummed the end of her pen on an empty page of a steno pad.

"I wrote my wish to find someone who would love me and that caused Leo to appear. So, if I write a wish for the three of us to go to his time, then it will probably work." She looked at her mother and her excitement faded. Her shoulders had dropped, and she looked like a guilty criminal waiting for judgment. *"Mamá, ¿Qué pasa?"*

"Nada."

"It's not nothing. What is it? You look terrible. Are you sick?"

"I guess I am." She smiled but it was forced. "I have been sick for a long time. So long that you felt the need to wish for someone to love you. I have been blind and now I can no longer go back and give that suffering little girl the hug she deserves." She reached for Celestina's cheek. "The little girl who loves me unconditionally."

Celestina was tired of feeling sad, and tired of crying for their past, but the tears still came as her heart tightened, as if it was being squeezed. If only she could tell her childhood self what was to come, she wouldn't feel so bad now. However, her mother had her own troubles, and, like her, had trauma she needed to get over. They would push their troubles out of their lives together.

She removed her mother's hand from her cheek, stopping her finger from drying her tears. "*Mamá,* what matters is now. It's better late than never, because it would be my biggest regret to never feel your love at all."

Her mother's forehead scrunched up before she pulled Celestina into a tight hug. "I'm happy for giving birth to you, *hija*. Why don't you just send that fool back to the future and live here with me? Just the two of us."

"*Mamá!*" she said with a smile as the air of sadness lifted from them. "You know I can't. I love Leo. And you won't be stealing him from me."

Maria Josefa broke away from the hug and raised an eyebrow. "*Hija*, I want a man. Not a boy."

"He's a man. Leo is a man among men."

"And your *papá*?"

"Urk," was the only sound that escaped her lips. She couldn't counter her mother. *Papá* would always be the first man she loved. She couldn't put one over the other. Her mother laughed, and she grimaced. "*Mamá,* that's cheating!"

"How could I be cheating by telling the truth?"

She groaned. When someone knocked on the door, she jumped from her seat and skipped to answer it, happy to get out of her mother's trap.

There were only two people who visited on a regular basis: Isabela and Leonardo.

She found three people when she opened the door. Isabela and their boyfriends, who, except for height and hairstyle, looked way too similar.

"Isabela, Alonso, welcome. *Pásate*." She opened the door wider.

Isabela marched in without hesitation and greeted Maria Josefa with a cheerful hello. The two of them chatted while Alonso stepped inside. She left the door open, and when she turned to walk back, Leonardo wrapped his arm around her from behind. He rested his chin on her shoulder. "Don't I get a welcome?"

His low, rumbling voice woke every part of her body, the fiber of their clothes offered no barrier to the heat traveling between them. He kissed the side of her neck, and she closed her eyes as she leaned on him.

"You'd better stop seducing me," he whispered, "or I'll carry you up to your room right now."

Do it, said the stupid part of her mind, but she hung on the weak thread of sanity and replied in a raspy voice, "Stop it."

He nipped the bottom of her earlobe, and she stifled a moan.

"Ahem!" Isabela stared at her.

She straightened up and slammed Leo's chin with her shoulder, feeling his pain as he grunted, his hand moving to his face as he crouched.

"Leo, *perdón.*" She sat in front of him, putting a hand on top of his head. "Oh, *perdóname,querido.*"

He let go of his reddening chin and looked at her. "*¿Que?* What did you just call me?"

Before she could repeat it, Isabela pulled her up. "She called you *querido*. Satisfied?"

Leonardo looked heartbroken. "You hag, you just ruined our moment."

Isabela snorted at his exaggerated pout and funny frown. "Celestina, I seriously don't get what made you fall for him. He hasn't got a single serious bone in the body. Having him is like living with a clown."

Celestina smiled. She fell in love with him because no one else knew how serious he could be.

Her mother showed up from the living room. "What are the three of you doing in the hallway?"

"We're coming!" Isabela said, pulling her along.

She looked back at Leonardo and smiled when he mouthed "*Te amo.*"

Alonso and Isabela stayed until lunch before saying goodbye. They made it sound casual but Celestina knew by how tight Isabela embraced Leonardo, as Alonso tapped his back, that it meant much more. They looked like a family, which they were. And they knew. They knew they may never see each other again.

Isabela turned to her. "I will miss you, *mi amiga*." She pulled her into another hug.

"Me too," she replied, struggling not to invite her to come with them.

"I wish I'd befriended you sooner. I wish I knew how good it was to be your friend."

Celestina blinked tears away. She wished the same. "I'll see you again, Isabela."

The three of them watched the couple until they were out of sight. Her mother moved back into the house. "I didn't bother packing. I'm sure you'll get me modern clothes, right?"

Celestina glanced at Leonardo. The heat they'd shared earlier had faded during Isabela and Alonso's stay, but whenever their gazes met, a fire of desire flashed in his eyes and she burned for him. "We should get this over with," she said, turning to follow her mother.

Leonardo caught her wrist and spun her to him, slipping his arm around her waist. "I love how these skirts move around your beautiful legs," he whispered, sending electricity around her body. "I'll miss them."

"I'll bring some with me to wear on special occasions," she replied. "And besides, I'd like to try mini-skirts."

"Sounds great." He buried his face at the connection between her neck and shoulder, and bit. She moaned but found the strength to push him away. He smiled, placing a light kiss on her lips. "Don't worry too much. It will be all right. I'm there, and your mother will be with us."

"You're right. Let's go?"

She left him with her mother in the living room and went to get the bottle from her bedroom. By the time she returned, they were throwing sharp words at each other, though with smiles plastered on their faces.

Scary, was the only thing she could think of and felt like a fool for getting jealous of her mother even for a minute.

"Okay, let's get started!" she said, putting an end to their bickering.

A few minutes later, the three of them were surrounded by Celestina's handwritten wishes, with every piece of paper containing a different wish. She kept trying to create one that would make both Leonardo and her mother happy. Wanting to please them both, she did her best to write it again and again.

"I'm telling you this is better," her mother said, standing in the center of the room. She shoved the newest note to Leonardo.

He tore it up and raised an earlier one. "This is better. Let's use it. Celest, let's put this in the bottle."

She glanced at her mother, who looked like a bullied kid. No, this won't work. She grabbed the paper from Leonardo and tore it. "Mothers always come first."

Her mother's eyes widened above a smile.

Leonardo's shoulders dropped, and Celestina sighed at his mortified look. The two of them made her feel like the oldest of the group.

Children. She was with a couple of children!

She rubbed her temples, then tore another piece of paper and sat on the couch, ready to write, but stopped when the two of them stood behind her. Using the pen, she pointed to the small sofa. "Look, both of you sit over there and wait until I'm done."

"But then we won't see what you wrote," her mother protested.

"That's the point," she replied, commanding Leonardo with a glare. He trotted back to the sofa, and her mother did the same. They sat at opposite ends, in silence.

"Done!" she said, rolling the piece of paper. She handed the wish and heart bottle to Leonardo, who looked startled.

The moment he took the paper from her, he shot up from his seat, shaking his head. "This isn't working!"

"What isn't working?" she asked.

He closed his eyes and groaned, then looked at her. "God, I've already said this several times."

She stared at him. "What?" The hairs on her neck prickled. "What are you saying?"

He shook his head, looking exhausted. "We've done this five times now."

Her breath caught. "What? I...don't get what you're saying."

"I also knew you would react that way." He softened his voice, as if soothing her jumbled mind. "Celest, I'm saying that I've gone forward in time five times."

Her mother laughed. "So, you're saying you've been to the future and back five times? We just started doing this."

Celestina shifted to the edge of her seat. "Let me guess, you did it again and again because I keep pressuring you to try again?"

"Yes," he said, nodding. "The sensation is the same as when I got here, but only for a second. I always come back right after you wrote something and said 'Done.'"

"The moment I let go of the wish," she said.

"Right."

She looked at her pen, still doubtful. "Okay." She took the folded note from him. "If you truly have been using the note—what does it say?"

He looked hurt. "You don't believe me?"

"I do, but please understand how hard it is for me. If what you said is true, how come only you remember what happened?"

"My daughter's right," her mother said.

"You're right." Leonardo nodded, and the smile on her mother's face faded. She clicked her tongue and kept quiet as she waited for him to repeated the words she'd written. "Send us with Leonardo to the future. All of us, not just one."

She crushed the paper in her hand. What was she doing wrong? "Could it be because it doesn't include the year?" She took another piece of paper and wrote: *I wish to travel with Leonardo and Mamá to the year 2020.* She looked up at him and felt a heavy weight on her chest when he shook his head. "Again?"

He nodded.

A sense of unease gnawed at her, knowing he'd traveled to the future. How far did he go? Who did he encounter before returning? Is this the time to ask? She looked at him and opened her mouth.

"I saw some people getting out of their car," he said. "I was there just for a few seconds, but enough to know it was the future."

She clenched her jaw. What is going wrong? What do they have to do to make it work? Will they ever succeed in going with Leonardo to the future?

Chapter 29

LEONARDO

As *Senõra* Josefa went to the kitchen to make dinner, I glanced at the clock and the pool of notes around us. I sat in front of my dejected girlfriend, sick in my stomach after being pulled through time on seven occasions. Instead of long bursts of memories and voices like when I first traveled, the shorter time was similar to dreaming of falling, then waking up before hitting the ground. But that wasn't what worried me the most.

Celestina was right. Why doesn't she remember going back? And why did I keep returning to the point when she was done writing?

Dinner provided a welcome break from the stress and tension of trying to figure it all out, but when it was over, we still couldn't come up with an answer. Alonso, who I'd woken when I returned home, went back to bed without saying anything, though I'm sure he saw the disappointment on my face.

Next day, he still said nothing. Just acted like nothing had happened. Isabela looked happy to see me, then glum after glancing at Alonso. I caught his slight shake of the head from my side view.

It was five in the afternoon when I told him I'd pay Celestina a visit.

"*Oye*, Leonardo," he said, "why didn't you use your key last night? I gave it to you so you could use it again in the future."

I shoved my hands into the pockets of my jacket, felt my phone, charger, earphones, and the keys. Hold on, the keys from the future? The note inside the bottle was from the past when I took it out. Like a gear clicking into place, an idea popped into my head. What if it wasn't the note as we thought, but its origin?

I grabbed him into a quick hug. "Thanks, *Abuelo!* You're the best!"

His face melted into a beaming smile. "Don't come back again!"

I smiled back and turned for the door. "I'll try!"

I sprinted past the road to Font Vella, down to Celestina's home. If the door wasn't locked, I wouldn't have bothered knocking. When it opened, I hugged her. "Celest, I think I know how to use the bottle to travel back."

Her mouth hung open as she stared at me. "How?"

I dangled my keys. The tiny pompoms bounced and the metal clinked. She watched with confusion.

"Let's go inside, I'll explain it then."

Celestina and her mother looked at each other after I was done explaining my theory.

"So, you're saying that the message on the note isn't the reason, but the item's last location?" Celestina gave me her now-familiar expectant look.

"Right," I answered, nodding.

"That means we need something from the future to put in the bottle," *Senõra* Josefa said.

"I think so."

She shrugged. "Too bad. Looks like we'll be staying then."

I wasn't overthinking it. She sounded happy, but not as much as me as I took out the keys. "This is from the future."

"But that's too big for the bottle," she said, no longer bothering to hide her smile.

I pulled out my earphones and raised them with a triumphant smile. "Ha! But I got this!" I ripped the earbuds from the cord. "This will fit." I turned to Celestina. "Should we give it a try?"

"Of course. I'll get the bottle." She flicked a look at her mother and headed to her room.

Senõra Josefa sighed. "You're clueless."

"I'm not," I retorted, tired of her always having to get the dig in.

"You are. Can't you see that Celestina is worried?"

I knew. I saw. And I felt it too. But I knew why. "That's only because she's apprehensive about the future."

"She's not. She's worried that it might not work for all of us."

"Why won't it?"

She gave me a disapproving look. "How can you be sure it will work?"

I'm not but we will never know unless we try. "We can try holding each other and not letting go."

She opened her mouth but Celestina's arrival stopped her.

"*Mamá,* please, let's stay positive. Okay?"

Her mother sighed, giving me a slow shake of her head. "All right."

Celestina placed the heart bottle in my hand, and my blood rushed as I unscrewed the metal cap. Excitement, worry, and fear flooded every part of me, leaving my fingertips buzzing. When I looked at her weak smile, all the emotions shot straight to my heart and sank like a block in the pit of my stomach. If it works, we will all be in the future. Am I truly ready to watch this sweet girl struggle to adjust to life over there? Worse, what if her worries are proved right? What if I'm the only one who arrives in the future?

I gripped the bottle tight, and when Celestina placed her hand on top of mine, I started shaking all over.

"Let's take things one step at a time," she said.

I let out a deep breath and nodded. She was years younger but sometimes her maturity beat mine hands down.

"Te amo."

She beamed. *"Y yo a ti."*

Senõra Josefa stood with us, forming a triangle. "Enough. How should we do this?"

I lifted my earphone cord and put it in Celestina's hand. "I'll hold the bottle. You put the cable in." I wrapped my arms around her waist. "I'll keep my hand here." She blushed, and I couldn't help but smile at the disgruntled look on Maria Josefa's face. "*Señora,* you may want to hold Celest's other hand."

"That's Celestina to you," she corrected.

I smirked. "Celest."

"Mamá, Leo, *basta!"*

I kissed her cheek, and *Senõra* Josefa, in silence, held out her free hand. Celestina dipped the cord inside, inch by slow inch. We waited but nothing happened. The light I expected to see didn't appear.

"The cap!" I nearly shouted, unwrapping my hand from Celestina's waist and putting the top in her hand. "You do it."

A collective anxiety filled the room but Celestina still gave me a smile as I placed my hand back on her waist. She twisted the cap on the bottle until it was tight, and I prepared myself for more disappointment.

Then it happened.

The bottle glowed, but, unlike the first time, the static electricity trailed up my arms into Celestina and her mother, with both of them jerking and screaming. *Senõra* Josefa let go. Seeing us both in pain, she grabbed the bottle from me, but like an electrocuted person, my fingers locked around it. I couldn't even open my clenched mouth to say that something was wrong, or offer any kind of comfort to Celestina, who clung to my neck, screaming in agony.

"*Hija,* let go of him!" her mother shouted as she pried my fingers one by one from Celestina's waist. She was a desperate mother determined to save her daughter. Once she succeeded, she wrapped her arms around Celestina and pulled with all her might. My consciousness faded in and out, from the present to a place I didn't recognize.

"Leo!" Celestina called out, struggling to free herself from her mother's grip.

"Celest!" I remembered crying as I reached out to her, but I only caught the locket dangling from her neck before I fell into the familiar space filled with unfamiliar voices and images.

My heart broke as I came out of the light and saw the locket and the empty heart bottle in my hands. I kissed the locket. "Celest, I promise I'll go back again. I'll find a way and bring you here with me."

I looked up, ready to get back home, but staggered backwards on finding myself in an unfamiliar place. A couple of stunned girls stared at me, screamed in fear, and ran away.

Dread spread through me like wildfire as I looked around. I'm good at finding ways to humor myself but I couldn't at this point. Not when I was surrounded by people in uniform, marching the alleys like thugs. The sweltering heat was too much and I had to take my jacket off. I made my way to the nearest paper stand, ignoring the snide comments of those around me regarding my clothes. The paper seller gave me a derisory smile while sizing me up. His gaze lingered on my polished shoes, and he smiled with approval, then offered to sell a paper to me, but I turned without replying after reading the date: August 3rd, 1936.

"August third, nineteen-thirty-six? *Guerra Civil Española,*" I mumbled, shivering. Not only was I sent farther back in time, I was in the middle of the Spanish Civil War.

I walked down the main street of Alicante city, not knowing what to do, all too aware that I didn't know a single soul.

Damn it. I wanted to cry—I really did—but, as if mocking me, someone was sniffling inside an alley. I followed the sound and froze at the sight of a girl shuffling along, in clear destress. A moment later, she slid against a dirty wall, holding her ripped dress close to her. If she let go, it would fall to the ground, leaving her exposed. She was barefoot, and blood dripped from her inner thigh, bringing my attention to a trail of red spots running to where the alley ended, where pieces of fabric lay scattered.

This poor soul had suffered a horrible experience, most likely rape or serious sexual assault. It didn't matter what time in history I was in, sexual abuse still occurred, and women still bore the brunt of it. I had no doubt they were pressured by society into not reporting it to the authorities, with shame so often falling on them instead of the rapist. Gritting my teeth, raging that I hadn't noticed anyone suspicious come out of the alley before her, I stepped closer and placed my jacket around her.

She went rigid. *"¡No me toques!"*

"Sorry, I won't touch," I said, stepping away, leaving my jacket on her shoulders. She didn't hear me, shaking and cowering, begging me not to hurt her any more. I looked around, relieved that no one was passing close by.

"*Señorita,* I won't hurt you." I approached again and crouched in front of her. "I'm trying to help." Brushing aside her messy hair, I froze at the tearful face looking back at me, turning my blood cold.

I nearly blurted out her name when she looked at her shoulders and thanked me. She was young, no older than fourteen, but there was no mistaking her. Maria Josefa.

"Can I bring you home?" I asked.

She whimpered and shook her head, then thanked me before making her way out of the alley.

I stepped up to the corner and watched her walk toward the old neighborhood.

Oh, man, what am I to do? Inside that young girl—too young to be a mom—was another girl who would find herself abused and unloved for years to come.

"*Puta madre*, I'm too late," a man beside me said.

I stared at him. He didn't seem much older than me and wore a dark-gray suit almost the same color as his eyes. He had a long nose and—just like Maria Josefa—looked way too familiar. Then it came to me and I snapped my fingers. Except for the dark curly hair, he looked just like the iconic Italian-American actor Rudolph Valentino. I'd only seen one of his silent films but I couldn't forget the name. One of my old girlfriends wouldn't stop yapping about how sexy his eyes were.

He turned to face me, his brows furrowed. "*¿Qué?*"

"Ah! You're Ángel!" I glanced at the band of soldiers passing by and tried not to show that I was almost overwhelmed at seeing him in person. "You! You raped her."

His gaze fixed on the bottle still in my hand. "Why do you have that?" he demanded, and, in one swift movement, he snatched it from my hand and pinned me to the wall. His forearm pressed into my throat, so hard I couldn't even cough or protest as my lungs screamed for air. "Where did you get this?" He lifted the bottle.

I stomped on his foot as hard as I could, then snapped a punch under the chin. He staggered back, and I gasped, sucking in all the air I could get. I grabbed the bottle from him but he shot a kick into my abdomen, knocking me back into the alley where the crime against Maria Josefa had been committed.

My gut hurt, and in that micro second as I lay on the ground, I couldn't understand why I enjoyed action and martial-art movies so much. The real thing was no walk in the park. But no way was I letting him get the bottle again. Still curled into myself, I looked out of the alley and saw a man pushing his woman companion away from us. I needed rescuing but war had made people wary of anyone. I reached for my chest, ready to hide the bottle in my jacket, and stopped. My jacket was gone. I gave it to Maria Josefa.

"My phone!" I roared.

"What?" Ángel glared at me.

I tightened my grip on the bottle. "You're not getting this from me. Rapist!"

"Woah!" he cried, now on the defensive. "I didn't do it! It was another me."

"Yeah, right." I shifted back, sitting up. "So, are you saying that you're Celestina's *papá* now?"

"Celestina?" His face paled. "You met my daughter?"

This Ángel was Celestina's time-traveling father. "I've got no time for this. I need to get my phone back from my jacket. Maria Josefa has it." I got up and walked out to the street, taking in the horrible effects of war. Military walked around like kings of the streets and weary people sculked at corners. I saw grim faces everywhere I looked, or men with guns. Even the children holding their parents' hands seemed to have lost their spirit.

"I can help you," he said, looking at the woman pointing in our direction. *"Venga."*

We walked in the direction Maria Josefa went, me with my hand on my gut, and a horrifying fascination at the brave protesters walking the street beside us, carrying a big black *antifascismo* banner.

Ángel pulled me away when I edged closer to them. "You don't want to be mistaken as part of their group."

My heart leaped when I spotted my jacket on the sidewalk, and I almost cried when I realized my phone was still in the pocket. But there was no sign of Maria Josefa.

Ángel cursed himself over and over for being too late to help her. He looked so dejected as he sat on the side of the road, so I sat beside him.

"You know that if you manage to prevent the rape from happening, Celestina won't be born?"

He shook his head. "Newbie. Traveling back and stopping events from occurring doesn't change the future."

I stared at him for a moment, working it through my brain. "What do you mean?"

"I'm only creating another timeline where Josefa wasn't raped." He hadn't answered my question. "I want a future where I can properly pursue Maria Josefa and make her fall for me. A future where I make her happy instead of living miserable, or where she ends up dead."

A chill ran through me. "Dead?"

"I killed her in my timeline. I didn't mean to but I did. And that's why I'm jumping from one timeline to the next, trying to save her from myself. But, even here, I'm too late."

"Why do you need to do all this? *Senõra* Josefa already loves you in the future."

He stared at me in disbelief. "When?"

"Well, I've come from nineteen-fifty-seven, and she—"

"Let's go!" He pulled out the heart-shaped bottle.

"Huh? Hey, when did you take it back?"

He dropped a couple of tiny stones into it as I realized that I still held my bottle to my chest. What the hell?

A moment later, I was pulled once again into the dark tunnel, and we landed back in Beniardá.

"This is a bottle I inherited from my family," he said, as if we hadn't just flipped through time. "I destroyed it from this timeline, after my other self was sent to jail for murder. That's why it's strange that you have one too."

"I got this from Celestina. I broke the one that brought me here."

"You shouldn't have been able to travel at all. But there's no time to waste. Let's go meet my dear daughter and future wife."

I grabbed his arm. "I forgot to tell you. They think you're dead."

He stared at me for a moment, his face reddening as his eyes widened. "*¿Qué?*"

Chapter 30

LEONARDO

February 24th, 1957

I brought Ángel to *Abuelo's* house, using my key to get in. The interior welcomed me like home, with the smell of cooking filling my head and reminding me I was hungry. I looked around the living room and handed Ángel the pen and paper he'd asked for earlier. He set about writing.

"This is good enough," he said after a few minutes, laying the pen down. He folded his letter into an envelope, along with a photograph. I'd seen the photo so many times over the fireplace, and I couldn't hold back a snort at the secrets and connections coming to life around me. It was like watching a movie, and I was its first viewer. Fascinating.

Ángel looked at me. "*¿Qué?*"

I looked away. "Nothing."

Despite his initial shock over his supposed death, he seemed to have got over it.

"Josefa is a stubborn woman," he said. "I can't easily assume that she will listen to me. This is for security reasons. If she doesn't listen,

I'll leave it in the house and torment her by making her think about it over and over before coming back."

He laughed like a maniac, which reminded me of the rapist version of him. I clenched my hand, tempted to jump up from the sofa and punch him, but pulled back. Don't be stupid—he wasn't the one who did it. As much as I hated to admit it, I understood Maria Josefa. Falling for a man who looked and sometimes behaved like the man she despised must have been hard.

I looked at the clock. Ten before two. *Siesta.* I got up from the sofa. "Ángel, we need to leave, Alonso will be home soon. It would be best if he doesn't meet you."

He nodded and walked out with me, and I gave the house one sweep over before closing the door. I missed them already but I couldn't stay forever.

"You'll help me get back to my time, right?"

He nodded. "I already told you I would. No worries."

"With Celestina," I added. Like the first time, he remained quiet. Like I would let him stop me. Besides, I was confident she would come with me.

The closer we got to the house, the harder my heartbeat. How is she now? How many days have passed since I vanished? Will she cry again, or be pissed at me?

As we approached the house, my heart froze at the sound of screams. Ángel and I glanced at each other and ran to the front door. Isabela tumbled out, her teary eyes widening at the sight of us.

"You!" She pointed at Ángel, looked back at the house, then back at him. "But...how?"

"Bella, hurry!" Alonso shouted through the screams and banging.

Isabela looked at me. "Leo! Go help Alonso. Please, don't let him get hurt. Please!" She sprinted up the road then, not looking back.

What the hell is going on? More grunts and screams filtered from the house. My heart thundered on hearing Celestina begging someone to stop. I raced for the door, but Ángel was inside before me. The living room floor was strewn with broken bottles, with much of the furniture upturned. Ángel leaped at a man and dragged him to the floor.

"Leo!" Celestina called out. She stood in front of Maria Josefa, who looked like a petrified child, crouched with her hand over her head, screaming. Celestina didn't look too good herself. Her shaky hand held a large kitchen knife, and blood dripped from her finger. A bruise darkened one of her cheeks, and her upper lip looked swollen. Alonso was slumped on one side of the fireplace, holding a handgun and panting with exhaustion. Like me, he stared in disbelief at the two men attacking each other. Two identical men.

Two Ángels, equal in every way. They swung their fists and legs in the same way, causing each other an equal amount of damage. The only way I recognized the one who came with me was that he wore a gray suit, while the other wore denim overalls.

Suited Ángel punched the other one and looked at me. "Get my family out of here!"

Maria Josefa, who seemed to have come to her senses, stopped screaming, "Ángel, you came back."

Overalls Ángel threw a kick at our Ángel, sending him flying toward Alonso. He puffed his chest out as he leered at Maria Josefa. "Of course I did."

Our Ángel's earlier maniacal laughs were nothing compared to this criminal. Rage flared in me. He wasn't only looking at Maria Josefa, who screamed again, he was grinning and licking his lips as his gaze traveled over my girlfriend's body.

I grabbed the closest thing to me—a broken leg from the coffee table—marched up behind him and swung as hard as I could. The wood splintered, the vibrations shooting up my arm. As the man collapsed, everyone stopped and held their breaths.

"That hurt!" he said, getting up from the floor.

Celestina's eyes widened in horror, and the blood drained from me when he jumped at her. Everything happened so fast. One second, he was on the floor, the next, he pried the knife from Celestina's hand, gripped her shoulder and pointed the blade at her throat. Tears streamed down her cheeks. Ángel and I rushed in but the rapist pressed the point into Celestina's neck. For a moment everything in my life stopped, including my heart, until I saw her still breathing.

"Come closer and I'll kill her," he said. "I will drive this thing straight through her beautiful neck." He licked the thin line of blood off her skin. My whole being ached to beat him but no one moved. Alonso pointed the gun at him but didn't fire. We all stood still, unwilling to risk it.

"Let go of my daughter!" Maria Josefa shouted as she leaped onto his back like a cat. She bit his ear, sending blood spouting out.

He screamed and let go of Celestina, then thrashed around to get Maria Josefa off his back, slamming her into the wall.

"*¡Mamá!*" Celestina cried out and, for a second, I thought he'd killed Maria Josefa when she landed on the floor, blood oozing from her mouth. But then her eyes snapped open and she spat out the piece of his ear. Everyone paled, and I was both impressed and disgusted. With his attention focused on Maria Josefa, he failed to notice when our Ángel lunged at him, pinning down his hand holding the knife.

He looked back at me. "Leo, get my family out of here. Now!"

"Leo, go!" Alonso shouted, struggling to get up.

I grabbed Maria Josefa and Celestina by the hand and pulled them out of the house.

"Both of you stay here," I told them and stepped back inside. Celestina protested, and Maria Josefa begged me to help Ángel.

I nodded, relieved to see Alonso's friends running toward the house. A gunshot echoed through the hallway, evoking screams from the women and nearly giving me a heart attack. As we stood there in shock, another gunshot rang out. I ran back in and stopped dead in my tracks at the sight of Overalls Ángel sprawled on the floor with a small, reddening hole in his forehead. Our Ángel stood over him, holding the gun. Alonso stared at him, his eyes wide, then looked at me.

"Leo, hurry. Let's get him to the hospital."

Before I could tell him there's no way to save the dead, our Ángel shook his head. "No, I'm fine."

"You're shot!" Alonso said.

Ángel gripped his stomach, and blood oozed between his fingers. He threw the gun aside. "No one touch it." He turned when Alonso's friends entered the room, all of them looking shocked at the sight before them. Isabela, out of breath, rushed to Alonso's side and inspected him.

"Get the bottles," Ángel said, pointing them out.

The two heart-shaped bottles lay in the corner, complete, even after flying out of our clothes during the fight. I brought them to Ángel. He licked the blood on his lips, put one bottle in my hand and wrapped my fingers around its neck.

"This is my family's treasure. Only those in our bloodline can control it with a drop of blood. Sometimes, desperation brings miracles. And right now, you and I are desperate." He made sure I had a good grip on it. "Don't worry about things here. Go back to your time and let history play out once more." He put his bloody fingers on my shoulder, grunted in pain, then placed it back over my hand. "You can also return if possible."

"If possible? What do you mean?" I asked as the air distorted around us.

"Good luck," he said, then collapsed.

Electricity whirled around me just as Celestina and Maria Josefa walked inside.

"I'll come to you," she said. "See you in another time."

"I love you," I mouthed, and let myself get sucked back into the void.

I materialized in 2020, the same day I'd left, and in the same place. I knew because I stood right behind my other self and watched as the heart bottle broke. When the bright light sparked, he attempted to break away from the pull.

"Oh, no you don't," I said under my breath and pushed him. As weird as it was, before he could turn, I watched as I—the other me—vanished. What a strange feeling. Is this what time travelers in the movies felt each time they saw themselves? Dead and living Ángel flashed in my mind. The memory of seeing his lifeless body made me queasy. What did Ángel feel after killing himself? Was he satisfied? He hated himself after all.

I pushed the thought away and headed home, holding the heart bottle close. My slow pace turned to a jog, and I was sprinting by the time my *abuelo's* house came into view.

"*¡Abuela!*" I called out, slamming the door behind me.

"Good timing, *hijo.* The food is almost—"

I pulled her into a gentle but tight embrace and she laughed, wrapping her aged arms around me.

"What's gotten into you?" she asked with a hint of a smile.

I kissed her cheek and stepped back, still holding one of her shoulders with my free hand. "I never truly appreciated how amazing you are, *Abuela.*" I shrugged. "I just want you to know that."

Her smile wrinkled the corners of her tired eyes, then she slapped my shoulder. "You're still eating *paella marisco.*"

I laughed, then groaned. "Do I have to?"

"*Si,* you must."

Abuelo descended the stairs and, for a second, I saw the sturdy young Alonso.

"What are you staring at?"

I smiled. "I'm proud to have taken after you."

"Hmph," was his only response, then he frowned when his gaze landed on my clothes. "Is that blood on you?"

I looked down at my arms. Blood covered my shirt. Even the bottle in my hand had dried blood smeared over it. "Uh, yeah. Don't you remember how it happened? I just came from the past. That reminds me, I need to get back again. I must prevent Celestina's biological father from shooting Ángel. I also need to bring Celestina here with me—" I stopped at their incredulous look. "Why are you both looking at me like that? What's going on?"

Abuela touched the bottle in my hand, and I gripped it hard. Something was wrong. I could feel it in their demeanor—their expression—their look of pity and sorrow.

Why? They should know by now that I just came back from the past.

"Why don't we eat first?" *Abuela* suggested with a soothing voice, which this time agitated me.

"*Por favor*, please, tell me what's going on. Did something happen in the past?" I stared at *Abuela*. "Did Celestina drop by?"

She cried, and it took all my willpower not to fall on my knees and beg her to tell me those tears weren't for Celestina. *Abuelo* came down the rest of the steps and placed a hand on *Abuela's* shoulder. "Let's go into the sitting room and talk."

My mind blanked out but I followed them. The hope of seeing Celestina again—even as an old woman—fell away with every step I took behind them. Please say she didn't disappear again.

Once we were sitting face to face, my grandparents dropped a bomb worse than her disappearance:

Celestina was dead.

Chapter 31

LEONARDO

It felt like the end of the world as I listened to my grandparents' stories. They had no recollection of anything I was telling them. Neither of them recalled meeting me in the past, and the fire after Valentine's still happened at *Abuela*'s house. Rodrigo dated no one, and my parents died in the same horrific manner, saving me.

"Celestina died the day her father got out of jail."

I shook my head when *Abuela* said she had been so hurt after losing Celestina that she denied the truth, as an act of self-protection, telling me during my childhood that her friend vanished without explanation. "I didn't want to tell you the truth that my best friend...died," she said, and my heart throbbed as she shook. She covered her face and cried for Celestina.

"No, *Abuela.* I was there. *Señora* Josefa saved her."

She looked up. "No one else was there other than the three of them. I was the first to arrive and saw that woman! She had a heart of stone, *hijo.*" Her hands shook. "She never shed a single tear for my friend. Celestina took a bullet, saving her! All she ever wanted was that woman's love, and she died trying to earn it. *Mi pobre amiga.*"

I slumped in my seat. My grandparents were telling the truth. They had no reason to lie. It wasn't even because I changed history. Nothing had changed!

In the week that followed, I don't know how I dealt with everything. I locked myself in my room, lost in my grief—having a pity party on my own.

I couldn't keep myself locked up forever, but the prospect of going outside and seeing everything as it existed before my travels—as if nothing had changed—killed me. No matter how much thought I put into it, I still didn't get it. I couldn't. My grandparents said I was gone for only an hour. Was everything a dream? Celestina's touch. Her smile. Her love? I looked at my clothes crumpled on the chair, with the unwashed bloodstain. And the heart bottle stood there on my side table. I clenched the locket, which fell out of my pocket the night I trashed my room, searching in desperation for evidence of our time together. No. I knew it wasn't a dream or an illusion. She was real.

Ángel's words when we met in 1936 flashed through my mind. A timeline where Maria Josefa was dead, but Celestina? How could she be dead? We saved her. I won't give up. I won't! I went through so much to meet her. Doing a bit more to get her in my arms wasn't a problem. I opened the locket and ran my thumb over her portrait. Ángel said "if possible," meaning it wasn't impossible. Call me crazy but I knew I'd find a way back. I closed the locket and placed it beside the bottle.

I put my spare wireless earphones in my ears and, as if cheering me on, the first track my phone shuffled to was Boy Meets Girl's

Waiting for a Star to Fall. So fitting. So many people loved her but she was the last to notice.

Hold on. My phone!

I scrolled through the gallery. My heart swelled at what came up. There it is. Everything. My phone was living evidence that our memories were real.

Too shaken by the news of Celestina's death, it hadn't occurred to me to show the videos and photos to my grandparents. They're even in here. There's me plopped on the sofa, with Celestina holding the phone, filming the two of us as she kissed me. She whispered to me, and I laughed before cupping her cheeks and kissing her. The camera spiraled and only our voices teasing each other remained. I don't know how I kept the tears back, or how I had the strength to let the next video play, but when I rose from my bed, it felt like I'd been asleep for such a long time. Well, now I was awake and ready to give fate a good beating.

Destiny? I don't care, I'll create my own. With Celestina beside me.

After watching all the videos and looking at the photos, I changed into dark pants and a hooded jacket, then stepped out of my room with renewed hope in my heart.

Abuela was busy in the kitchen and instead of greeting her with a morning kiss on the cheek like I normally would, I tiptoed my way out of the house. I took a deep breath after closing the front door behind me, needing to calm down before confronting them with my evidence.

I turned the music on and jogged down the path toward the house owned by the only woman who possessed my whole heart. There was a better road to get there now, but I chose the one I took with her, even though it had become a haven for weeds.

I expected the house to be there and even steeled myself to see Maria Josefa's old self, but what I found was an abandoned home, the front door broken and the furniture old, worn, or broken. Maria Josefa didn't bother putting the place back together. If she remained the way she was the first time I met her, this was no surprise—she would be too busy drinking to notice anything.

Over the next few minutes, I looked around the interior, searching for anything I could use. I cleared wood splinters from the sofa and smiled, remembering the first time I sat on it filming Celestina having a fight with the fireplace. I ran my fingers over the fabric, stopping when I touched something stuffed down the side of the cushion. I pulled it out and stared at the familiar photo through the cracked glass. The frame was different but it was the photo of Celestina and Maria Josefa with Ángel.

I stared at it, my heart thumping in my ears. Why is this here? I removed the photo from the broken frame, flipped it, and caught my breath at the writing on the back:

Regret truly comes when it's too late. I'll show my love
to both of you in the next life – Maria Josefa

Did she kill herself after writing this? A cold chill ran down my spine. The walls, the silence, even the surrounding mess—everything seemed to observe me. It crept out of my skin. I got up but remained still for a long moment, then walked toward the door, not really feeling the floor, as if I was walking on thin air. My brain seemed to shrink and expand at the thought of Maria Josefa's ghost haunting this house, but it didn't stop me from noticing a small drop-pearl earring among debris on the hallway table. I grabbed it before running from there like a frightened child.

"If I didn't know what happened, I'd be panicking now," *Abuela* said as she walked out of the kitchen and saw me leaning against the door. I was cold, shaking, and out of breath when I got home. Coughing, too, from running nonstop, but satisfied.

"And if I didn't know better, I'd think you lived in the kitchen," I said, grinning. She waved me away and walked back toward the oven. I followed her. "You were a lot more fun to tease when you were nineteen."

"Like you'd know how I was back then."

"Oh, I know, *Abuela*. Like the fact that *Abuelo* hated it when someone else called you Bella."

"Did he tell you that?"

"Yes, when I met you both in the past. You really don't remember? We were together for six months, from nineteen-fifty-six to nineteen-fifty-seven. I was there when he proposed to you in his bedroom."

She stopped and looked at me. "*Hijo,* how many times have I told you? Your *Abuelo* proposed to me the first time he cooked for me."

I shook my head. "Why are you lying to me, *Abuela*? What really happened after I left? Did Ángel get arrested for killing himself?" This came with a laugh, though it was mixed with a hint of bitterness at the thought that she was choosing to lie to me. "Is it because of my parents' accident? I told *Abuelo* about it but the accident still happened. Is that why you're both lying to me? Do you hate me that much?"

"No one is lying to you!" *Abuelo,* who never raised his voice at me, now looked like he was about to punch me. He pushed me away from the kitchen door and put a hand around *Abuela's* shoulder. "No one in this house hates you."

Abuela's tears trailed down her cheeks. "We love you, *hijo.* We can't hate you or lie about something so big."

I ignored the guilt eating me inside, pulled out my phone and scrolled through my files. When I reached the video of Celestina and I, while she and *Abuelo* approached us from behind in the video. I showed it to her. They were there for only a couple of seconds but it revealed my truth. *Abuela* covered her mouth with a shaky hand.

"How can that be?"

"Because I was there. In the past. With you!" I looked at *Abuelo,* who remained calm and silent as he watched the video.

He sighed, rubbing *Abuela's* shoulder. Ah, now you're ready to tell the truth? But, instead, he asked me to tell them again about everything that had happened in the past. "Also, tell us why you think we hate you so much. Enough so we would deny you your happiness."

And so, sitting in the living room, I recounted everything I'd experienced in the past, including Rodrigo's date.

Abuela shook her head in disbelief. "I'm sure Rodrigo's one and only love is working in the field."

That made me laugh a bit. And, just as young Alonso advised me in the past, I told them of how I blamed myself for my parents' death and for robbing the life of their daughter.

"How can we possibly hate you, you foolish child!" *Abuela* said, hugging me, her warm tears wetting my cheek.

Abuelo gave me a disapproving look. "My daughter died saving you, her son. There's no way I would hate you for it. Remember that. If you've had doubts about that for such a long time, you should have been a man and confronted us. Stupid kid." I burst out laughing, which didn't go down well with him. He glared at me. "You want me to beat you?"

He could have done it in the past but I doubt an eighty-nine-year-old could do it now. Still, I shook my head and explained what he'd told me back in the 50s. It dragged my mood right down. "What the hell is the point of me going back if I can't change the future?"

They looked at each other—the look that only comes when two people have lived together so long they don't need words to know what the other one is thinking.

"I'll go prepare *merienda*," *Abuela* said and left the room.

Abuelo cleared his throat. "I have no reason to doubt what you experienced. If you really returned to the past and met me and your *abuela*—"

"Bella," I said to test him, and his eyes narrowed.

"Okay. You've proven your point." I held my laughter and waited while he gathered his thoughts. "The future that developed as a consequence of you going back to the past, that future exists, but it's not our future."

He'd said so little but my head was already reeling. Even after seeing it for myself, I still had difficulty grasping the concept of parallel existence. Ángel had explained it to me in brief, but I couldn't grasp it. "*Abuelo,* do you know how parallel existence works?"

He pointed at the TV. "If you're watching a news channel, do you think other channels exist?"

"Of course, but—"

"Can you see the movie channel while you're on the news channel?"

"No, of course not, but I could if I wanted to."

"How?"

"I'll change the channel."

"Using what?"

I struggled to keep my annoyance down. The answer was obvious but I said it anyway. "The remote."

"Exactly. Instead of the remote, you used Celestina's bottle to change the channel of time."

"I..."

"If you switch to other channels, does the news channel stop airing?"

"No," I replied, grimacing at the pain thumping around my head.

"To see other TV channels, you must switch there but the news channel will still exist. When you went to the past, you went to another channel." He shrugged as he looked at me, the action gentle. "You can't make two channels play at the same time."

I swallowed as the dots joined. "You mean to tell me there's no way for me to change what's already happened?"

He nodded, and my whole body felt empty, like a shell sitting there with nothing inside. I shook my head, looking up at the ceiling. "If I can't save Celestina and prevent my parents' death, what the hell is the point of all this?"

"You can't save the dead. The past is a battle you can't win. You can simply create opportunities for new futures."

A spark of hope flared in my heart. "You mean that, even if I can't change this future, I can still experience a future where I exist in the past with Celestina in it?"

He gave me a sad smile as he nodded.

"But if I manage to go back and stay...?"

"Follow your heart, *hijo,*" he said, using an endearment he rarely used on me.

Abuela walked in carrying a food tray for all of us, and dread spread through me. There's no way I can leave these two on their own, but, then, can I really go on living without Celestina?

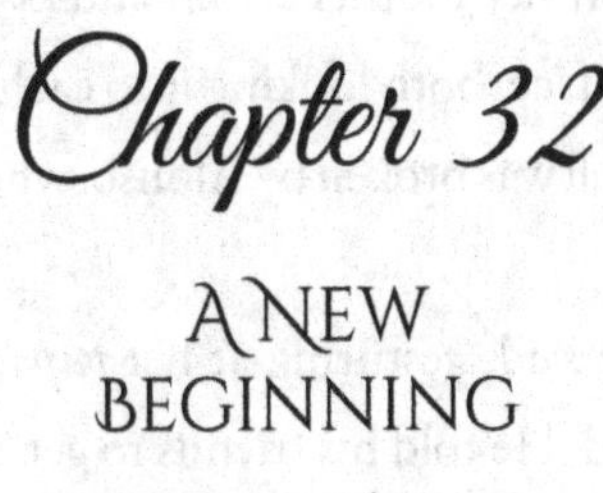

Chapter 32

A New Beginning

February 24th, 1957

Celestina stood in the middle of a mess of broken glass and dead and hurt men. Her mother continued crying, and her father pressed a hand against his bleeding abdomen.

"I love you," Leonardo had mouthed as he'd vanished with one of the heart-shaped bottles. She'd promised to see him again—to go to him—and she would. One way or the other, she would find him.

"Are you all right?"

She looked at her *papá* in time to see her mother slapping his hand away from her face. The scene hurt her. Since childhood, it had been one of her dreams to see the two of them in love, and, even now, her mother couldn't show her feelings.

"You idiot!" her mother cried at him. "You're more hurt than me."

Her *papá smiled.* "But it hurts more to see you in pain."

"Shut up." And with that, she let him pull her into an embrace.

The afternoon sun made the chaos seem tranquil as Celestina watched her *papá* lift her mother's chin and kiss her. She returned the kiss, holding his face, both looking into each other's eyes.

But then the spell was broken by Alonso, who groaned as Isabela helped him up.

"He's shot," he said, gesturing at her *papá*, whose pants were now soaked in blood. He told his friends to get the car ready.

The horror on her mother's face reflected her own concern. Her body felt icy and light as she made her way across the room toward the two people she treasured so much. "*Papá*, you need to get to the hospital."

"*Si, mi* Ángel," her mother agreed, nodding with vigor. "We must bring you to the hospital."

Her *papá's* face softened at the way her mother addressed him, then hardened. He looked back at her rapist of a father, lifeless, lying a few feet from them. "I must leave," he said, cupping her mother's cheeks and waving away any protest. "Someone needs to be responsible for his death, and me being here will raise too many questions. I must go. I love you both." He kissed her mother, then turned to her and squeezed her hand. "I'm so proud of you, Celest."

He lifted the bottle, which glowed, and, just as Leonardo had, he vanished. She and her mother both turned to her biological father and seemed to have the same thought. Rage reflected in her mother's eyes as she marched to the corner of the fireplace, grabbed the kitchen knife and stomped toward the corpse, only to be stopped by Alonso and Isabela. But her mother's fury was so strong she dragged them with her.

"Let me go! I'm going to slice that scumbag into pieces!"

Two of Alonso's friends rushed to help. One held her back as the other took the knife from her hand.

Celestina, seeing red herself, grabbed a wooden leg of their broken table. She walked in a daze toward the man who had ruined her mother's life. Ruined her childhood. And only returned to do it after they'd struggled hard to fix it.

"He's got no right to wear *Papá's* face," she said.

"Celestina, stop!" Alonso shouted. "If you touch that body, you'll probably be a suspect for killing him. Your *papá's* sacrifice will be in vain."

Hate and disgust coiled inside her. She despised the man so much, she didn't know what to do with it. But the sight of his lifeless face made her want to throw up. Bile surged into her throat, its force so strong she could only let it pour from her. As she gagged and coughed, sounds of someone else vomiting came to her.

Juan Martin entered. "Alonso, a group of *guardias civiles* are on the way." He threw one glance at the body and went pale. "Excuse me, I'll be outside."

Alonso and Isabela let go of her mother, who went to her and pried the wood out of her hand. "*Hija,* let's go. It's over. Let's get out."

Celestina looked at her red eyes, her face still wet from tears, and spattered with blood from that man. "I hate him. He shot *Papá.* He's the reason *Papá* disappeared again."

"I know." New tears flooded her mother's eyes.

"*Mamá,* I hate the blood that keeps me alive. I hate his blood." She clutched her chest. It hurt so bad, she clawed at her skin. The hate which had nowhere to go now directed itself internally. This rapist truly was her father, and maybe she was as bad as him, because she couldn't feel any pain as she dug into her neck.

Her mother looked horrified at first but then grabbed her hand and pulled her up. "*Basta, hija, basta.* It's enough, we're free." She took her face in her hands and forced her to make eye contact. Her *mamá's* eyes were as clear as she had ever seen them. "*Te quiero, hija,* and that monster could never change it. That blood coursing through you is the same as the man I love. The man who saved us. The man who came back to say his goodbye."

Celestina's nose ached inside, and her eyes stung as her mother pulled her into a hug.

Alonso touched her shoulder. "Let's get out." Isabela, who seemed to be just hanging on, nodded.

A short time later, the *guardia civil* arrived at the house. The next few hours were a mess of answering questions while cars came and went. *Policia local* and other government authorities showed up, filling the sleepy village with activity. Everyone wanted to know what happened, and many were ready to help.

Celestina couldn't believe that she'd ignored such kind people almost all her life—friendly people who offered their homes to them. Her mother seemed to think the same thing when they looked at each other.

Señora Juliana pushed the crowd aside and took both of her mother's hands. "Celestina is my daughter's friend," she said, glancing at her. "The two of you can stay in my house."

"You can stay in my house," Alonso said, coming closer.

Isabela, still assisting him, nodded. "That's right, use the house until you both figure out what to do."

Señora Juliana frowned at her daughter. "You want another woman in your fiancé's house?"

"Celestina and *Señora* Maria Josefa can stay there while Alonso recuperates at our house," Isabela said.

"*¿Que*?"

"I want him close to me. I need to nurse him back to health."

Celestina looked at Alonso. The signs of battle showed on every part of his body: the crumpled clothes, the cuts and bruises, his demeanor. But despite all of that, he looked content with Isabela under his arm.

A mixture of gratitude and envy crept into her heart. Alonso reminded her of the man she wanted so much beside her right now. But like her *papá*, he was out of this time.

A detective from the city approached them. "*Señora*, can I talk to you?" Her mother nodded and left with him.

By the end of that long day, she and her mother lay huddled together in Alonso's guestroom.

"*Mamá,* what are we going to do now?"

"We will be fine." She rubbed her shoulder and soothed her like a baby. "And I think we will see your father soon."

Celestina stiffened. "I'd rather drown myself than take part in his funeral."

Her mother's hand stopped. "I don't consider him your father at all. I'll cut his body to pieces and feed it to crocodiles if I can."

"Now I feel bad for the crocodiles," she said in all seriousness before they laughed together. She hugged her mother. "I'm sorry for all your pain, *Mamá.*"

"Having you here now with me, your love, is enough. If I could go back in time and change history, I would choose to love you sooner."

"Then you should have asked *Papá* to do it."

"I did but, as you can see, you're still here. A future which exists can't change, *hija.*"

"What? Then what's *Papá* been doing? Leo's return?"

Her mother rubbed her shoulder again. "Our future isn't here yet. It can still change. Leonardo's return changed our future, which will now differ from the future he knows, but our history in his future is the same." Her brows creased as she took a sharp breath. "I'm not the best at explaining this, *hija.* Ask Leonardo or your *papá* when one of them arrives. I'm only copying your *papá's* words."

"*Mamá*, I don't think we should hope too much. *Papá* was badly wounded. What can he do to save himself?"

"Leonardo will help him." The conviction in her voice stunned Celestina. "Remember when I said that Leonardo was with him the last time I saw him?"

Because of all that had happened, she'd forgot that part. The thought that she'd get one of them back eased the lingering ache in her heart. If it was her father who returned, she would still have a chance to travel, because he would, for sure, have a bottle with him. No, hold on, his bottle was the one he gave her that time. So that means only Leonardo has it.

"I don't think I can enter our house and not see him, *Mamá*. That man's death tainted our home."

"I feel the same, but enough thinking for tonight, *hija.* Go to sleep. We have a lot of things to sort out tomorrow."

She nodded, snuggled into her mother, and let the tiredness of her body and mind overtake her.

Chapter 33

LEONARDO

October 24th, 2020

Lying on my bed with Pandora's *La Usurpadora* blaring out of my earphones, my tears fell on my pillow as the singer sang about giving her heart and making him experience heaven. It was easy to get lost in their velvet-like voices as I drowned in my emotions and memories. I didn't realize *Abuela* was beside my bed until she touched my shoulder.

"*Abuela.*" I was deep into my own dream that her face overlapped with her nineteen-year-old self, and I nearly said her first name.

She looked around my room and stopped at my bloodstained clothes, still unwashed. "I knocked, but you didn't answer. But I saw that your light was on and figured you were still awake."

"You need something, *Abuela*?" It was rare for her to drop by my room at night.

She smiled at me, her expression telling me she knew what was bothering me. "*Dame la mano, hijo.*"

Wondering what she was up to now, I kept quiet and gave her my hand. She placed a small drop-pearl earring on my palm. I stared hard at it and shot up.

"That's my most-treasured item," she said, "but I only have one of the pair." She nodded once at the earring. "I lost the other when I was seven years old. I later saw it with Celestina. She told me she saw me lose it but was too shy to approach me." She chuckled. "I let her have it, and now I'm letting you use this to get back to her."

"*Abuela,* do you understand what you're saying? Leaving you here and going back means possibly never seeing me again. I can't—"

She shook her head. "*Hijo,* I have your *abuelo*. He's the most loving man I could dream of having beside me. You're a young man who found love in another time. Go there, to her. Give her the love she deserves. Make my best friend happy."

"But—"

"No more excuses. My only condition is that you let us properly see you off this time."

I nodded, no longer daring to say a word. I had cried enough. But I put the earring back in her hand and pulled out the drawer of my night table. I showed her the one I found.

She touched the pair of earrings with shaky fingertips. "You were at her house?"

I nodded, reached for Celestina's family photo and handed it to her. Her mouth opened, her bottom lip trembling. "So, she wasn't lying about her *papá* looking like her biological father.

"Turn it," I said. She did and, as I expected, cried.

She clenched her hand, wrinkling the photo. "Stupid woman. If she loved Celestina, she should have shown it before things went wrong. Why wait until it's too late and then follow them? Stupid woman."

So, Maria Josefa did kill herself. I got up and wrapped my arms around my *abuela*, letting her sob against my chest. I kissed the top of her head. She was shorter than her younger self, but still the same lovable *Abuela*.

"I'll try to bring Celestina back here with me. Hopefully you won't be the little villainess that you were."

She broke free from my embrace. *"Yo? Villana?"*

"Si, Abuela."

She squeezed my cheeks and I smiled, feeling lighter. "Should I include those for tomorrow's laundry?" She nodded toward my bloodstained clothes.

"Yes. *Gracias, Abuela.*" My gratitude was not only for the clothes.

Two days later, wearing the clothes I used the first time I went back in time, now washed and free from bloodstains. I stood in my bedroom with my grandparents and stuffed my jacket with things I needed: my cellphone and charger, face mask, and an extra copy of the house key. Yesterday, I also bought a small bottle of sanitizer and a pair of new stud earrings for this trip. Who knows, I might find a way to return. If not, I'll just give them to Celestina together with the locket, which I'm also bringing with me.

"Say hi to my best friend," *Abuela* said, her eyes glistening with tears. She hugged me and kissed my cheeks. "I will miss you, but I wish you all the happiness, *hijo.*"

Abuelo tapped my shoulder. "I'll take good care of *my* Bella. So, don't worry and go." *Abuela's* cheeks turned red. I wanted to be able to do that to Celestina when we were as old as them. "Now, go before she changes her mind and keeps her *nieto* here." His demeanor softened but his eyes turned serious. "But if you can come back to us, we want to see you and your girlfriend. Maybe even our great-grandchild."

My heart drummed at the thought of a child with Celestina. She was only twenty years old, and I doubted she'd wish to have a child right away. But when she decided, I was sure she would be one of the most caring mothers in the world. Warm and gentle, and strict. I couldn't hold back my smile.

"You're grinning like a fool," *Abuela* said.

My happy spell broke. As I stared at her, in my mind, I could see the nineteen-year-old Isabela in front of me.

"Enough fooling around, get going," *Abuelo* said, cutting the staring contest between me and *Abuela.*

I nodded, dropped the earring into the heart bottle, then squeezed my eyes shut. Nothing happened, but when I opened my eyes, my grandparents were fading. *Abuela* hugging *Abuelo* was the last thing I saw before plunging into weightless darkness.

This trip was getting more and more comfortable for me. But it was the longest time I'd been inside before I saw the light and was spit out to it, like it was angry at having to do this again.

I stumbled into an unknown yard. "What the hell?" I yelped when the bottle popped out of nowhere and tossed itself at me. Huh? Could the portal actually be alive? I laughed at myself. I have to stop watching sci-fi and fantasy films. Then again, traveling through time is the perfect fantasy.

A little girl stepped out in front of me, and I almost jumped to my feet, gawking. *Abuela?* Could it be? It was, but she couldn't be older than six or seven.

I looked at the bottle. Shit, it brought me back too far. You stupid thing! I swear, when I get things the way I want them, I'll pulverize you.

"*¿Quién es?*" young Isabela asked, but I couldn't tell her I was her grandson, so I pulled the hoodie of my jacket over my head and ran off.

Beniardá looked different. Font Vella wasn't in its place, and a horse stable stood where Rosetta's house would be. But from the area above the hill, I saw Celestina's house. My heart leaped. I hid the bottle inside my top and squirted my hands with sanitizer, then broke into a run. I had a better chance of finding a way into the right time if I was there. And, besides, I remembered Celestina saying that her *papá* still came to her at this time. I might get Ángel to help me again.

As luck would have it, the first person I saw when I reached the house was Ángel. He stood with Maria Josefa, who looked so much like Celestina in her twenties. They were facing each other, and didn't notice me approaching them. Then I saw her horrified expression as she looked at an envelope pressed into her hand by Ángel. It was smeared with blood.

"Promise me, you must read this letter and take good care of our girl," he said between heavy breaths. "Remember, she's my daughter, not his. Stop living in the shadow of his crime." He grunted, then straightened up to plant a kiss on lips. She froze for a second, then shoved him away, and he stumbled to the ground.

I moved before I could think. Ángel is alive. I thought he had died. I can save him.

"You—what are you doing here?" he asked, struggling to get up, holding his bloodied abdomen.

"Good, you recognize me. That means I'm not in the wrong timeline."

"You can't—"

"Papá?"

He froze, open mouthed, at the child's call from inside the house. My heart thundered but I couldn't risk being seen by Celestina and add an extra timeline. I pulled out the stud earrings from my pocket and dropped the pair in the heart bottle. When I grabbed Ángel's hand, the bottle glowed.

Maria Josefa flicked a look at me, then frowned, "No! Don't take him! Give him back!" she shouted, but the light swallowed us both.

We dropped into the center of my room. My grandparents, on their way out after having just said their goodbyes, turned back. The moment *Abuela* saw Ángel, she screamed. "You criminal! Get away from Leo—"

"Abuela, espera!" I got up, leaving Ángel to writhe in pain, and stopped her from ramming him with the vase. *Abuelo* assisted me. "He's the man in the photo. The guy I told you about in my story."

Both of them nodded, then we looked at Ángel, now quiet.

Abuela gasped. "*Ay, dios mio!* We need to rush him to the hospital!"

Abuelo, composed as ever, cupped her cheek. "*Calmate,* Bella. Leo and I will bring him to the hospital. You stay."

That calmed her.

We wasted no time in driving to the nearest hospital in Benidorm. Because the elderly were more vulnerable to the pandemic when in a crowded place, I put my face mask on and entered the hospital alone, carrying the unconscious Ángel over my shoulder. He was rushed to the operating theater, and I was left to sign as his guardian. I filled the questionnaire as much as I could, and inventing a story that he was the victim of a stray bullet and I had no idea where it came from.

Less than an hour later, the doctor told me that Ángel was stable but still unconscious. "He has a strong chance of making a full recovery."

Relieved, I couldn't wait to tell Celestina about it. After paying the hospital deposit, I got back in the car, filling *Abuelo* in on the way back to Beniardá.

He looked at my top. "You sure love having blood on you."

I let out an awkward laugh. "I will not trouble *Abuela* again with this, I promise."

He smiled. "Trouble her, she loves spoiling you."

I laughed. "Admit it. You're spoiling me too."

He huffed and looked out of the window, leaving me smiling like a fool. As much as I love being *Abuelo*'s friend in the past, I preferred being his grandchild.

Once we were at home, I asked them if they had anything I could use to travel back in time again. The earring brought me to *Abuela's* childhood because that was where she'd lost it.

"I need something from February nineteen-fifty-seven." If I could bring Ángel here, there should be no issues bringing Celestina—her mother too. They can live here, with me—with us.

"I know something," *Abuela* said and disappeared into their room. She came back with a set of sewing needle. "I bought this right after the fire. Because I wanted to sew something to remember my friendship with Celestina."

I took one of the needle, which clinked when it landed at the bottom of the bottle. As I waited, a strong sense of deja vu enveloped me, with the three of us watching for the bottle to do something.

"Nothing's happening," *Abuelo* pointed out, and I almost yelled "I know!" but bit my lip.

"Maybe we should try something else?" *Abuela* suggested.

"Good idea," *Abuelo* said, and the two of them left me. A strange voice in my head told me my luck had run out—that I could no longer use the bottle. Why? I don't know but it was a miracle I could use it in the first place. The bottle belonged to Ángel's family.

My grandparents returned with different items to use. But no matter what I put inside, it failed to react in any way. It looked like an ordinary bottle now. The thought of smashing it even occurred to me.

"If only there was someone who could tell you how to use it right," *Abuela* said, and I stared at her.

"Of course, there is! He's in the hospital." I kissed her. "You're the best."

"I know," she replied, smiling wide as she threw a side glance at *Abuelo.* He tried to play it cool, but I knew he was waiting for the same thing.

"You're both the best grandparents a grandchild could wish for."

"And we can't ask for a better grandchild," *Abuela* said. *Abuelo* nodded.

We laughed, and I calmed down a bit, looking forward to speaking to Ángel again. This time, I'd make sure to bring Celestina here. No matter how many tries it took, I would steal her from death.

Chapter 34

LEONARDO

With the bottle safely tucked inside my jacket, I took the elevator up to Ángel's hospital room. For the first time, I saw his full name, on the patient information, which hung on the side of his bed: Ángel Castro Rivera. I had put *De La Mota*, which was Celestina's chosen name. The fact it had been changed meant he'd woken up and corrected it.

I locked the door behind me and walked with caution toward the visitor's chair.

"I'm awake," he said, his unexpected comment almost sending me airborne. He blinked a couple of times and took a deep breath. "So, this is twenty-twenty."

It wasn't a question, but I answered anyway. "Yes, bringing you was the best way to help you stay alive."

He nodded to himself. "What a disappointment. I expected much more."

"What? Being in twenty-twenty saved you." I couldn't believe I was forced to defend my time to him. "Technology has evolved so much compared to where you come from. What do you mean by disappointing?"

"Evolved? Ha! This is a joke compared to what could have been. They placed the first object in space in nineteen-fifty-seven and landed on the moon's surface ten years later. But a half century on and everything seems the same. The car isn't even flying."

I opened my mouth to protest but stopped. I'm not the brainiest but I know when I'm about to lose. "It's great to see you're doing well," I said instead.

He nodded again, this time at me. "Thanks to you."

A heavy silence fell between us. I took out the bottle, placed my jacket over the back of the chair, and sat facing him. It was harder to open the topic of time travel than I imagined. He looked at my hand, and I placed the bottle together with my phone on the table beside his bed.

"How did your family get this?"

He shifted his position and looked at the ceiling. "I'm not sure. It belonged to my mother but she didn't stay long enough to tell me about it. My father was a violent man. He never hurt me but I remember him hitting her. I was about four when I first saw the bottle. She used it then with the intention of taking me with her but my father found us and pulled me away from her." He shifted again, grimacing as he settled. "She tried to stop the process, but you know how impossible that is."

I nodded but stayed silent, letting him go on in the hope of discovering how to use it to get back to Celestina.

"She left the bottle behind, and my father hid it for a long time. I was nineteen when he was killed during *Guerra Civil*. I was cleaning up his belongings when I found it, with my mother's letter. She explained in it what the bottle did—how it made her travel through time."

"How?" I asked, biting back my impatience.

He shook his head. "I don't know how she did it. For me, it just happened. I wished so bad to be with my mother, and it transported me but I ended up on another timeline. I don't know how to explain it. One minute I was at home, the next I was looking at myself raping a girl in a secluded alley."

"You mean you didn't rape Maria Josefa?"

He stared at me, his eyes hard. "I never saw her in my timeline. The other me from the timeline I ended up in seemed to travel through time too."

I groaned to myself. This timeline shit was confusing the hell out of me—giving me a headache—but I didn't interrupt him.

"When I caught him with her, I attacked him with the knife I always carried with me. But he used Maria Josefa's body as a shield." His knuckles whitened as he clenched his hand into a fist. The muscles in his jaw twitched. "I ended up killing her with my own hands."

I remembered him muttering about being too late when we first met. "So, you've been jumping around through time to stop him?"

"Yes."

"Are there timelines where you saved her?"

He nodded, the corner of his mouth lifting in a half smile. "Two. One where she got married and had her own family."

"And you're fine with that?"

"Of course. Because the other timeline had that asshole in jail. But he got out and killed my daughter. Then Maria Josefa, the woman I love, killed herself."

"This timeline."

He nodded. "But I now have new hope because of you."

I sat up. "That's good then."

He took a deep breath, though it didn't go beyond the pain in his gut. "Yeah."

"How do you know which timeline you're in?"

He gave me a curious look, then explained his difficulty controlling it—something about mental concentration and the bottle being the medium, which made it happen. It had taken twenty years of training, with many failures, to get where he wanted to go.

"Can you teach me?" I asked.

"I'm not giving you my daughter."

"She isn't your daughter," I retorted, not liking this switch in direction.

He smiled. "Any blood test will prove it."

"I bet you haven't even been to Maria Josefa's room despite being in love with her for so long." His glum expression pricked my conscience. I changed the topic. "Come on, teach me how to control the bottle. I really want to bring them here with me."

"If only taking them away was that simple."

"What do you mean?"

"Do you think I never tried bringing them with me?"

"But you took me with you. And I brought you here."

"Yeah, but have you ever tried bringing two people with you?"

Damn it, he's right. Trying to get back here with Celestina and her mother sent me somewhere else instead.

"It won't happen," he went on. "Things will go wrong if you try. And you being able to use the bottle is already enough of a miracle."

"What do you mean by that?"

"My mother told me no one outside my family can use it."

"If it's exclusive to your family, then why did it work on me?"

He shrugged. "I'm only telling you what my mother told me but, as I said before, desperation can bring miracles. Maybe that's what happened to you."

I shook my head. "I was far from desperate when I first traveled back."

"Maybe you just didn't realize you were."

"How about you? Are you always desperate when you jump through time?"

"Always," he replied and looked me straight in the eye. "I'll return to Josefa's side, no matter what I have to do."

I nodded, understanding his passion. "Then I can also use my blood like you did."

He shook his head. "I wouldn't recommend it. Even though I can use my blood, I prefer to use objects because using blood without training can do more harm."

My lingering hopes of getting back to Celestina drained from me. I walked out of the room in something of a daze, only remembering when I was at the reception that I'd left my jacket on the chair. Ángel was asleep when I returned, so I just took my jacket and slipped out. There was nothing more to be said, anyway. I drove back home, panicked for a moment when I discovered that my phone and the bottle was missing, but calmed when I remembered leaving it on the table. Driving the long, winding road at night wasn't worth it. Ángel would take care of my things. I'll survive the few hours without my phone.

I woke up the next morning feeling like a fool, but I hadn't given up. If I couldn't use the bottle, for whatever reason, it didn't mean I could never get back. Ángel said it only worked in his family, but it didn't change the fact that I'd used it. It worked three times before, so maybe I just needed a break. Besides, who was to say I couldn't hitch a ride with Ángel?

With excitement in my gut, I readied myself and drove back to the hospital, leaving a goodbye note for my grandparents. I hadn't been able to find my charger too, so I'll have to stop by the nearest phone store to buy a new one after the hospital. However, Ángel wasn't in his room, and that knocked me. The bottle and my phone wasn't where I left it, and no one I asked had seen him leave the hospital. A voice in my head whispered that all hope of going back was lost, but I ignored it. I went to the reception desk to inquire more and discovered that he'd left a note for me:

I'm sorry. To be honest, I'm not sure if you can't travel back anymore, but I need the bottle. Thank you for everything, but you should find someone else in your time and live a good life.

I crumpled it and did well not to fall as I staggered out of the hospital.

"Damn you!" I shouted as I almost collapsed onto a bench. It would have been better if I'd left him to die. I should have kept the bottle.

I watched leaves dancing on the ground, swirling in the light breeze. The sunny day seemed to mock me as I slumped on my seat and cried in silence.

"Damn you, Ángel. Damn you."

Chapter 35

AFTERMATH

February 25th, 1957

Celestina woke up the next day without her mother beside her. The room was bathed in sunlight, its rays streaming through the curtains. For a moment, she wondered where she was, then it all came back to her and she shook her head at the memory of everything that had happened. It felt so long ago and yet so close. Two men in her life said their goodbye minutes after each other, heading to two different times.

Her stomach churned at the thought of her biological father—his dead body in her living room. She brushed it off and got out of bed.

"*Mamá?*" she called out when she went downstairs and didn't see her. She followed the sound of kitchenware and soft voices and found Isabela cooking, with Alonso behind her.

Isabela swatted Alonso's hand when he wrapped his arm around her waist.

"*Un poquito?*"

"Wait," Isabela replied with a smile in her voice.

"Buenas dias," Celestina said. Isabela turned, and Alonso moved away and sat at the table. "Have you seen *Mamá*?"

"Not yet," Isabela answered. "*¿Quieres desayunar?* This is almost done."

Celestina shook her head. "*Gracias,* Isa, but I'll have breakfast with *Mamá.*"

"I saw her talking to *Señora* Catalina earlier," Alonso said.

"Thank you." She was grateful to him for letting them stay at his home and for the information.

She went to find *Señora* Catalina, who told her that her mother rented one of her houses in La Nucia. That surprised her but not as much as discovering that she had already left.

As she walked toward her home, she dreaded what she would find. She stood at the doorway, her heart aching at the sound of her mother's cries calling her *papá's* name. When she rushed in to comfort her, she stopped dead in her tracks, her heart lifting at the sight of her mother with the man who looked just as he did that day he left when she was seven.

"*Papá!*" she called, and both of them opened their arms toward her. Her face almost hurt with the intensity of her smile, which only happened when she was wrapped in his embrace, and an overwhelming sense of happiness made her wail like a child.

Her *papá* kissed her hair and whispered to her and her mother. "*Mi preciosas*, I promise to take good care of you both from now on. We will start a new life together."

Though she smiled, the happiness in her heart lessened with the thought of one more missing man in her life. She broke away from their hug and looked at her father. "*Papá*, you were with Leonardo before coming here, were you not?"

Her mother glanced at her *papá* and her, her anxiety clear in her eyes. She knew right then without being told that her parents had other plans for her and Leonardo.

Chapter 36

Meeting Leonardo

December 31st, 2020

Celestina's heart nearly stopped when she materialized in the middle of a crowd at the Levante beach. However, no one seemed to notice, with everyone's head up with their phones filming the fireworks. She wasted no time. Leonardo must be nearby. In all her travels, this was the first time she had such a strong gut feeling. She walked around the area but saw no one who looked anything like him.

She groaned. Her gut feeling couldn't be trusted—she should have known after so many failed jumps. With her shoulders slumped, she walked out of the crowd and went to cross the street. A man bumped into her, and she shrieked with horror as her heart bottle slipped from her grip.

"Whoops!" he said, catching it. "Sorry about that."

She froze.

He stared at her. "Miss?"

Her mouth fell open. "Leonardo?" She couldn't believe it. Impossible. She threw her arms around him. "I've missed you so much!"

"Leo, *¿qué está pasando*?"

They both turned to face the beautiful pregnant blond frowning at them. Leonardo lifted his hands, still holding the bottle. "I don't know, she just hugged me." He shrugged. "Miss, please let go. My wife might get the wrong idea."

"Wife?" she asked, staggering back. "Y-you're married?"

"Yes."He smiled and put his arm around the woman, who smiled at Celestina.

How could he get married? I told him I would find him. Why couldn't he wait for me?

She took a deep, shuddering breath. Anyone with eyes would see her heartbreaking in that moment.

"*Hola*, I'm Elena. Do you two know each other? I don't remember meeting you before." She flicked a suspicious look at Leonardo.

"*Yo,tampoco cariño,*"Leonardo said. "Have we met somewhere before? You look familiar."

Celestina straightened, her mind clearing. Could it be that she was in the wrong timeline again? She pointed at the bottle in his hand and he gave it back to her. "Have you seen this before?"

He hummed as he studied the bottle. "Oh yes, I've seen that bottle." He nodded several times. "*Abuela's* friend was holding it in one of their photos together." He turned to his wife with a half-smile. "You remember Celestina in the photos?"

Now that she looked closer, there was something off about this man in front of her. The air around him seemed different. He wasn't as jolly as she remembered. This Leonardo seemed more stoic.

Elena smiled at her. "Are you Celestina's grandchild? Once Leo mentioned her name, I saw the resemblance. You look so much like her in the photo."

Celestina forced a smile, relief easing the pain in her heart. "Where is Isabela now?"

"Oh, she traveled to Switzerland with my uncle, but they're due back tomorrow. Do you want to come with us? You can chat with my parents instead."

Celestinasmiled and shook her head. "I know the way. I'll come another time."

He truly isn't my Leonardo. However, seeing him eased her loneliness and motivated her to keep trying.

"Great. I'll tell *Abuela,*" Leonardo said and gave Elena a loving look. "I think we should get going."

Elena kissed him, then looked at her. "Nice to meet you, ah...?"

"Celest," she answered.

"Happy New Year, Celest."

"Same to you both."

She waited until they were out of sight before weaving through the crowd. In a secluded area, she eased the lace, which would take her back to 1958, into the bottle. Her search would continue.

Chapter 37

LEONARDO

September 5th, 2021

"Wohoo!"

Everyone screamed as the fireworks exploded like beautiful flowers in the sky above the impressive sculptures made of wood and papier-mâché. *Fiesta las fallas* was a joyous event traditionally celebrated in March in the Valencian Community. Initially postponed due to COVID, the celebrations had been rescheduled to this time. In a sea of excited and happy faces, I seemed to be the only gloomy one in the crowd. There was no way I could be happy, because the only woman I deeply loved wasn't there to share it with me. I could have been with her if I hadn't been so stupid as to leave the bottle with Ángel.

"Leo, *hombre,* smile a little," Danielo, my best friend and business partner, said. "I didn't travel from Valencia to see you still sulking, even during a festival." He pointed at the emotional faces of the creators of the now-burning sculptures. The kids were wiping their tears. "You look worse than them. Come on, show that cheerful smile everyone loves."

I give him a smile that most probably made me look like a growling dog. It was hard to feel even a shred of joy. He shook his head and went on with the same dialogue about me needing to get depression therapy, or even just speak to someone about whatever was going on. But other than my grandparents, I couldn't talk about traveling back in time and missing my girlfriend from the 1950s. They'd send me to a psychiatric unit, maybe with my grandparents if they defended me.

"Leo, you've been this way for almost a year now. Can't you at least tell me a little of what happened to you?"

I gave him a side glance and sighed. "I fell in love."

He whistled. "You fell hard this time. I've never seen you so down after a breakup."

I smiled a bit at the thought of Celestina. "We never broke up."

"Oh." He nodded, then turned back to the fireworks, knowing well that he wouldn't get anything more from me.

After my initial bout of self-pity, anger, and ultimate depression, I tried everything I could think of to get back in time. In the eleven months since Ángel left with the bottle, I've attempted so many stupid experiments. I locked myself in my room, studying books on time travel I borrowed from the library or bought online or in any shop that sold one. And that says a lot about someone who hates to read anything longer than five hundred words.

Christmas and New Year went by without me even noticing the season changing, or how my grandparents worried over me. I couldn't blame them, what with me spending so much time isolated in my room. I also watched documentaries and tried anything they suggested. After viewing *Somewhere in Time*, I tried something

Richard did. I locked myself in my room for a week, hypnotizing myself, convincing my mind that I was in 1957. No surprise that it didn't work. My mind wasn't as strong as Richard's, and I couldn't get back to the woman I loved.

Two months ago, after watching the 2001 *Kate & Leopold* film, I went out to the ocean and tried to let the waves take me away, hoping the tide would carry me back in time. It didn't go as planned, landing me in a hospital bed instead.

"You're going insane," *Abuela* told me when I woke up in the hospital. They said my stomach and lungs were filled with salt water, and I wasn't breathing when the rescuers pulled me out. "Please stop doing this. Celestina wouldn't want you to die trying to meet her."

Her tears woke me from the long sleep I seemed to have put myself in. She was right—I was so obsessed with returning, I nearly killed myself. I realized then that I couldn't keep doing this.

I tapped Carlo's shoulder. He was busy scrolling through his Instagram after, no doubt, sharing the celebrations in his story.

"*¿Qué?*"

"I'll stay with my grandparents for a little longer to fully recuperate, and after that, I promise to be the Leonardo you always knew."

He smiled. "Take as much time as you need. Just don't take too long. No one can make a traveler smile as much as you. Speaking of, why don't we hire a model to market us?"

I stared at him. "A model? Can we afford it?" The travel agency wasn't doing well, and I was useless in my current state. I don't know how Danielo did it but he managed to keep the company afloat.

"I think we can," he replied. "I doubt the model I had in mind will charge much. Celestia—"

"Celestia?"

He laughed and walk away, through the excited crowd. I followed, rolling the name around my mind, thinking of Celestina, but then I lost interest when he told me the model was a rising influencer.

"She just started last year but now has a huge online following. So, what do you think? Should I negotiate with her, or do you want to? Her sweet retro charm will be perfect for rural travelers."

I shook my head, not ready to face the online world just yet. "You do it."

"Great! Welcome back, Leo. This is so exciting!"

Chapter 38

FAMILY

June 3rd, 1967

Celestina sighed after materializing with her heart bottle in the middle of the dining room. Her mother almost choked on her food and her *papá* nodded his approval.

"Congrats, I see you've made it through your travels. Can you finally control it?"

She nodded and observed the fine lines on her mother's face, the few white strands of her father's hair, and the young boy gawking at her. He was a one-year-old the last time she saw him, about three hours ago for her. "Angelito, you've grown."

He seemed taken aback and looked at his mother and father.

"Celestina, *tus hermana,*" her mother said to him.

He looked at the enlarged frame of them on the wall, then at Celestina. "You look prettier than in your photo." He said it in such a cute way, she had to embrace him.

"Sit down, *hija, comer con nosotros,*" her *papá* said.

Her stomach rumbled when she looked at the food. She went into the kitchen and filled a plate, then took the seat beside her brother. “How old are you now?”

“Nine,” he replied, with a smile that looked so much like their *papá.* For a long time after they’d moved to La Nucia, her parents refused to let her travel through time. The year with them had been fun, and she’d waited until her *papá* established a new identity, and for her mother to become pregnant before pressuring them about the bottle once more, her thoughts never far from Leonardo.

Angelito was three months old when her mother gave in and helped her convince her *papá* to teach her how to use the bottle. It took a few months before she could make a jump, but most places she ended up were anywhere but the time or location she wanted to be. She jumped back and forth between past, present, and future, but after two years of this, she still hadn’t reached Leonardo’s side.

He was the only one who kept her sanity intact each time she failed, though every time she made a failed jump, it felt as if a piece of her soul had been chipped away.

Now, at twenty-two, she had experienced so much—encountered so many people—even meeting Isabela’s son, with her grandson. But even though he looked like Leonardo, he wasn’t the one she’d fallen in love with. And now, here she was with her aging parents in 1967. She was tired of searching for ways to jump into the correct timeline, and her *papá* could only do so much to help. It was up to her to put what she learned into action. She looked at the bottle and punched a forkful of food into her mouth, struggling to taste it with the pain in her heart at how much she missed Leonardo.

"What?" she asked her family when everyone looked at her.

Her mother went back to her food. *Papá* smiled at her with compassion in his eyes.

"You look like you're about to cry," her brother said. "Is the food bad?"

The emotions she'd been holding down got the better of her. "Yes, you're right, Angelito, it's terrible." She continued eating, the food soaked up the flavor of her tears.

Her mother glared at Angelito, and *Papá* rapped him on the head.

"*¿Que?*" He rubbed his head, then looked at her. "*Hermana,* let's go out. I know a good restaurant here in La Nucia. They have great food. You'll want to stay with us forever." He sniggered. "I'll show those girls how low their standards are compared to my *hermanita*."

Celestina and her mother exchange glances, and her father gave the boy another light slap on the head.

"*Papá,* are you trying to make me stupid? You keep hitting my head."

"You're behaving stupid, so I'm trying to shake the intelligent part of your brain off the shelf."

Father and son bickered, and soon Celestina found herself laughing along with them all. Her first dinner with her family in a while went better than she'd hoped. They were the best.

"We kept your room as it was," her mother said as Celestina opened her bedroom door. "No matter where or when you end up, this will always be your home."

A smile tugged at her lips and she hugged her mother. "You always know how to warm my heart."

"So, you're staying?"

"*Mamá,* you know my heart will always be with him."

Her mother clicked her tongue and stomped out of the room, not unlike an ungracious child. Celestina chuckled and looked around the space. The pastel interior consisted of light pink, light brown, and white. Her single bed was between two green plants under a large window. The round mirror was framed with brown wood, and the manila chair had a light-pink pillow. Everything soothed her.

She placed her heart bottle on the white cabinet under the mirror and looked at her reflection. Two years didn't change her appearance much, but she felt a lot older.

"You will find him. You will," she told her reflection before heading to her wardrobe. She pulled out her pajamas and changed into them.

She was half asleep when her eyes shot open at the sound she hadn't heard since scrolling through Leonardo's phone, so long ago now. The song was about a man who thinks a girl is too good to be true. She got out of bed and followed the music, until she knocked on her brother's bedroom door.

Angelito opened it, the music filtering out, bringing so many memories with it. "*Hermanita, ¿qué pasa?*"

She shrugged, then gestured inside his room. "The song. What's the name of it?"

"You heard it before?"

"Yes, from Leonardo's cellphone."

His brows furrowed. "What's a cellphone?"

"It's a—" She looked up at the ceiling, not sure how to respond, and explaining something she couldn't show seemed tedious. "It's a future thing."

"Cool!"

"*Si, si. Por favor*, tell me the name of the song."

"That's Frankie Valli. He's famous right now."

"*¿El título de la canción?*"

Angelito smiled. "Can't Take My Eyes Off You."

Her heart lifted, and she took a deep breath to steady herself. "It's beautiful."

"Won't you go out with me tomorrow?" he asked as she turned to go back to her room.

She faced him, ready to turn him down but changed her mind at his expectant look—like it meant so much for him. If she was being honest, a part of her was jealous when he was born. He was an adorable baby, and she loved him but also envied him for the love he received, from her, *Papá*, but most of all from *Mamá,* because she had neglected her throughout her childhood.

The boy didn't deserve any negative feelings from her so she smiled at him. "Sure, but you must pay for me. All right?"

He curled his mouth up. "Can we split?"

She laughed, then kissed his forehead. "I like a man who knows when to ask for a woman's help. Goodnight, *hermanito.*"

He blushed and said goodnight before closing his door. She heaved a sigh. He was the best brother she could ask for but she doubted she was the best sister he could have.

At three in the afternoon the next day, Sunday, Celestina walked with her brother along familiar streets, with both old and new businesses lined up on each side of the road. Men and women's clothing was way different from ten-years back. Ten years—it felt short but also a lifetime ago. She looked at Angelito. "Sorry for being a missing person in your life. And I'll probably be worse in the future."

He grinned. "I understand. *Mamá* and *Papá* explained everything to me. It's just—"

"Just?"

He took her hand and shook his head. "Never mind. *Vámonos,* I want to introduce you to everyone."

She gripped his hand, saddened at the thought of him having to grow up without her, and wanting to know what he was going to say.

He brought her into the *cafeteria* and walked around like he owned the place, greeting the customers and chatting to the workers who, in turn, treated him like an important person.

"Impressed with me now, *hermana*?" he asked, laughing

She messed up his hair. "*Sí,* very impressive."

He flattened his hair back in place and entered the kitchen. Again, he exchanged greetings with everyone. The cook told him Imelda was in her room.

"My daughter has been waiting for a while."

"Gracias, Tito!" Angelito said and introduced her before making his way up the stairs. Celestina followed, intrigued.

They entered a room filled with a rainbow of colors and stuffed toys. A girl who looked like a doll seemed displeased to see her with Angelito but her attitude made a hundred-eighty-degree turn when he introduced her.

Her parents delivered food for them. The two kids interacted happily and spent a long time telling Celestina about their days and school life, which sounded so different from her own childhood. After almost an hour, they got up and left the young girl on her own again.

They went to get an ice cream from a local store and sat on one of the park benches in La Nucia. The enormous fig tree created a beautiful canopy—a perfect shield from the stifling summer heat. Celestina wiped the melting ice cream from her hand. "Angelito, what were you trying to say earlier?"

His brows furrowed as he looked at her. "When?"

"The time you didn't complete what you wanted to say."

"Oh." His shoulders slumped.

Her heart sank at the sadness on his face as he told her how guilty he felt about being born. He was almost in tears as he explained.

"Why would you feel like that? Everyone loves you. Our parents adore you." Her voice cracked. "*Mamá* has treasured you ever since you were born." She cleared her throat and rubbed his shoulder. "So, never think you aren't wanted."

"You don't want me."

Her world stopped spinning for a moment. But she was an adult, and dealing with a boy who could pass as her son should be easy, except it wasn't. A twenty-one-year age gap was a lot for siblings. "Are you stupid? Of course I want you. I love you." She pulled him into her arms, not caring that his ice cream smudged her top. "Don't ever doubt how much I love you."

"But you also hate me. You've got to."

She distanced herself but still held his shoulders. "Why?"

He took a deep breath and swallowed hard. "Isn't finding Leonardo only an excuse to get away from me because you can't stand seeing our parents' love toward me?"

She couldn't decide whether to laugh or cry at his words. "Has this been occupying your head the whole time?" He nodded, failing to hold back a sob, which had his shoulders shaking. She hugged him again. "I truly want to find Leo. And if I could, I would be so proud to introduce him to you."

He sobbed on her chest and confessed at how much he missed having her around. "I never complained because I thought I deserved to be abandoned by you."

"You crazy boy. No kid deserves to be abandoned."

"But *Mamá* abandoned you when you were a kid."

"She didn't. And our situations were different. *Mamá* thought differently then."

"Mamá, ¿estás bien?"

"I'm fine, José Antonio," Isabela said to her five-year-old son who had noticed the change in her mood, what with all her sighing. She kissed his forehead and locked the final stitch for her newest creation. "Look. Do you like it?"

"¡Sí!" he answered, tracing the back of his hand across the blue suit, adorned with white butterflies flying from the jacket hem toward the breast pocket. Being the last item she would sew for Rodrigo's wedding, she had enjoyed putting the extra effort into making it. José Antonio was the ringbearer, and no matter how much she wished to sew a dress for a girl, she needed to show off how adorable her son was.

"¿Es mio?"

She smiled at him. "Yes, it's yours."

"I want to show *Papá*!"

"We will, *cariño*."

He bounced around the room, full of excitement, while she draped the jacket over her sewing mannequin and pulled it out of her store window. She sighed. They were doing well. She had a thriving shop, and Alonso's farm was a success, with multiple contracts with restaurants in Benidorm, where they had lived for the past six years. They'd got married two years after Celestina's family moved to La Nucia. They would have loved for her to attend, but she was gone by then. After living in Beniardà for two more years, they moved to the city and built their family there.

She felt accomplished, and thought José Antonio's birth would make her complete. But not having her best friend at her wedding, and now preparing for Rodrigo's wedding, she couldn't help but feel a bit annoyed and sad. She didn't crave much, only wanting to share her happiness with the woman who shared some of the most unforgettable moments of her life.

When she looked at her son, a swirl of emotions bubbled beneath the surface, knowing this little boy admiring his suit was supposed to be a girl named Mariposa. Mariposa, who would one day give birth to the man who introduced himself as her grandchild.

Alonso was right, their future wasn't Leonardo's future.

And he stole her best friend. She frowned. Or was it the other way?

Alonso walked into her shop and turned the sign from *abierto* into *cerrado.* "Bella, *hijo,* I've come to collect you both."

She smiled at him. "Hey, you don't get to do that!"

He walked up to her, leaned down, and kissed her lips. "I just did." She opened her mouth to protest but he kissed her again. "Let's go home. I have a surprise for you."

She almost squinted as she stared at him. He had only become more charming with age. "What is it?"

"A surprise."

José Antonio pulled Alonso's hand away from her. "*Papá mira! Es mi traje.*"

"What a nice suit. I bet you'll look even more handsome next to me."

"Sí?"

"Sí." Alonso kissed their son's cheek, and Isabela's heart swelled with contentment. Right, with or without her best friend, when these two were together, her life felt complete.

The three of them rode in Alonso's car back to their chalet on the mountainside of Benidorm.

"So, what's the surprise?" she asked once he'd parked the car in their garage. The chalet wasn't the biggest home but proved sufficient for a family of five. It was gorgeous, with a colonial touch, surrounded by shrubs and flowers, and a spacious garden with a pool.

"You'll see," he said, giving nothing away. "Why don't you go inside first?"

"*¿Por qué?*" José Antonio asked, but Isabela left Alonso to explain it. She walked, buzzing with apprehension and excitement.

As she advanced up the hallway, she scanned ahead to note anything missing or additional but saw nothing.

He was probably playing a joke on her again. She shook her head, smiling to herself as she rounded the corner. When she looked up, she froze in place, her mouth agape, staring at the woman she hadn't seen in a decade getting up from their orange-brown sofa.

"*¿Que tal?*" Celestina said.

Isabela covered her mouth. "Your dress is out of date." It was all she could think to say, and they both laughed.

Chapter 39

FRIENDS

"Why did you bring your son?" Isabela asked as they watched Alonso and the two children playing in the garden.

Celestina adjusted herself on the pillow she was sitting on. They were on Isabela's roof, looking over the farm and across the city, with more than double the number of tall buildings she remembered from before. "My son? You know Angelito's my brother."

Isabela laughed. "He might as well be your son. There's a bigger age gap between you and him than there is between you and your mother."

"Solo trece años."

"Don't give me that excuse. We both know you were twenty-one when he was born, not thirteen."

"Your point?"

Isabela hung her head. "Nothing. Sorry, I just feel sad sometimes when I look at Alonso."

The hint of pain in her friend's voice made Celestina stare at Alonso. He lifted his son away from Angelito's hand but then put him down and lifted her brother up to his shoulders and made José

Antonio chase them. She couldn't see why it would make Isabela sad. "You don't like him having fun with other kids?"

"It's not that—"

"Then what?"

Isabela leaned back, her eyes narrowing.

"Okay, sorry, but what's making you sad? You'd better be quick about it because, once I leave, you'll never know when I'll come to visit again. If ever."

"Nice try." Isabela smiled. "But teasing doesn't suit you. You suck at it."

Celestina nodded once but stayed quiet. Her travels didn't teach her how to handle depressed friends. But at least she'd made Isabela smile.

"I want a daughter," Isabela said.

"Ah. Did you tell him that?"

"No, but look at how happy he is. It's obvious he isn't interested in having another kid."

"Oh." She couldn't see the 'obvious' but it wouldn't be right to say that. It would only make Isabela insist more.

"Why do you look surprised?"

Celestina forced a blank expression but it was too late.

"You know something, don't you?" Her eyes widened as excitement replaced her sadness. "You've been in the future—farther than this year! You've met...me."

Celestina struggled to keep her expression neutral. Oh, dios mio. She hated how perceptive Isabela could be when it came to time drama. "I did."

"Then tell me what I was like. Did we have another child?"

"I don't know. I didn't have enough time to chat before leaving." No way was she telling her they had a daughter. She wanted this future to develop without interruption. Angelito and José Antonio's laughter pulled her attention to them. Yes, she wanted to see what future those two were heading into, with no meddling from her.

"Not going to happen," Isabela said, and, for a second, Celestina thought she'd read her mind. "Can you believe he said that? What kind of man refuses to have more kids?"

"He must have a reason." She tried to look anywhere but her friend's face.

"He said I tortured him enough when I gave birth to José Antonio. He doesn't want to experience that fear again."

Celestina smiled. "How sweet. Leo must have inherited it from him."

"You do realize that, even if I give birth to a son, Leonardo is still my grandson."

"Of course. I'm sure he got a lot of his charm from you too."

Isabela pushed her shoulder. "I missed you, *bruja.*"

The 'witch' reference made her chuckle. She poked her friend's side. "Me too, *maldita.*"

Alonso and the boys looked up at them as they burst out laughing.

Over the next hour, until it was time for them to leave, Celestina told Isabela everything she went through, skipping the part where the Leonardo she met was a lot different from hers. It came as no surprise considering Leonardo from this timeline grew up with his parents, not with his grandparents.

Isabela sympathized but the couple couldn't do much more than listen.

"I'm not experienced when it comes to time travel," Alonso said when they were saying goodbye, "but have you tried traveling to where you think he might be at the moment? Time is a mysterious dimension, and it's hard to understand how you and your father can break through it, but you might as well try. What if you both are in the same location, at the same time? Maybe then, instead of jumping, it will be like walking through time—like walking over to another dimension."

She and Isabela stared at him, and Angelito looked at him with admiration.

"That's the most you've ever said to another woman," Isabela said.

He lowered his head and whispered something to her, which made her blush. Celestina didn't want to imagine what it could be but the way her eyes undressed him told her more than she needed to know.

"Thank you," she said, breaking the moment.

"I didn't know you had such a cool friend, *hermanita,*" Angelito said once they were in the car.

"You mean you haven't seen them before?"

He shook his head.

"I guess it's no surprise," she mumbled. Her parents weren't too close to the couple but she kind of expected them to meet from time to time.

"*Mamá* sends them birthday cards and calls Isabela on the phone."

She nodded, thinking about what Alonso had said. She'd been so focused on getting to Leonardo but always ended up in the past, watching him with an earlier version of herself, or in the future where that Leonardo wasn't hers. She never considered thinking about location, only of time. But Alonso was right, if only she could think of where her Leonardo would be, she could time it.

"He's so cool."

She stared at her brother. "Who?"

"Alonso, of course. He's as cool as *Papá.*"

She parked the car and held both of his shoulders. "Listen, Angelito. No one is as cool as *Papá,* remember that."

"Not even Leonardo?"

She let go of him. "That's another story. Leonardo is special."

He nodded to himself. "I'll be cooler than *Papá.*"

"Uh huh."

"*¡Lo juro!*"

"*Sí, sí,*" she replied, stepping out of the car with a smile but stopping dead when an idea of how to find Leonardo came to her.

After dinner, when Angelito was in bed, Celestina walked down to the sitting room. As she expected, her parents were there, chatting with wine in front of them. It was a habit they'd developed after her mother stopped breastfeeding Angelito. Time for bonding after a stressful day.

Her mother saw her first and slapped *Papá's* hand from pulling the shawl off her shoulder. They both looked at her.

She backed away. "Sorry, I didn't mean to—"

"No, you're not interrupting," her mother said, her face flushed, either from the alcohol or the interruption.

"You were. But I don't mind." Her *papá* smiled, with no trace of guilt, as if getting caught flirting wasn't a big deal. Her mother's face darkened, and *Papá* motioned her to sit. "*Siéntate*. Do you want a glass?"

She sat in front of them but refused the wine. "Do you guys have it?"

"Have what?" they asked in unison.

"The cellphone."

They looked lost.

She did her best not to roll her eyes. "*Papá*, the flat thing you took from Leo in the future."

Her mother's face brightened. "Yes, I remember! Where did we put it again?" She tapped the air with her forefinger. "I got it! I put it together with our old stuff. I've been waiting to give it to you. I even thought of throwing it away." She shrugged. "It's not working."

"The battery probably needs to be charged."

Her mother raised an eyebrow. "There's a battery inside that flat thing? How does it look?"

"Can I have it?"

"Sure, I'll go get it now. Wait here." Her mother almost jumped up in her eagerness to leave the room.

Her father cleared his throat and sipped his wine.

"Papá."

"Hmm?"

"Were you with Leo before you returned to us after *that* man died?"

"This question again. Why do you want to know?"

"Because I may know how to get to him."

Her father gulped the rest of the wine. "*Lo siento,* he was not. I took the phone after nineteen-thirty-six."

She slumped into herself at that. "Oh, that's okay." The quiver in her voice said otherwise. She'd hoped he was with her *papá* because that might make her search easier.

Her father cursed under his breath and sighed. He refilled his glass with wine. "I can't keep lying to you."

"What?"

"*Sí,* he was with me before I returned. I was talking to him in the hospital room before I left. That's when I took his phone and the bottle."

Instead of anger, happiness filled her heart. "When was it, *Papá*? The date?"

He shook his head, his shoulders almost at his ears.

She gripped the hem of her dress. *"Por favor, Papá, dímelo."*

"Even if I wanted to, I can't tell you, *hija.* I don't remember."

"You're lying!"

"I'm not." He looked like he'd been slapped. "I-I didn't bother about the date because I planned to jump as soon as I had the chance. When Leonardo walked in with the bottle and left it in the room, I returned as soon as he departed."

Her mother came back with Leonardo's phone. It had been beaten with time. "Here you go." She handed it over, looked at her downbeat expression, then at her *papá's* dejected one. "What happened?"

"*Hija,* please—"

"Nothing," Celestina stated. She got up, ignoring the pain in her father's face, and kissed her mother's cheek. "Goodnight." With that, she left the room without throwing another glance at her *papá.*

Celestina expected it but was still disappointed when she couldn't turn on the phone. Of course, there was no way a phone's battery would last so many years. With her heart in a mess, it would have been wonderful if she had a charger. She glanced at the bottle on the table beneath her mirror. I could jump forward and buy a charger but it means interacting with people—something she tried hard to avoid. She was grateful for the timeline Leonardo created for her but didn't want to change anyone else's fate.

The hurt on her father's face when she ignored him flashed in her mind. She couldn't help it, needing to escape from the room before blurting out what was on the tip of her tongue: "I'm not your daughter," which would for sure tear them apart. No, she didn't want that.

Her *papá* wasn't guilty, but there were moments—like today—when not getting what she needed from him turned her into a selfish person. And hearing he tried to lie brought it all out. He could do nothing to make her doubt his love for her as her father, and she knew he lied to keep her with them, yet it didn't stop her lashing out at him.

Her mother held the phone since she was seven but she never blamed her for keeping it a secret.

A knock on the door snapped her out of it. She put the phone down on her bed and opened the door. Her still-dejected *papá* stood in front of her, his arms behind his back.

"*Hija,* can we talk?"

She left the door open and walked back to her bed and sat. When she lifted the phone, she didn't miss his reaction, his gaze glued to her hand. He sat on the chair, looking around her room. "You didn't change anything."

His forced lightness hurt her more than she expected. "No, there's nothing to change. It's perfect as it is."

He swallowed. "Celest, I'm sorry for lying the first time you asked but I really don't recall the date. Please believe me."

"I know, *Papá*." His gloomy expression brightened a bit. "I'm sorry too. I know you only wanted to protect me but I really want to be with Leonardo, and that blinded me for a moment."

He shook his head. "I've been in love with your mother for a long time. I understand what you feel, which is why I want to give you these."

She looked at the several dangling cables in his hand. "Are they—"

"Chargers?" He smiled. "Yes, they are."

She threw herself into his chest and they tumbled out of the chair. "Thanks, *Papá*. You're the best!"

"I'm not. If I was, you would stay with us."

"*Papá,* you know what I mean."

"I don't know which one will fit that phone but it won't take long to figure it out."

She tried four, with none fitting, and held her breath as she placed the small end of the last one into the phone. It worked, and she almost jumped into her father's arms again. She shoved the plug into the wall and the charging sign lit up the screen. It was the best thing she'd seen all day. She released a loud breath and looked back to her *papá*. "But why did you take his phone?"

"I've been to different places, and if there's one thing I learned, it never hurts to bring a souvenir back." He chuckled. "I have quite a collection of things from the future." He shrugged, his brows arching. "When you meet him again, tell him to be more attentive of his pockets. It was so easy to steal things from him."

Her eyes widened. "You mean, this is Leo's charger?"

He smiled, and she laughed. Even if the phone didn't work, she could squeeze the cable into her bottle and reach him.

Her mother popped her head in, carrying a midnight snack. "Can I come in?" she asked, directing the question at her father.

"Come in, *Mamá*."

Angelito squeezed in. "Me too, *hermanita*?"

"Yes, you too."

"You should be asleep," their mother scolded.

Angelito grinned, "And miss a cozy, midnight family gathering? No way." He turned to the phone charging beside her, his eyes widening. "That's the phone you mentioned, isn't it?"

"Go to sleep!" their mother repeated, and they all laughed again.

Chapter 40

FINDING WAYS

October 25th, 2020

The first thing Celestina did when she materialized was look around and heave a sigh of relief. She was in Benidorm on Playa Mal Pas, the charming little cove between the bigger beaches of Playa de Levante and Playa de Poniente. She opened her orange shoulder bag, which matched her 1960's attire—an orange-striped skirt dress. Leonardo said no one would pay her too much attention, even if she wore her mid-50's clothing, but she wanted to be safe and blend in from the moment she arrived.

She walked up the small steps from the beach and turned where a sundial stood. Fifteen minutes before five in the afternoon. No wonder no one was on the beach, with everyone probably at home or in the restaurants for afternoon meals. She felt lucky. As she faced the clear blue sea, she smiled at what could be mistaken for a sinking ship—the Benidorm Island.

A wave of nostalgia hit her as she looked to the left towards the Balcon del Mediterraneo. It was hard to believe the site where she had a date with Leonardo over sixty years ago still looked the same. She could almost see them walking there, viewing the sea, the beach filled with fishing boats. Her gaze landed on a couple on a balcony. She was too far from them to see their expressions but their body language and pointing told her it was time to run. They must have seen her pop out of nowhere.

She dropped her heart bottle in her bag, beside the cellphone, and strode away until she was out of sight, then ran as far as the nearest park. Parque de Elche. Leonardo was right, it'd been at least ten minutes, but no one cared about her presence, though she was the only person not wearing a mask over her mouth and nose.

"*Perdon,*" a woman said, but she was too captivated by the tall buildings and wondering about the absence of fishing boats.

This was the furthest she had gone, and it disturbed her how few people were around. When she jumped to 2018, the park was packed with people, especially since it was summer.

Where are the tourists?

"*¿Señorita?*" the woman called out, tapping her shoulder.

Celestina whirled around and faced the woman. Like everyone, she wore a mask but she guessed they were around the same age. They were almost the same height too. The woman's eyes widened, as if recognizing her, which was strange. Could it be she traveled back in the same parallel she left? Was she in the wrong time again?

Dios, please, no. She tilted her head at the woman, fighting off the panic building inside her. "*¿Si?*"

"Uh, you shouldn't walk around without..." The woman pointed to her mask.

"*¿Por qué?*"

The woman's smile was unseen, but her eyes brightened. "Because it's mandatory." She stepped back but leaned in. "You could get a fine if the police see that you're not wearing a mask."

"What?"

"Wait." She rummaged through the pocket of her tight jeans. They looked too constraining, but the woman didn't seem to mind. She produced an extra mask identical to the one she wore. "Here, put it on."

Celestina only looked at it for a moment, then remembered what Leonardo had said. The government had issued lockdowns because of a pandemic. *"Gracias,"* she said before putting the mask on. After breathing through it twice, she wanted to rip the thing off her face.

"I'm Xiomara, *¿y usted*?"

"I'm Cele—" Should she be giving her real name? She still wasn't sure if this was where Leonardo lived. And even if she was in the right timeline, she had no official ID. "*Soy* Celestia."

Xiomara nodded and complimented her name. After a few more awkward exchanges, she said goodbye, but Celestina followed her.

"Xiomara, wait."

Xiomara did, and Celestina decided not to waste time.

"I don't have any cash with me, but I have some jewelry I can sell. Do you know a place that's open?"

Xiomara's eyes brightened again. "You're so much like him."

"¿Que?"

Xiomara waved her hand. "Nevermind, you just reminded me of someone."

She nodded, relieved at why she felt as if Xiomara knew her. "Ah, about the jewelry..."

Xiomara grabbed her hand. "Leave it to me. I'll guide you around and make sure to make you feel at home."

Celestina laughed. "Thank you." She was going to look for a room after getting some cash.

Xiomara reminded Celestina of Isabela. After selling some of her jewelry, her new friend invited her home. They chatted over a welcome snack, with both women enjoying each other's company. Xiomara suggested that she should stay in her spare room. Celestina accepted the offer but insisted on paying a little until she could find a job.

She made an extra effort to understand how things worked in 2020. Xiomara was both amused and weirded out regarding her ignorance of modern technology. She'd nearly dropped Leonardo's phone when it beeped nonstop.

Xiomara laughed and teased her about it, but then she frowned. "You don't know how to use a phone?"

"I only know how to play music and videos."

"You're joking."

"No, I'm serious. My boyfriend gave this to me before I came here."

Xiomara's eyes widened, and she burst out laughing. "Even my grandmother knew how to use it more than that. Let me guess, you're not on social media."

"What's that?"

"Oh, my god! Which cave did you grow up in?"

"What?"

Xiomara snapped a dismissive wave and helped her set up a Facebook and Instagram profile. It was also thanks to her new friend's tutorials that she confirmed that she was indeed in the right timeline. Leonardo's Instagram had some photos still stored on his phone. His sim card, however, was blocked.

Again, despite her puzzling excuses, Xiomara helped her get a new sim. It took her a month of reading and searching the internet—a fascinating thing—before she came up with a solid plan.

First, she applied for a new birth certificate, then a national ID. Thank goodness she didn't have to sign official documents with her thumbprint. It all sounded easy, but it was a slow-moving process, causing her regular anxiety, and she felt like a fraud. It didn't help that Leonardo wasn't reacting to her social media messages. When her IDs came through, she got a job as a part-time waitress, began to relax, and enjoyed her time on Instagram.

At first, she posted about all things '50s, as a hobby. She dressed and fixed herself up in the style, and talked about that time. And for some reason, her followers grew so much that people wrote articles about her account. Strangers were coming to her for advice about '50's fashion, then advertisers got in touch with her. Three months later, she became a 'micro-influencer,' as Xiomara called it. More sponsors came and, after another month, she earned enough to quit her job and focus on promoting products and clothing brands.

With Xiomara assisting, her followers and engagement kept growing. Things were looking good, except that she still had no luck contacting Leonardo. His messenger was inactive, and had so many unread messages from people she didn't dare to open.

One Friday morning, Celestina was drinking coffee on the couch in their white living room, made homely with an array of potted plants, when the silence was broken by Xiomara bursting in, still in her pajama, with a crazed, excited look.

"Celestia, you won't believe this!"

Celestina had been checking if Leonardo had read her messages or if there was any new activity. Nothing. His account looked abandoned.

"What is it?" she asked.

Xiomara poured herself a black coffee and walked toward her, holding her phone out. On the screen was a message to the email address they'd created for her online accounts.

> Dear, Miss Celestia. We saw a couple of your videos, and we would love to interview you. We would be delighted if you would appear on our show next week.

It was signed by a woman who presented herself as a fashion host of *Canal Oro* TV station.

Celestina sipped her coffee and looked at her friend. “Should I?”

“Should you?” Xiomara laughed, “Of course you should!” Xiomara, whose dream was to be a celebrity manager—now working as both her assistant and manager—babbled about all the opportunities and benefits they could get from appearing on the show. Celestina was passive about it until Xiomara pointed out that the show was popular with young people and would be shown nationwide, meaning Leonardo might see her.

Chapter 41

FINDING YOU

September 21st, 2021

Thanks to the *Canal Oro* show, Celestina got invited to more TV and online interviews. She even had a modeling contract for clothing brands and a fashion show. She gained more than half a million followers by the spring of 2021. Xiomara also quit her job and focused on managing her and establishing a small company for them.

For a while, Celestina was stuck in a whirlwind of publicity and work—enough to distract her from thinking of Leonardo, until nighttime came. She sighed, taking in the messy living room of their new place.

Xiomara looked up from unpacking one of the boxes. "Before I forget, I found an email from earlier this month asking if you would like to model for their company."

She looked at her. "What kind of company?"

"It's a travel agency. The owner reached out, hoping you'll help promote them for countryside travelers. The agency is legit but I doubt they can offer much. They were very upfront with it."

Her tummy fizzed. "Leonardo owns a travel agency. Is it him?"

Xiomara checked the email again. "His name is Danielo Rubio Morales. Are you interested in the job?"

"I'd love to help them, but if I model for a travel agency, I want it to be Leo's company first."

"Got it. I'll tell them we can't do it."

"Thanks," she said, disappointment weakening her voice.

Xiomara frowned. "What's wrong? Don't tell me you've changed your mind about this place. We already paid for it!"

She laughed and shook her head. "It's not that. I'm just thinking of meeting him soon." She reached for Leonardo's old phone.

Xiomara shook her head. "I don't get it. So many men are begging for your attention. Yet your heart stays with a man who doesn't even read your messages."

"He has his reasons, I'm sure."

"I'm looking forward to the day I can meet him. You'll let me meet him, right?"

Celestina smiled. "Of course."

When Xiomara lifted the heart bottle from the box, Celestina almost jumped up, taking it and cradling it. "I'll mind this."

"What's up with that bottle? You're holding it like a lover."

She laughed. "It is precious. It's my father's gift and the one that connects me to Leo."

Xiomara huffed and went on with what she was doing.

A year had passed since her arrival in Leonardo's timeline, and she was now a successful, independent woman. She gazed at his photo on the phone.

Just wait a little more, Leo *mio*.

Chapter 42

LEONARDO

February 11th, 2022

After closing the door of my grandparents' house, I looked around, sure someone was watching me, but no one was on the street but me. I plucked some wildflowers growing at the side of the house. They reminded me of Celestina—small, proud, and beautiful. I liked how they remained strong, even when no one wanted them in their garden.

I placed brand new wireless earphones into my ears and played Jason Donovan's *Too Many Broken Hearts*, then jogged toward the cemetery. It was a route I'd taken every morning for the last two years, rain or shine. By now, I knew every crack on the road and the position of every tombstone. Heck, I was sure I could navigate my way with my eyes closed.

The cemetery was a lot different than in the past. It now looked like a garden—a place to rest. Beniardá was changing, more so since the start of the pandemic. They'd renovated many roads, but the most evident was the colorful 'BENIARDÁ' monument in the parking plaza, which lit the night. Everything was moving forward, even if I kept looking back to the past.

Jason Donovan's song provided some comfort, with a pinch of pain. Like the song, I also needed Celestina's body and soul. However, my dream was broken. Even if I didn't want to give up the fight, there was no way for me to reach her.

I stopped in front of her grave and crouched to put the wildflowers at the base of her headstone. It was engraved with her family name on top, followed by her name and Maria Josefa's at the bottom. My own name should be next to hers.

"Happy Birthday, *mi cielo,*" I whispered. "Celest, I—" I cleared my throat as my voice broke, and turned the music volume down. It was now playing MLTR's *The Ghost of You.* I blinked away the tears pricking the corners of my eyes and went on. "I'm leaving Beniardá. I can't stay here anymore, *mi cielo.* I have to see if I can restart my life. I can't do that here. I feel you in the air. I see you on every street. I hear your voice in the wind."

A shaky chuckle escaped my lips. I always found it silly when people talked to graves out loud, and even more with stupid lines. "Yeah, I know it sounds bad. Cliché, like in some cheesy romcom movie. My exes always wanted me to use lines like that, but I never did. I swear. But, with you, I truly want to bring down the moon, offer it something in some mystical way, and ask it to let us be together."

I straightened and took a deep breath, "But, sadly, the universe is against me. I love you—I always will—and never will I ever give my heart to another person. I never told you before but I lost myself each time I looked at you, Celest. But when I'm not with you, I get lost. And I don't know if I'll ever find myself again without you here with me. But I have to live my life. I need to move on. If there's a next life, I hope you and I can be together from the beginning."

With that, I bent, ready to do something people might think ridiculous, but before my lips touched the cold headstone, the snap of a twig behind had me standing tall. As brokenhearted as I was, I didn't want to be caught in such a position. I remained there, looking at Celestina's name, waiting for the person to pass, but it didn't happen. The back of my neck burned, and that feeling of being watched I'd had earlier returned. Someone was behind me, and it creeped me out, like in a horror movie. I hate horror movies. Having someone behind me at such a private moment was bad enough, but they're refusing to move on made me want to scream.

With my heart thundering, and Thunder's *Love Walked In* swirling through my head, I turned, ready for a confrontation. But the sight I met drained all the energy from me. I would have laughed at the irony of the singer saying the person they love appeared like a vision, when I was giving up because I'd lost the reason to want them, only that reason was now standing just a foot away. No sign of laughter. The air, the sounds—everything stopped at the sight of her.

"Celest," I tried to say, but no sound came out of my mouth. I stood there, unable to believe my eyes. Tears trickled down her cheeks as she covered her mouth with her hands. She was dressed in modern clothing: blue jeans, black shoes, and a casual white blouse beneath a cream blazer. But her curls were wild as ever, making her even more beautiful. So many things rushed through my head, all at once: How did you get here? When did you arrive? I missed you so much. I'm sorry I couldn't go to you. I'm happy to see you. Where have you been? Why did you only get here now? So many words circled my mind, but only one found its way out:

"Celest."

She nodded.

"You're here. I-I'm not dreaming."

She shook her head, and before she could complete "I'm home," I had her wrapped in my arms, feeling her heat through the layers of fabric between us. "It's really you, my Leo."

I released her and cupped her cheeks. "Yes, I am. Who else would I be?"

She sniffed. "I missed you, dummy."

I reached for her hair, still not believing she was with me again. In my time. "Well, I missed you, too, Purrball."

She pushed my arm and laughed. "I never thought I'd be so happy to hear such an insult."

"It's not. Purrball is a way of addressing cats. My Filipino dad told me."

"Cats? Do I look like a cat to you?"

I snorted back tears, without success. "Close."

She pouted. As I looked at her, love filled my heart to the brim. She was with me. She was really with me. I ran my fingers through her hair, wrapping her curls. "Celest, I never meant it as an insult. It has always been my way of saying I love you."

Her lips curled in a soft smile. "Then Purrball to you too!"

We both laughed. I pressed my forehead to hers, our noses touching. "I missed you so much," I whispered, but it lacked the feeling I wanted to convey because, what was inside my heart contained so much more than any words could express.

She rose up on her tiptoes and kissed me. “I’m sorry for making you wait.”

“Thanks for finding me.” I kissed her back, deeper, hungrier.

We were breathless by the time we broke away from each other. The gray fog that ruined my perspective for the last two years lifted at the realization that everything I wished for was with me. I grabbed her hand. “Come with me. You must meet my grandparents.”

She stiffened.

I studied her wary face. “What’s wrong?”

She grimaced. “I...don’t know how to face them.”

I grinned. “Position yourself correctly and make sure you don’t have your back to them, and that your eyes can see—” I yelped when she pinched my side.

“Stop fooling around. I’m serious.”

“It’s going to be okay. I won’t ever let go of you again.”

“And I’m not going anywhere without you, because I, too, am lost without you.”

The cheesy lines I had spouted at her grave—the other her—returned to me and heat crept up my neck.

She laughed. “*Oh, Dios mio*, you’re blushing!”

“I’m not,” I said, though my head felt like it was on fire.

“You’re even redder n—”

I sealed her lips with mine. I was going to explode with shame if she kept going. “Shut up or I’ll make you suffer.”

A mischievous glint lit up her eyes. She laced her fingers at the back of my neck and kissed me back. "Maybe that's exactly what I want."

I groaned. This woman was driving me crazy, and I doubted I'd ever get over it. I peeled her hands away from me. If this kept going, my desire for her might see me doing something no graveyard should see.

When I put my hand on my jeans' pocket and felt the locket, I couldn't hold back a smile. I always had it with me, and I was glad of it now. With the chain unlocked, I moved behind her and slipped it around her neck.

She gasped, holding the locket as she turned to face me. "You had it with you?"

"Yes, waiting for its owner's return," I pointed my heart, "And this as well." Her eyes widened as I took her hand and got down on my knee. "I still don't have the ring, but I'll ask you again—"

She pulled me up and cupped my face in her hands. "*Sí*. I'll marry you."

I chuckled. "Couldn't you wait until I'm done before answering?"

"Waiting is something I've done for a long time."

I shrugged. "Point taken. Besides, this is getting weird—I hope this will be the last time I'm proposing to you in a place like this. Or else I'll send out a wedding invitation with a title like 'Romance from the Grave,' and that sounds awful."

"Oh, how I've missed your terrible jokes!" She laughed, and I let her finish before inviting her to leave with me. She nodded and held my hand as we made our way back.

As we walked, she told me everything that occurred after I left: her journey to find me, and how she arrived back in 2020 with the help of the photos from the phone I'd lost.

She sighed. "Searching for you in the right timeline was a nightmare. If I hadn't succeeded in getting here, I think I would have gone insane." She squeezed my hand as we neared the church. "I jumped from one time to another in my search. Between parallels too."

I thought she was going to cry when she told me about her encounters with me—a different kind of me. Some were dead from a car accident, some disabled, and the last one before me was married.

"His wife, Elena, was pregnant!"

The topic was too heavy for my simple mind, so I grabbed the one concept I understood the most. "If you arrived two years ago, why didn't you come and find me? It must have been hard living in our modern time on your own."

"This modern time is why I didn't come and find you."

"Eh? I'm confused."

She laughed. "First, I needed to establish myself here. I had to get myself registered. And do you know how long everything takes with all the lockdown restrictions? At first, I even felt like I'd walked into the worst year ever. It was horrible."

I gave her my full attention as she told me how she'd acquired a new identity using Ángel's name and her friend's help. "I'm now officially Celestia De La Mota Rivera. I'm a freelance model and influencer. I have my own website, and my Instagram is thriving. Besides, I followed you, and even sent you private messages at first. Why didn't you recognize me?"

"I haven't been near my social media since—"

"*Papá* ran away with the bottle?"

I nodded and looked at her for a long moment. The new independent her.

"Celestia," I said, engraving her new name into my heart. I loved it. It suited her. Wait a minute, influencer? Instagram? Celestia? Is my wife-to-be the Celestia who rejected our travel agency and crushed Danielo? I shook it off. It's not important right now. I stopped in front of my grandparents' house and traced my fingers across her cheek. "Celest, *mi cielo, para siempre.*"

"Before until forever, I'll always be yours, and you are mine."

"Only yours." I dropped a butterfly kiss on her lips and opened the door, then pulled her in with me. The million questions in my head would have to wait. We had a lifetime ahead of us to get all the answers.

"*Abuela, Abuelo,* I'm home!"

Epilogue

IN ANOTHER LIFETIME

Benidorm, Summer 1968

Alonso watched his wife sigh as José Antonio waved from the backseat of Rodrigo's car. He put an arm around her and hugged her to him.

She looked at him. "I love him so much. Thank you for having him with me."

He leaned down and kissed her lips. "No, thank you for surviving everything to bring him here with us."

"And I'll do it over and over if it means living a wonderful life with you both." She smiled at him and leaned into his chest.

Years of being together, and Isabela was still the only woman who could warm his heart with her smile. He'd been ecstatic when she became pregnant but walked on eggshells afterwards thanks to her mood swings, cravings, and nausea. At one point, she cried because he put the ketchup bottle on the wrong side of the fridge, and he spent hours trying to soothe her. It was tough, but didn't come close to life after José Antonio came along and her raging hormones took over. He shivered at the memory. "Let's not have any more kids."

"What?" She looked into his eyes. "How did you know I was about to ask—"

"You always bring it up whenever kids are mentioned."

She pouted. He kissed her, smiling inside at how ageless she seemed in his eyes. She would never say it but he knew her tears when the nurse put a baby boy in her arms weren't of pure happiness. Thanks to Leonardo, they were convinced they'd be getting a daughter. Although, seeing they had a son didn't surprise him. It took Isabela a few hours before she warmed up to José Antonio.

Their son was one year old when Isabela mentioned having another child, much to his horror.

She ran her fingertip across his chin, then trailed it down his neck. He took a deep breath as she popped the first button of his shirt.

"Al, just one more baby, okay?" she said, her voice soft.

He almost agreed right away but the hellish labor during his son's birth replayed in his mind. At the peak of her pain, Isabela even blamed him for her suffering and cursed everyone in the room.

His mouth became dry, his palms sweaty, as she pulled him back into the house. She pushed him onto the sofa and straddled him, her heat spreading to him as she caressed his chest.

"Don't you want to see Mariposa?" She dropped a kiss on his lips, then his neck.

His reasons, the logic, the fear, faded with every kiss. But he still managed to ask: "Do we have to?"

"We must." She kissed his neck again, then nibbled his earlobe.

He swallowed, knowing he could never turn her down. Never. He held her waist and let his desire run free as he claimed her lips and carried her toward the bedroom.

Dear readers

I hope you enjoyed this story- if you did, I'd appreciate it if you could take the time to rate and review it where you purchased the book and on popular platforms like Bookbub and Goodreads or wherever it's possible.

Your review means a lot to me, especially knowing that you enjoyed my stories enough to share it with others motivates me to keep writing.

Thank you so much for your support.

Warm regards,
Jessie Winterspring

Author's Q&A

- **When did you start writing *In Another Time*?**

I started writing this story in November 2019 for NaNoWriMo. I didn't reach my 50,000-word goal, but I got very close, haha.

- **How long did it take you to write it?**

It took about five months, but I didn't write every day. If I had, who knows? Then again, even if I had tried writing daily, I doubt I could have done it. Inspiration doesn't always make an appearance.

- **What inspired you to write this book?**

A beautiful tree on the side of the road. We were driving on the autobahn in Germany back in 2006. It was during one of our many cross-country road trips from Spain to Norway. It was one of those comfortable silences inside the car. I was humming to an '80s song from our CD when the car slowed, and my sight landed on a large tree. It had lush leaves, and the way the afternoon light shone through them was almost magical. I saw it then: a man finds his mother's letter.

Yes, it's a bit different from the book, but that's what usually happens to my ideas once I write them. In fact, the story was originally supposed to be about a love letter that dragged him back in time and straight to his grandparents' front door. Together with his mischievous, young mother, they would create a plan to make his bad-boy father fall for her by making him jealous. But then I saw *Back to the Future* and loved it, so I completely lost interest in my original idea after that. I didn't bother writing notes for it, but the story lived in my head all those years. I wrote many other romances before finally writing it in 2019.

- **What comes first: the plot or the characters?**

The character. I saw Leonardo, my main protagonist, before the plot.

- **Are your characters entirely fictitious, or have you borrowed from real-world people you know?**

Yes and no. Almost all the characters are fictional, except for Rosetta, the cat-loving character. She's a minor but important character. My friend inspired her.

- **What are your favorite moments in the book?**

Leonardo and Celestina's "first date" at the reservoir. It's the part where Leonardo broke his hand, and the moment when his first attraction to her hit him, as he saw her pain through her smile.

- **What was the hardest scene to write?**

Leonardo's flashback to his parents' death. I wanted to hug him as he cried like a boy—thank goodness Celestina did it, haha.

- **If you were to write a spin-off about a secondary character, who would it be?**

Maria Josefa and Ángel's romance. It's so tempting because it would be such a challenge for Maria Josefa. It's hard to imagine falling for a man who raped you, even if it was his other self. But it's so heart-wrenching, that I'd probably never write it.

- **Do you listen to music or other sounds while you write?**

I normally prefer complete silence, but with In Another Time, I played "Love Walked In" by Thunder and "Do That to Me One More Time" by Captain & Tennille. I had them on repeat while writing the chapters! Haha.

- **Did you submit your work to Agents?**

Yes, but I quickly withdrew it in favor of querying small presses and publishers. When a publisher requested the full manuscript, I backed away and decided to go indie.

- **What made you decide to go Indie, whether self-publishing or with an indie publisher?**

Lack of patience and the need for control. I followed an author back in 2019 when she first got an agent. It took years before she finally posted, excitedly telling her followers that a publisher had offered her a contract. She posted this in mid-2022, and the publication date was set for 2025! No, that's not for me. I don't want it! It took me four years to revise and edit with editors; there's no way I can wait that long for publishers. Other reasons involve control, but the long wait is definitely one of the top ones.

- **What can we expect from you next?**

I'm currently working on two time-travel stories. The working titles are:

1: *"One More Time."* It tells the story of a childless couple. After forty years together, he thought their relationship had become boring—until he saw her lifeless body and his life crumbled. He realized then that she was his most prized treasure, and he would do anything to bring back their mundane life together.

2: *"The Escort Girl's Time Reversal."* She was working as a high-class escort when a politician's son spotted her and took her in. He was kind, handsome, and charming, and she fell head over heels and did everything he asked—even killed for him—only to die by his hand. While dying, she suddenly woke up on the day he had originally asked her to kill his father. She doesn't care how or why time reversed. This time, she will have her revenge, and she will make sure it's super sweet.

I've started writing both, but I'm progressing at a snail's pace because I can't decide which one to prioritize. I received advice about using generative AI to speed up my writing, but NO THANKS. I can accept using it to ask things about history and science facts, or even mathematical solutions because I'm as dumb as I can get with math. But that's all. I've written stories way back to 2001. I'm not going to get lazy now and let a technology that was trained using writers' work in an unethical manner take over.

Special Thanks

Thank you to the people who helped me in my journey of writing this book.

To my beta readers, KB, Claire Gonzales, and Auburn Edge. Your honesty and valuable feedback were greatly appreciated.

I want to thank my first editors, Lena Kinder and Lara Alonso Corona. Lara, you assisted me not only with Spanish words, but I also learned a lot from you. Also, I've just realized that your middle name is Alonso while writing this. Haha!

Thank you so much to Eamon O' Cleirigh, I initially reached out to you because I wanted a male perspective on my book before sending it out into the world. However, you turned out to be a fantastic substantive editor, line editor, and proofreader rolled into one. Words are not enough for me to express how lucky I feel for having found you. Thank you for catching so many embarrassing flaws in this book even after so many edits before you. You're a big reason I feel confident about this story now.

And last but most important is my beloved husband, who listened to me talk about this book since the idea hit me back in 2006. Thank you for nagging me to write it and for taking care of our son whenever I childishly threw tantrums as I tried to reach my goal of completing this book until the early hours.

With love,
-Jessie

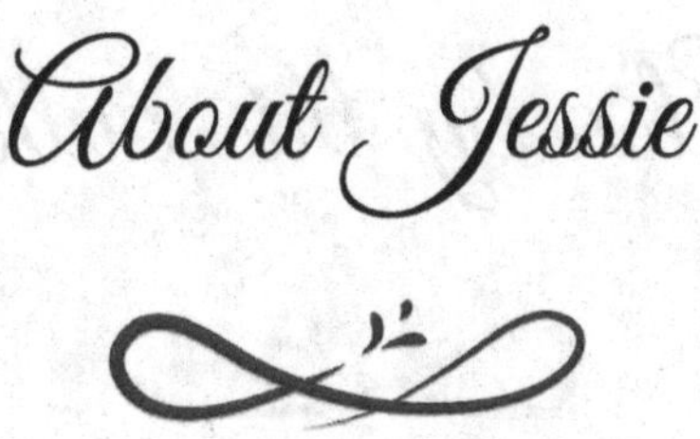

Jessie Winterspring is a Filipina time-travel romance writer living in Spain with her family. When she's not reading or daydreaming, she's crafting stories about ordinary people caught in extraordinary circumstances. Since actual time travel is still out of reach, Jessie does the next best thing—she writes it.

In Another Time is her debut novel.

When she's not writing or reading, she's likely chasing after her son or baking cakes. She shares short stories and musings on her blog and is most active on Instagram @jessiewinterspring.

Visit her at jessiewinterspring.com

Also by this author

Love, Die, Live short trilogy

A story of loss, love and reincarnation

1: Live for Me | 2: Die for Me | 3: Love for Me

The Flame Squad series

Individual short stories of the Flame Squad members, a vigilante group.

1: Sly Prince | 2: Shadow Prince | 3: White Crow Princess

100% standalone short reads

Sweet Bloody Secret: A Short Vampire Romance

Tomorrow is Yesterday: A short time travel romance

Under Her Spell: A short Christmas YA romance

www.ingramcontent.com/pod-product-compliance
Lightning Source LLC
LaVergne TN
LVHW031428170726
843492LV00010B/2902